Peace Like A River

D0190899

Peace Like A River

ELAINE SCHULTE

LIFEJOURNEY
BOOKS

LifeJourney Books™ is an imprint of Chariot Family Publishing,
a div. of David C. Cook Publishing Co.
David C. Cook Publishing Co., Elgin, Illinois 60120
David C. Cook Publishing Co., Weston, Ontario
Nova Distribution Ltd., Newton Abbot, England

Published in association with the literary agency of
Alive Communications, P.O. Box 49068
Colorado Springs, CO 80904

PEACE LIKE A RIVER
© 1993 by Elaine Schulte

All rights reserved. Except for brief excerpts for review purposes,
no part of this book may be reproduced or used in any form without
written permission from the publisher.

Cover design by Turnbaugh & Associates
Interior design by Glass House Graphics
Edited by LoraBeth Norton

First Printing, 1993
Printed in the United States of America
96 95 94 93 5 4 3 2

CIP Applied for.
ISBN 0-78140-358-8

The California Pioneer Series

The Journey West
Golden Dreams
Eternal Passage
With Wings As Eagles
Peace Like a River

With special gratitude to Nancy Ballard Stenger,
a dear school friend, who did research for me in Indiana.

In memory of our
sisters and brothers
who brought His love
by orphan train

Prologue

*S*end *me a sign, Lord, a great star in the sky, Thy voice calling from the heavens into this wilderness of California*, Benjamin Talbot prayed. *I know full well I'm not to ask for signs, but this is an exception . . . an exception to take me from this dismay and aridity of faith.*

He lowered himself gently onto the wooden seat curving around the willowy pepper tree. Most evenings when he settled here in his courtyard at the house he had named *Casa Contenta*, he felt as at peace as any old widower could hope to feel. Tonight, however, the letters in his pocket felt as if they might burn a hole through his vest and white shirt. Instead of being of God, the letters seemed to have come from the very forces of evil.

Amazing how the past could catch up with a family, even from the faraway eastern seaboard, he mused. He had prayed on and off all day about the matter, ever since the letters had arrived at his San Francisco warehouse, and he still hadn't come to terms with the news. Now the question was how his family—especially his niece Abby—would accept such unforeseen tidings. And she would be coming by any moment.

He'd no more than thought it, than Abby strolled into the clay-tiled courtyard, tucking stray strands of blond hair back into the bun at the nape of her neck.

"What a glorious, glorious evening!" she observed with her usual exuberance.

Benjamin glanced at the rays of sunlight beaming through the graceful branches and realized that he'd scarcely noticed. "Yes, a fine evening." His eyes turned to her.

She was thirty years old now, a beautiful woman with four children—not the seventeen-year-old innocent she'd been in 1845 when he and his adopted son, Daniel, had arrived at Miss Sheffield's School for Young Ladies in New York to bear the bad news: her parents dead and their estate bankrupt. The letters in his pocket now held new complications . . . complications that some would find downright disgraceful. If Abby allowed it, they were complications that could damage her joyous life.

He patted the seat beside him. "Sit down, Abby. Is Daniel coming along?"

"He promised to be here in a moment," she answered, settling her blue calico frock around her as she sat down beside him. "And you know Daniel's promises."

Benjamin nodded. "Your husband is a man of his word."

"For which I am most grateful," she replied happily.

Benjamin glanced with her toward her white stucco house, one of four Spanish houses on the family compound he had bought when they arrived by covered wagon in '46. It was still early enough in the evening for her children and their growing band of cousins to be laughing and playing within the compound's white stucco walls.

"'Rambunctiousness,'" she said, entitling the scene as she often did with her artist's gift of encapsulating people and their surroundings in a word.

"Yes, 'Rambunctiousness.'" After a moment, he considered the letter in his hands and hoped she wouldn't mentally title its contents "Shock."

She turned back to him and asked, "Whatever are you frowning so about?"

"Best to explain it once, to you and Daniel together," he answered. "Ah, here comes Daniel now."

She shot him a curious glance, but instead of asking further questions, she turned to give her husband a radiant smile as he crossed the courtyard toward them. "I do believe Daniel is growing more handsome, if that's possible," she confided.

"Yes," Benjamin agreed, "he's aging gracefully."

Daniel's eyes remained as deep blue as ever, and the few gray hairs in his dark beard only added distinction. Most important, he and Abby had as fine a marriage as anyone could wish, and Benjamin hoped that the letters in his pocket would not in any way strain it.

"A family consultation?" Daniel asked with his broad white smile, which he directed first to Abby and then to Benjamin.

"Indeed," Benjamin answered. "We have two letters from New York."

Daniel settled himself beside Abby on the wooden seat and eyed both of them with interest.

Benjamin wished he knew how to soften the blow, but in the end, straightforwardness was best. He turned to his niece. "Abby, the letters concern your father's five . . . illegitimate children."

Her blue eyes widened and her lips parted. "With . . . with Father's il-illeg—" She stopped, then finally forced out, "with my . . . half-sisters and half-brothers?"

Benjamin nodded unhappily and was sorry to see her drop her head into her hands in dismay. "Doubtless you hoped that chapter of your life was not only closed, but that the entire book had been burned. Life doesn't always turn out like that, though. Old wounds are often reopened."

Head still in her hands, she nodded in sad agreement. At length she straightened up and looked at him. "I've tried hard to put them out of my mind forever . . . and I'd almost succeeded. Yet I've often suspected they might show up."

"What do the letters say?" Daniel inquired.

Benjamin took the thickest letter from the envelope that had come by Butterfield Overland Stage and spread open the crinkley white pages. "I read it several times already, but I'd like to read it with you again myself." He handed it to Abby so they could all read together.

February 5, 1858

Dear Mr. Talbot,

I can't bring myself to call you Uncle Benjamin, although that would explain who I am. In 1845, when you took care of your late brother's (my father's) estate, you met my mother, Roxanna Murray. I am Charlotte, the eldest of their five children.

I am sure it was a terrible shock to you that my father had another family, but it has made life difficult for us, too, especially after our mother died four years later of consumption. We had no other family, and didn't have your address, so we were taken to Grayton Orphanage north of New York City. None of us was adopted out, since most people prefer sweet little babies. At that time, I was ten, Langsdon nine, Rolland four, Glenda three, and Emelie two.

In 1853, when I was sixteen, the orphanage found me work as a housemaid in the city. For the last two years, I have worked for the Stafford family, who are very kind people and have taken an interest in my education. Mr. Stafford is a banker and has offered to write a letter to you, as he understands my plight.

Also two years ago, the other children were sent to families across the country by orphan train, and we have lost track of each other. Langsdon was taken by a hard family of upstate New York farmers and left them when he was eighteen. He is now established in banking. He got your address and learned that Rolland, Glenda, and Emelie were placed in homes in Indiana. He fears they might be as miserable as he was, and so I am writing in hopes that we might all be welcome with your family in California.

We have very little money and would need some help to travel to Indiana to look for the other sisters and brother. Would you help us? We understand you are Christians, and we hope you would "do unto others as you would have them do unto you." We thank you for considering this matter, which is of great importance to us.

Sincerely,
Charlotte (Callie) Murray Talbot

P.S. I hope you will not find it unsettling, but Mother had us named Talbot just before her death.

Benjamin watched Abby's face as she finished the letter. It was as white now as on that fearsome day she'd learned of her parents' deaths.

Daniel slipped an arm around her, and for an interminable moment, she sat speechless against his shoulder. Finally she asked in a shaken voice, "How could they be named Talbot?"

Benjamin drew a resigned breath. "Unseemly arrangements are often possible if one has sufficient money or the right contacts in high places."

For all he knew, his own brother had legitimized them since he'd been a man with contacts in high places himself. Or Roxanna Murray, a most persuasive woman, could have managed it as easily as she'd managed to be well kept in a fine house and neighborhood with a housekeeper and a British nanny for the children. She'd not only been a beauty, with her sapphire blue eyes and jet black hair, but was as alluring as Eve in the Garden of Eden. If ever a woman could tempt a man to folly. . . .

On the other hand, he felt pity—actually compassion—for the misguided woman, despite her obtaining a goodly sum of money in a court appeal following his brother's death. Benjamin drew a deep breath. After charming such a hard-bitten judge, it would have taken only a modicum of Roxanna Murray's charm to talk a minor official into a simple matter like changing her five children's surnames.

"There's no need to rush into a decision, Abby," Daniel assured her. "We'll take time to consider it." He turned to Benjamin. "You said there's another letter?"

Benjamin handed it to them. No need to read this one again. It purported to be a letter of recommendation from a Mr. Stafford, a banker and her employer, and it claimed that Callie Talbot was bright, responsible, and of good moral character. In a word, she was recommended. She'd even taught their young grandchildren the rudiments of education and would make a suitable governess for small children.

When they'd finished reading it, Benjamin said, "I'm sorry to say I'm not convinced that Callie's employer wrote this letter. The quality of writing paper doesn't seem right for a wealthy banker. Look at it," he added, fingering it, then holding it up to the light. "I believe it's the same paper on which Callie wrote her letter."

"Do you think she wrote both?" Abby asked with astonishment.

"Perhaps," he answered, "and perhaps neither. I dislike mentioning it, for although we found Roxanna Murray to be beautiful and most charming, she was less than trustworthy. It is sad but prudent to assume that her child might be lacking in trustworthiness, too."

He gave the letter to Daniel who examined it carefully, then slipped it into the envelope with a frown.

Abby spoke with soft resignation. "Whether it's true or

not, they are my blood relations."

"Yes," Benjamin answered. "No matter how wrong your father was in taking a . . . " He hesitated, unable to utter the word *mistress* before her. " . . . in having another household, they are all of them our blood relations."

Abby was taking it considerably better than he'd expected. If it had been her arrogant father speaking, he'd have laughed off the matter and told them in no uncertain terms that they were being provincial. He'd doubtless remind them too that their family was, after all, descended from British royalty, which to his mind excused all impropriety.

"I remember the two of you coming to my rescue at Miss Sheffield's," Abby said thoughtfully. "When I thanked Daniel for his help, he told me it was his pleasure to repay others in a small way for the help he'd received when he needed it—and that someday I might have an opportunity to help someone else myself. Perhaps that time is now."

"Perhaps," Benjamin responded, and pressed his lips together to guard his tongue.

"How did this young woman, this Callie, get our San Francisco address?" Daniel asked.

"The letter was sent to Independence, and Adam forwarded it," Benjamin said, referring to his eldest son. "Their mother must have given them our old Missouri address."

"I don't know—" Daniel began.

"I do," Abby said, lifting her chin decisively. "I think we should invite them. I think we should do unto others as we would have them do unto us."

"That's very commendable," Benjamin replied, "but, first, we should be cautious and pray earnestly about it. With so many no-accounts coming to California, it might be wise to have a circumspect investigation conducted as well."

"Do you truly think so?" Abby asked.

"I do," Benjamin replied. "It's not an easy thing to say, but since it concerns that side of the family, I do. I felt sorrow for Roxanna Murray, bearing five children without so much as a husband's surname, and I feel sorrow for the children, but I am also apprehensive. One concern is that Callie's letter bears a postal box on its return address. It strikes me as a most unfortunate possibility that her children might have acquired not only their mother's guile, but also her ferocious greed."

Abby's blue eyes widened with such dismay that he added, "On the other hand, my dear niece, I'm certain that the Lord is pleased with your decision. Who knows but that God has chosen you to be the instrument of their salvation? We each have a duty to act in the arena in which He has placed us."

He smiled, thinking of his older sister. "As your Aunt Jessica often and rightly claims, 'We are blessed to be a blessing.'"

On the other hand, Lord, he thought, *though I know very well we are to give thanks in all matters—and I do in this now— these letters still strike me as most unpleasant tidings.*

1

"Miss Murray!" The butler called out with his crisp British accent into the cavernous white kitchen. "Miss Charlotte Murray!"

Callie turned from her seat at the kitchen table, hearing her name over the servants' chatter and the clatter of eating supper. She rose into a growing silence, almost overturning her chair. "Yes, Mr. Stane?"

"You are wanted at the *front dowah!*"

The other servants' eyes turned to her.

"At the front door?" Callie Talbot repeated uneasily. Who could be calling for her? She had no family or friends outside the household here in New York City.

Mr. Stane gave a disapproving nod. "Warn your young men to come around to the servants' quarters hereafter."

Young men? her mind repeated through the surprised whispers at the table. She had no "young men" either,. . ..not that she didn't have her chances with the brasher servants and tradesmen, none of whom she fancied. But there was no sense in contending with Mr. Stane, who ruled the entire household with his ostentatious accent and resolve. "Yes, sir."

Her best friend, Becca, whispered, "*Ach, du lieber!* Who is it, Callie?"

Callie lifted her shoulders with puzzlement.

Ignoring the servants' gazes, she followed Mr. Stane from the kitchen and across the white marble hallway that curved around the staircase as it led to the great entryway.

"A good thing for you that the Burlingtons are out," he muttered. "Speak to your caller at the dowah."

Callie wiped her damp palms on her apron and caught a glimpse of herself in the gold-framed entryway mirror: black uniform and white housemaid's apron, taller than most but not overly thin, auburn hair done up in a simple bun. A proper housemaid of twenty-one years, that's what she was—although sometimes it felt like a mere role.

Mr. Stane opened the door part way. His narrow back, rigid with reproof, blocked Callie's view of the visitor standing in the glow of lamplight. Who could it be?

"Regretfully, sir," Mr. Stane intoned, "you shall speak on the dowahstep, as you have no invitation to this house."

"As you wish," the man replied, sounding undaunted, "though your employer will not be pleased to hear of it."

Mr. Stane did an abrupt turn that befitted the queen's guard and allowed Callie to step to the door.

"Well, Callie," the young man at the doorstep said, "haven't you turned into a beauty?"

She was so startled to see her brother Langsdon standing before her, all grown up, that her hand flew to her mouth. It had been five years since she had seen him, though he'd written her for money when he'd gotten out of prison three months ago. Now here he stood, tall and handsome in a black coat and top hat like a fine New York gentleman.

His blue-gray eyes sparkled. "Cat caught your tongue?"

"It's only . . . only that I'm so surprised—"

"Aren't you goin' to chance invitin' me in, either?"

She glanced back and saw Mr. Stane standing at rapt attention at the stairway. "I'm not allowed to receive guests at the front door. If you'd go to the servants' entrance—"

"I certainly will not!" Langsdon replied indignantly and loudly enough for Mr. Stane to hear.

She was taken aback, but pleased, too. Langsdon might be a year younger than she, but he didn't appear to have what people called a servant's mentality.

"Then . . . I guess we could stroll in the park," she said, not knowing what else to do. "I'll have to run upstairs for my cloak and bonnet. It's cold this evening."

Langsdon shot a shaming glance at Mr. Stane and spoke loudly. "Cold indeed. As frosty outside as an old Britisher."

Callie drew back, half amused and half appalled.

"In the park, then," Langsdon said. "Fortunately the lamps are lit."

Langsdon gave her a slight bow, which she suspected was for Mr. Stane's benefit. All the time her brother was bowing, she had the impression he was taking in the fine crystal chandelier and the huge Persian rug below it, not to mention the oil paintings that lined the entry walls.

"I'll be out back in a minute." She closed the heavy door and turned to see Mr. Stane staring at her, his arms folded across his narrow chest.

"See to it that you're back soon," he said. He gave her one of those appraising looks that men often did—the kind she detested. "And see to it you return by way of the back dowah."

Callie nodded. "Yes, sir."

"It appears you've caught yourself a man of means. Not that you don't have the looks to do so. But I don't recall your having time off this evening. I shouldn't like to report to the Burlingtons that you sneak about with young men when they are out."

"I'll just be a few minutes," she promised.

He grinned, his thin lips stretched across his bony face.

"You may stay out a good bit longer than that," he said, "just so you aren't quite so *frosty* to me yourself."

"No-no, sir," she answered, swallowing her distaste. He was at least forty and lank as an old stick, but he thought himself quite dashing in his black butler's uniform. Well, she'd deal with him again when the time came. Right now she had to hurry out to see Langsdon. She'd sent him almost all of her savings when he'd gotten out of prison, and in his letter he'd written of a plan to get their family back together again. This must be the beginning of it. Just in case, she'd better bring more money.

Minutes later, she hurried out the door to the poorly lit back steps. She felt for the leather pouch in her inside cloak pocket. Reassured that it hadn't fallen out, she pulled on her gloves and shivered. Most of the last snowfall had melted, but it was still chilly out.

"Callie? Over here!"

Thankfully Langsdon had relented and come around back after all. Union Square Park was well lit with oil lamps and quite safe, but sometimes prowlers lurked in the darkness behind its mansions.

"Oh, Langsdon!" she whispered and threw her arms around her brother's neck. "I thought we'd never see each other again. And then when I didn't hear from you after your last letter . . ."

He patted her back. "Should of known I wouldn't let you down, sister. I got my faults, but leavin' my family in the lurch isn't one of 'em."

Tears of joy pressed behind her eyes. How could she have doubted him? "You're right, I should have known. But you have no idea how lonely I've been, even working in Father's old mansion. I wanted so badly to live here, but instead of it being a consolation, it's been an endless reminder of the hurt and embarrassment of our unfortunate past."

"Hush," he whispered, then held her tight and kissed her forehead. "That was for the benefit of your meddlin' old butler, who is watchin' this very minute from behind the second-floor draperies. Better to let him think you got a suitor than to have him guess the truth."

"But why not tell him you're my brother? And why not explain our plight? The Burlingtons are so nice since they've turned Christian. They might help us find Glenda and Emelie and Rolland."

"Maybe they will," he answered with a note of wariness. "Maybe they will. But this is no time to tell 'em."

He took her arm, and they strolled around to the side of the house. "Leave it to me, Callie. I've had long months in prison to think everythin' out. I have a plan . . . a complicated secret plan." He looked enigmatic, almost sinister, for a second. "There's just a few more things to tie up on it."

He darted a look at the upstairs windows. "Well, well. Your Mr. Stane is certainly on guard at every corner. He must run himself ragged. Tell me, Callie, is he . . . ummm . . . how shall I say it? Is he overly fond of you?"

She drew a disgusted breath. "He tried to kiss me last week in the library."

"And what did you do?"

"Why, I slapped him with the duster," she admitted. "And it was good and dusty too. He had to go upstairs to change his uniform!"

Langsdon looked amused. "A fine way to stop a man's advances. But you must not have much of our dear departed mother's tricks about you, Callie. She'd of handled it very differently, turnin' his interest to an advantage, one way or another."

"Mother's tricks?" she asked with alarm as they crossed the street to Union Square Park. "What do you mean by that?"

His smile was illuminated by one of the park's ornate oil lamps. "Artfulness, some call it. A bit of cunnin' in speakin' and actin' that's very useful to women. I still remember her battin' her long lashes at our father. You look a little like her, Callie. You've got her big blue eyes and dark lashes, but not her dark hair. Red hair is more showy, though."

"Auburn," she corrected him. "Not red like carrots."

"Auburn, then," he said. "And it might be that you're still teachable, too."

"Teachable? How do you mean?"

"Do you let men kiss you?"

"Why, Langsdon Murray, I do not!" she replied, shocked that he would even ask.

His lips curled up slightly. "Langsdon *Talbot.*"

"You're using Father's name?"

"I'll explain when I'm ready," he replied with a nod. "What's important now is for me to learn more about you. For example, tell me why you don't allow men to kiss you."

She shrugged under her cloak. She didn't like to think about it, but it was best to tell Langsdon now, once and for all. "I've promised myself that I'll never be like Mother."

"Oh, have you?" he asked with a flicker of amusement.

She nodded. "I have."

"And pray tell, why not?"

Callie sighed. "Just look at the disgraceful situation she put our family in. Worst of all, she didn't seem to mind in the least. I think she was proud of herself! I can't even bear to think of the word for us, but the neighbors surely called us by it when we were children. You know exactly the word I mean, and don't you dare say it!".

Langsdon smiled at her outburst. "But she and Father had passionate natures. Passion's in all people, but not all will admit it." He sounded smug.

Callie faltered in mid-stride, but he took her arm and

escorted her onward through the park.

Langsdon gave a laugh. "For better or for worse, I am my father's son," he told her, "even if you aren't quite our mother's daughter."

Callie didn't care to think about passionate natures. One had to fight against passions and temptations; that was the only answer. If everyone lost control of their passions, doing what they wished, the world would be an even more fearful place. She disengaged her arm from his.

"Please, Langsdon, I don't care to discuss this further."

"Then we won't," he said, "though I'm glad to see you're so 'well spoken,' as they called it in school."

"I read all I can from the Burlingtons' library," she said, "and when their grandchildren lived here last summer, they let me assist their governess. It was wonderful, truly wonderful."

"So you wrote," he replied without enthusiasm. "I'm like our father about education, too, and believe me, I fought hard to get what I could. It was all I could do to get those blamed farmers to allow me to attend school."

"But you did attend?"

"I did . . . and I was number one in the class, too," he bragged. "Right now I'm workin' at the New York Trust and Savings Bank."

Callie kept her eyes on the lamplit footpath as they strolled along. Best to let him believe he was well spoken, even if he did drop his g's. It was a habit he'd doubtless picked up from the street children at the orphanage . . . or in prison.

"I'm proud of you, Langsdon," she told him, which was true. "I'm proud that you've tried to better yourself. What is your position at the bank? Are you a teller?"

"Never you mind, sister. Just be assured that I plan to go high in this world."

She darted a sideways glance at him and, seeing how determined he looked, decided not to reply.

The crunching of their shoes on the gravel path was the only sound until Callie finally spoke. "You look like Father . . . as I remember him. Handsome as he was, only taller and broader in the shoulders."

"Earned muscle by muscle sweatin' like a workhorse on that slave house of a farm where the orphanage sent me," Langsdon complained.

"I'm sorry it was so hard for you," she replied, feeling almost responsible. She'd felt terrible, being the eldest child when her family was torn asunder, wishing desperately she could hold them together. "When you wrote about your hardships on the farm, I thought and thought how to get you out, but you were signed up until you were twenty-one. And then . . . to hear from you from prison . . ."

"Couldn't stand that farm another minute, so I bolted and ran," he said with anger.

"But to be imprisoned for running away when they were mistreating you so hideously—"

"No one mistreats me for long," he muttered.

Something about his tone frightened her.

After a moment, he added with lightness, "Big shoulders make the young ladies all the more attentive to a man, so it wasn't all lost."

"I suppose so."

"I know so. I know a great lot about women," he boasted.

Best to change the subject, she decided. "It's . . . it's too bad that the water in the park fountain is turned off now. It's so beautiful here in the spring with the trees leafing out and in June with the rhododendrons in bloom."

"Don't grow overly fond of it," Langsdon warned her, and looked quickly over his shoulder. "Don't grow overly fond of anythin' here."

She peered around too, glad that they seemed to be the only ones in the park. "What do you mean, don't grow overly fond of anything?"

"It's not all worked out, but I do think . . . now that I see you're so respectable . . . that it'll all fall into place. Trust me." Suddenly he asked, "Are you a believer, Callie? You know, a Christian?"

She was so taken aback that it took her a moment to answer. "If you mean do I go to church and such, no. But I do try to be a good person." What would being a believer have to do with finding their brother and sisters?

"You said that Mr. and Mrs. Burlington are Christians."

"Yes, indeed they are! They even have daily devotions for us now, in the morning before Mr. Burlington leaves for his office. It all happened so suddenly, his changing, that none of us knew quite what to make of it."

"What else can you tell me about them?" Langsdon asked.

Callie knew a great deal about their conversion since Christian leaders often came to dinner now, and she helped to serve when they had a crowd. "It began last summer," she said. "A businessman named Jeremiah Lanphier took an appointment as a city missionary. He often comes to the house—a tall, fine-looking man, full of good cheer . . . and a good singer."

"Yes," he said impatiently. "Go on."

"Well, North Church appointed Mr. Lanphier to start prayer meetings, and he sent out a handbill for others to join him Wednesday noons. I have a copy of the handbill in my room. The Burlingtons gave one to each of us. It's called 'How Often Shall I Pray?' and it's about praying when you see need. I don't remember all the words."

He studied her under the street light. "You kept it?"

"It seemed . . . important," she explained, embarrassed to

admit it to him. "It's important to know what others do."

"But you're not a Christian?" he asked again with suspicion.

"Why, I am not even baptized, and you know it!" she snapped. The entire subject of religion made her head whirl with anger and confusion. "You know they'll never baptize us . . . as if we could help Mother and Father not being married! And for all we know, she didn't even want to have us baptized!"

"It's no longer important, Callie," Langsdon said soothingly. "We got more important matters to deal with. Does your Mr. Burlington fall in with those businessmen gatherin' at the Fulton Street prayer meetin' every day?"

She drew a breath of damp night air. "He does," she replied. "It's been reported in all of the newspapers." Then, embarrassed, she realized that Langsdon probably hadn't read them in prison. He probably didn't even know that, in six months' time, Mr. Lanphier's prayer meeting had turned into a revival that was sweeping the nation.

She continued, "A few months ago, Horace Greeley even sent a reporter with horse and buggy riding around to the prayer meetings to see how many men were praying. In one hour, he could only get to twelve meetings, but he counted over six thousand men praying! They're closing down the big stores at noon to use them for prayer, and even the theaters. They say ten thousand people turn Christian every week."

He shook his head in the dim light, then smiled sourly. "Well, I don't aim to be one of 'em."

"Why not?"

"I got other plans," he answered impatiently. "Look here. Your Mr. Burlington must know Charles Loring Brace of the Children's Aid Society."

"Yes, Reverend Brace has been here to dinner. I-I wanted

to ask him how to find the rest of our family."

Langsdon's lips parted with alarm. "You didn't say anything to him, did you?"

"There was no chance for it."

"Good! Don't you go pryin' and ruinin' my plans," he warned. "I know their whereabouts already."

"You do?! Where are Glenda and Emelie and Rolland?"

He eyed her warily. "You won't tell?"

"Of course not! I promise! If I just knew where they were, it might give my heart some peace," she said, near tears. "I think of them all the time and worry about them hating their families like you—"

"In Indiana," he interrupted. "They're in a small town in Indiana."

"That far west! But how could you know? The Orphan Train Society records are supposed to be secret."

"I have my ways," he assured her and looked mysterious again. "If you see Brace, don't you dare ask about 'em. Don't call attention to yourself, either. It could ruin my plan for all of us."

"What plan, Langsdon? Tell me!"

He smiled at her avid interest. "You have to keep it secret."

"I promise. I won't say a word about anything."

He looked very sure of himself. "The main part of the plan is to get us to California, Callie. Clear across the country from our 'unfortunate past,' as you call it."

"All of us—to California?"

He nodded. "I've already written to our uncle, Benjamin Talbot, who lives there."

Callie's heart pounded wildly. "Whatever did you say to him? That we wished to come visit them?"

"Trust me," Langsdon replied. "Anyhow, I didn't write in my name."

27

"Then whose name did you use? And how . . . how can you expect a reply?"

"Trust me!" he repeated with impatience. An enigmatic look came into his eyes again, then he smiled. "I don't have it all worked out yet, but when we get to it, I'll know what I'm doin'."

"Has he answered?"

"Not yet. But from what I hear of him, he'll welcome us."

She felt almost too scared to think it might be true. "And all of us would be together again?" she asked.

"All of us together to start afresh, and me not havin' to stay here and spill my blood over darkies if war comes. I'd like to try my hand at findin' gold, although they say the easy pickin's are over. It's mainly hydraulic minin' now, washin' away whole mountain ridges. Lots of miners have gone off to strikes on the Kern River or to Oregon; some even to British Columbia or to the big strike in Australia. But me, I believe there's still gold waitin' for me in California."

She tried to stop thinking of Glenda, Emelie, and Rolland, and to fix her mind on Langsdon's words instead. Why were men so excited about gold rushes? As for him having to fight in a war people claimed would eventually come over the institution of slavery. . . .

Langsdon was studying her, and looked rather kind, the very picture of Father when he was in a good mood. "I suppose, like most women, you want a husband and children."

"Yes," she replied, feeling shy. "I'd like a real family more than anything in the world. All of us together first, and later, maybe, a fine husband who loves me and my family . . . and our own dear children."

"Then count on it," he promised. "You can count on a new life in California, Callie. Trust me. All I need is your money to help gather up the family . . . and your confidence." He smiled magnanimously at her.

"What will you do with the money?"

He gave her a hard, hard look. "The less you know, sister, the better it'll be for all of us in the end."

She hesitated, then reached inside her cloak for the small leather pouch. She handed it to him. "I do trust you, Langsdon," she said, though she had reservations. There was something forbidding about his glance that told her she'd better not question him further. And he was their family's only hope for being reunited.

"Good," he said, feeling the pouch quickly, then slipping it into his pocket. "All of it helps. And if you really trust me, I suggest you start battin' those long dark eyelashes at Mr. Stane. You'll need more freedom of movement, more chances to get out of the house."

"Only if you truly think so," she answered reluctantly. "I don't care for him one bit."

"Just do your best to beguile him, that's all."

At her distraught look, he added, "Flatter the old fool. Smile as though you think he's splendid. Only pretend, like an actress."

"I don't think I can do it," she admitted, sorry to disappoint him. "It is too much like lying."

Langsdon shook his head at her, then asked, "What days do you have off?"

"Only Sundays."

His tone was final. "You'll have to have more freedom so we can meet whenever we need to."

"But why?"

"You do want to have the family together again, don't you?" he asked.

"You know I do, Langsdon!"

He glanced around again, and she felt they must be in some sort of peril.

"Trust me," he said again. "You don't think my part in

this will be simple, do you?"

"I guess I hadn't considered it." She faltered, then drew a deep breath. "Maybe . . . I can do it."

The more she thought about beguiling the old butler, though, the less sure she was that she could endure it. On the other hand, now that there was hope, she wanted with all of her heart to get out of New York and gather their family together.

"It'd be useful too, Callie, if you'd begin talkin' like a Christian," Langsdon said, eyeing her with a certain eagerness.

"Talking like a Christian?"

He nodded. "You know, givin' out with 'What a blessing!' and an 'Amen' now 'n again." At her blank look, he asked, "Don't you listen to Mr. Burlington at them morning devotionals?"

"It's hard for me to understand some of it."

"Well, pay closer attention," he snapped. "And somehow you've got to meet Reverend Hansel." His voice turned quiet. "We'll have to be very careful of how we go about it."

Callie glanced about the park quickly again, but there was no one to overhear them. "Reverend Hansel? Who is he?"

"A minister who's said to be takin' an orphan train west to Indiana, then headin' for Missouri and California. We have to check on it all carefully, though. No mistakes. Keep your ears open!" He smiled at her. "It's almost too good to believe. You livin' right in the old Talbot mansion . . . and settin' you up with a bachelor minister, though he's probably a dried up, pinch-lipped prune."

Setting her up? Callie didn't understand it all now, but she felt sure it would soon make sense. Their only chance for success, it seemed, was in obeying her brother's orders the best that she could.

The next morning, Tuesday, she stood in the dining room with the rest of the servants for morning devotions. Mr. Burlington, a portly gray-haired gentleman, sat at the head of the long table with his big black Bible open before him. Mrs. Burlington, gray-haired and grandmotherly, sat at his side, giving him her full attention.

Callie blinked sleepily, determined to learn what she could, especially about talking like a Christian.

"This morning our scripture is a joyous one," Mr. Burlington said. "Psalm 100. Make a joyful noise unto the Lord, all ye lands. Serve the Lord with gladness: come before his presence with singing."

He looked up at all of them, and Callie felt as if he were looking especially at her.

"Know ye that the Lord He is God," he continued. "It is He that hath made us, and not we ourselves; we are His people, and the sheep of His pasture. Enter into His gates with thanksgiving, and into His courts with praise: be thankful unto Him, and bless His name. For the Lord is good; His mercy is everlasting; and His truth endureth to all generations."

He looked up at the servants with his newly found kindness. "Can any of you explain it?"

As usual, most of them shook their heads. Finally old Molly, who'd served in the house under Callie's father, ventured, "When Mr. Benjamin Talbot was stayin' here, he said folk in Israel knew about sheep just like the Irish, so they understood about God bein' a kind o' shepherd, and bringin' His lost sheep back to the home pasture."

The same Benjamin Talbot they'd be going to in California! Callie thought. *So that was why Langsdon wanted her to learn about religion. Perhaps they'd discussed religion in this very room.* She caught Mr. Stane watching her, and quickly glanced back at Mr. Burlington.

"Very good, Molly," their employer said. "Benjamin Talbot enjoys a fine reputation hereabouts, even though he moved west. His father was a renowned minister, so he knew about the Great Shepherd. Yes, indeed, we are the sheep of God's pasture, and He wants to bring us home to Him."

Mr. Burlington looked down again at his Bible. "We are to enter into His gates thanking Him for His mercy, not because of duty but because we love Him. It's an amazing thing that, after all of our meanness and forgetting about God, He will take us back and still love us."

He and Mrs. Burlington smiled at each other with joyous understanding, but Callie didn't feel good about it at all. If only she'd been baptized . . . if only her mother had married instead of ruining the lives of her children.

"Shall we sing 'Old Hundredth' now before setting about our day's work?" Mr. Burlington suggested.

He and Mrs. Burlington rose from their chairs, and led in the singing.

All people that on earth do dwell
Sing to the Lord with cheerful voice . . . .

Callie tried to recall the words from last week, but they escaped her. She pretended to sing along, not doing much worse than the rest of the servants. It was encouraging to know that God wasn't just full of hell and damnation, but that He loved people too.

When they dispersed, Callie headed for the back stairs, lifting her black skirt slightly as she started up the steps. She'd been so lost in her thoughts about Langsdon and gathering up the children to go to the California Talbots, that she'd scarcely noticed Mr. Stane behind her.

"Well, Miss Murray," he said, "that is a cheering sight for the beginning of my day." He was staring at her ankles most intently—not that he could see much through her black high-topped shoes.

She dropped her skirt lower and was about to give him her huffiest look when she remembered what Langsdon had told her. It took an effort, but she gave Mr. Stane a small smile and managed to bat her lashes just once.

"Well, now!" he said with amazement. "First a handsome young man comes to the front dowah calling on you as if he were the Prince of Wales, and now I get a civil look from you. You grow more and more interesting, my dear-rr Miss Murray."

It took even more of an effort to manage a secretive smile, but it was worth it to see his Adam's apple jump as if he'd gulped. She turned away to hide her surprise. If need be—if it meant everything Langsdon hoped for—maybe she could be beguiling.

"Mr. Stane?" Mr. Burlington called from the front entryway. "I'd like to discuss the day's plans with you."

Callie hurried up the stairs. At least for now, Mr. Stane wouldn't be after her. But what should she do if he cornered her again for a kiss? How could she keep him interested in her without his . . . touching her? She might be innocent, but she'd heard plenty from Becca, who had grown up with five older brothers. And though she was plump, she was so pretty and had such a merry heart that she always attracted men. Her latest beau, Thomas Warrick, seemed recklessly in love with her.

Becca, with her German accent, had warned Callie, "First a man, he likes to touch you. Then comes holding your hand, then kissing, and before you know it, you got trouble . . . and then he calls you a trollop! *Ja*, that's just how it goes. I heard from my mother and my brothers, and they say they will kill me if I am a trollop!"

Mr. Stane's advances toward Becca had loosed a volley of German that had scared him off. Of course, Becca could get by with it, being Mrs. Burlington's highly prized seamstress and personal maid. Ordinary housemaids, Callie reminded herself, were easily replaced.

Upstairs, she opened the cleaning closet and stared blindly at the rags, mops, pails, brooms, and dusters. Suddenly a thought hit: *she didn't believe in kissing until she was married.* She nearly laughed out loud. One thing Mr. Stane prided himself on, besides his imagined dash and good looks, was that he'd never, in his words, "been snared into wedlock."

In her amusement, she almost banged the wash pail against the wall as she got out her cleaning supplies. Wouldn't the mere mention of marriage stop Mr. Stane flat?

By noon, she'd finished cleaning the Burlingtons' richly furnished bedroom and the rest of the upstairs rooms.

At the mid-day meal in the kitchen, Mr. Stane said, "May I remind you that Saturday evening the Burlingtons will be having a dinner-rr party for over one hundred people."

Callie almost choked on her mouthful of stew. She'd entirely forgotten—and this might be of importance to Langsdon and his plan. Once she'd swallowed and could speak again, she dared to ask, "Who's coming to the dinner?"

"The usual straitlaced Christians," he replied mockingly, "which means we shall all have to be especially puritanical."

"Now, now, Mr. Stane," Molly chided. "I notice it's the Christians who are the kindest employers. And I once had two Talbot brothers in this very household to compare . . . one a believer and one far from it. Believe me, there was a great difference."

Callie spooned up a bit of beef. It was disturbing when Molly spoke of Father and his family having lived here in the mansion, especially since she had such mixed feelings about him.

Mr. Stane turned a superior smile on the old servant, then apparently decided not to dignify her remarks with a reply.

Beside Molly sat her husband, Joseph, the carriage driver. "Mr. Stane," Joseph spoke up. "Ye be a fair man, an' we know ye'll be fair in yer judgments on Christians."

Becca, who attended a German Lutheran church every Sunday, let out a doubtful "Hmmmpf!"

Callie peered at Mr. Stane from under her lashes. He was giving her a coy glance, his bulgy gray eyes glittering, and she quickly looked back down to her stew.

If only she could learn if the man Langsdon wanted her to meet was on the guest list. Whatever was his name? Ah . . . Reverend Hansel. In any event, she must let Langsdon know about the dinner since the orphan train people were likely coming. Already she could see one reason she needed more freedom of movement—to get messages to him.

Finally she decided on an indirect question to the butler. "Will Reverend Brace and the orphan train people be amongst them?"

"*Among* them," Mr. Stane corrected her. "Yes, *The Reverend Mr.* Charles Loring Brace will be *among* them. Do tell us, Miss Murray, why you are suddenly interested in the orphan train people."

She shrugged. "It seems a strange thing, taking New York City's orphans and sending them out to live with families in the west." Her mind flew to Langsdon. "Probably working them half to death on farms out in the wilderness. . . ."

"Good riddance to the whole ragged, thieving lot, I say," Mr. Stane answered.

Her temper rose and, with it, her voice. "I'm sure that not *all* of them are thieves, Mr. Stane!"

He glanced up at her. "I forgot you lived in an orphanage," he said by way of apology. "I was thinking of the ragged street brats that steal the shoes off your feet. I'm sure you're not one of that ilk."

She pressed her lips together, then said, "I am not."

"You've done very well for yourself, Miss Murray, consid'ring your background."

How much did he know? she wondered, darting a hasty look at him. He had an overly elegant way of eating, just as he did everything else, and seeing his pinkie finger curved high over his tea cup, as well as his ingratiating smile, she was irritated enough to forget all reason. "I need to go out for an hour this afternoon, Mr. Stane," she stated firmly.

"To what purpose, if I may ask?"

"It's private."

He leaned back and gave her a long smile. "Perhaps we should discuss it directly after dinner in the li'bry?"

She nodded and swallowed hard, aware that others at the kitchen table were watching them.

When everyone began to talk again, Becca leaned over to whisper, "Be careful, *ja*, Callie?"

Callie whispered back, "*Ja*, I will be careful."

What she had to remember was that whatever transpired, this was important for getting her sisters and brothers together—important for their new life in California.

2

Benjamin Talbot glanced over his letter to the New York investigators for a last time. His handwriting had grown scratchy and less slanted, but his instructions were straight to the point. Learn what they could about Callie Murray Talbot. Investigate Langsdon Murray Talbot, employed at a New York bank. Find out about the other children, who were supposedly dispersed to Indiana by orphan train.

If only he knew Callie's employer, Stafford, he might contact him, too. On the other hand, such a letter might cast unwarranted suspicion on Callie and cause her to lose her position. According to the newspapers, work in New York was still difficult to find because of last year's financial collapse. It was best to combine prudence with compassion.

Benjamin folded the writing paper and slipped it into an envelope. Tomorrow his letter would go by Butterfield Stage to St. Louis, then sail across the Mississippi and up the Ohio River by ship until it was transferred to rail . . . and then it would take some time for such an investigation to be completed. In the meantime, he had to answer the letter from Callie, who seemed extraordinarily forthright about their lives. He selected a sheet of writing paper from his desk drawer and took his quill from the inkstand, all the while deliberating how to strike a kind but careful tone.

Finally he put quill to paper and began, determined to be equally forthright.

Dear Callie,

    Our family was surprised to hear from you and sorry to be informed of your mother's untimely death. A mother's passing is always one of the most difficult, and even more so when her children are young.

    We understand your heartache, especially with the three younger children scattered to Indiana by orphan trains. On the other hand, we feel that the orphan trains have been a humane way to help orphans find new homes in the country, and we give them our support. I understand that most of the children are happy in their new homes, and regret to hear that Langsdon was placed with a hard family. Farming has never been an easy occupation, and it would, in all likelihood, seem all the more difficult for a young man who was reared in the city.

    With regard to your request, we are indeed Christians and will pray about the idea of further helping you. For the moment, I am enclosing a bank draft to help ease your current financial situation until we know you somewhat better.

    Would you be so kind as to write and tell us what your expectations would be if you were to come to California? I hope this request does not sound too harsh, but many emigrants here have preceded you expecting to find gold on the streets. After reading your letter, I feel hopeful that this is not the case with you, but we've learned it is wiser to ask about one's plans in advance than for those coming here to be sadly disappointed.

    There are two Californias, according to our noted philosopher Josiah Royce. One is represented by gambling—gaudy, bold, powerful—and by liquor—

riotous and assertive. The other is made up of laymen, ministers, and churches—quiet and unpretentious, but conducting a remarkable work of relief and good will. "One," Royce says, "is as representative as the other: the one of the illness of society, the other of its health." These latter are those of whom our Lord said, "Ye are the salt of the earth." They are the salt of California.

As for our family, we try to be the latter. We live in the countryside on what is called a rancho. We are a goodly distance from San Francisco where we have a shipping and chandlery establishment. Some of the family is engaged in work there, and others raise cattle and crops on the rancho. We live quiet family lives, each of us having a full day's work.

Again, I hope that the bank draft will assist you somewhat until we hear more in detail about your expectations. May God bless you with His wisdom.

Sincerely,
Benjamin Talbot
P.S. We are greatly interested in the great spiritual awakening taking place in your city and would appreciate your sending news articles about it, if you can.

He replaced the quill in his inkstand, then shook a fine dusting of sand from the sand shaker over the writing paper to absorb the excess ink.

Likely he was an old fool for sending any money at all, he reflected, but such a modest amount would scarcely stir up much larceny in an innocent's heart.

Usually Callie enjoyed cleaning the library more than any other room in the mansion. She and the rest of the household were allowed to read whatever books and journals they wished—not that many of the other servants took advantage of their employers' kind offer. This afternoon, however, she entered the book-lined room with trepidation—and with the cleaning supplies, including the infamous duster, in hand.

She'd no more than begun dusting the periodicals on the library table, than Mr. Stane arrived, closing the carved walnut double doors behind him with a show of deliberation.

He raised his chin, his bony face imbued with his usual confidence. "Well, Miss Murray, I see you're hard at work."

"Yes."

He stepped toward her with an unctuous smile on his lips. "You are a fine worker, no question of that."

"Thank you, Mr. Stane. I do the best I can."

He hesitated, as if for effect. "The question I bring has more to do with your standoffishness. Your employers think you consider yourself superior to the rest of the staff."

Callie almost dropped her dust cloth. "The Burlingtons said that?"

Mr. Stane raised his thin eyebrows. "Not in so many words, but a good butler understands ev'ry expression that crosses his employers' faces, ev'ry nuance. And as you know, I pride myself on being a very good butler-rr."

She was willing to grant him that, since visitors often remarked about his excellence and some had even tried to lure him into their employ. He was wrong, though, about her being standoffish. "It's true that I'm reserved by nature," she countered. "I shall apologize to them, or at least try to explain myself so they understand."

He shook his head slowly. "Discussing the matter with them would be taking the wrong tack." He paused, his gray eyes gleaming as he stepped closer. "It would be far smarter to show *me* you're not quite so standoffish; then I can drop occasional hints to our employers that you are merely a reserved young woman, one who is more intelligent and better mannered than the rest of the staff."

"What do you mean, show you?" she asked warily. To avoid the predatory look in his eyes, she stooped to dust the ornate legs of the library table.

"I mean that you are one of the most beautiful young ladies I have ev'r seen, Miss Charlotte Murray Talbot."

His flattery flashed past her, but her mind repeated, *Talbot?* She stood up again. "How do you know that?"

"That you are beautiful?" he inquired. "Or that you are a Talbot—of sorts?"

"About my name."

"A good butler makes it his business to know all that he can about his staff. It just happens that I have friends in your old neighborhood who remember your mother and her five offspring all too well. As you might've guessed, with a prominent man like Charles Talbot involved, it was the kind of scandal that people don't easily forget."

It was exactly what she'd always feared—and confirmation that she and Langsdon must get out of New York City. She stood rooted to the floorboards while the butler made his way around the library table toward her.

"If your mother, Roxanna Murray, looked like you, I can see how she could carry off such a bold affair."

Suddenly his hands were on Callie's shoulders and he was kissing her neck.

"Mr. Stane!" she exclaimed, trying to push away. "Don't . . . I beg of you, don't—"

His voice turned husky. "Aren't you the very one who was batting her lashes and sending coy smiles at me this morning?"

"I didn't mean . . . ."

"What you didn't mean and what a man of my experience perceives you meant are two different matters," he answered. "I presume you are your mother's daughter."

"Mr. Stane, I am not like my mother."

He smiled with disbelief. "I saw you throw yourself into

the arms of the so-called gentleman who called for you last night. It's of no use playing the innocent with me, Miss Murray." Still holding her shoulders, he forced her to face him. "Didn't you request an hour off this afternoon?"

"Yes," she answered, pulling away as far as she could. "I have personal business."

"With your young man?"

"It is not at all what you think, Mr. Stane!"

"Surely you can spare just one kiss in exchange for an hour off. Is it such a costly price when it would give me so much pleasure?"

In the midst of her panic, the answer she'd thought up that morning came to her. Her voice trembled, but she got the words out. "I don't believe in . . . kissing until one is married. Are you . . . are you perchance proposing matrimony to me, Mr. Stane?"

His gray eyes widened, and immediately his hands dropped to his sides. "Whereveh would you get such an idea?"

She backed away. "You seemed to like me a great deal just a moment ago."

"Liking and marriage are two different propositions entirely. As for your hour off, you certainly may not have special priv—"

"I shall have to ask Mrs. Burlington then," Callie interrupted, backing away from him until she stood against the marble fireplace. "She would not want to hear *why* you denied me an hour off the very first time I've asked for extra time in the entire two years I've worked here."

Furious, he drew himself up to his full height, which was only a few inches taller than she. Slowly his glare changed to a devious smile. "You are even more beautiful when you are angry, Miss Murray. It puts color in your cheeks and a stiffness in your spine that makes your form quite provocative."

Her face grew hotter yet, and he laughed at her embarrassment. "Very well, have your hour off this afternoon."

"Thank you, Mr. Stane. I think I should take it right now, if I may."

He gave a nod. "Don't be late and . . . don't mention our little meeting this afternoon to anyone, you hear?"

Callie returned his nod, took up her cleaning supplies, and hastily departed from the room. It would be best not to tell Mrs. Burlington about Mr. Stane's attentions, but she certainly intended to tell Langsdon.

Twenty minutes later, wearing her black cloak over her black uniform, Callie entered a bank for the first time in her life. She fervently hoped that people in the New York Trust and Savings would mistake her for a young widow and give her the privacy afforded to those in mourning. Instead people stared at her, and she guessed her stubborn red curls must be peeping out of the edges of her black bonnet.

Quickly tucking loose strands of hair back under the bonnet, she glanced behind the bars of the five tellers' cages. Wherever was Langsdon? Could it be that he worked in a back office?

Suddenly a voice said from behind her, "Excuse me, madam. May I be of assistance?"

She turned and saw him looking very fine indeed in a black uniform.

Before she could speak, he shot her a warning glance, then took her by the elbow and escorted her to the front door. "Ah . . . the New York Trust Bank," he said loudly enough for others to hear. "Many people make the same mistake. Let me show you where it is down the street. No problem at all."

Outside on the busy sidewalk, he hissed, "What in blazes

are you doing here?"

She spoke quickly. "You have no idea what I had to endure with that Mr. Stane to get an hour off, so don't look so enraged. I came to tell you there's to be a party Saturday night at the Burlingtons', and the orphan train people will be there. I checked the guest list, and Reverend Matthew Hansel is on it. Also, Reverend Charles Loring Brace, who is head of the Children's Aid Society."

Langsdon's expression changed rapidly. He pressed his lips together, thinking. "Are the Burlingtons perchance using a caterer?"

"Yes . . . they always use Partridge House Caterers."

He smiled, then pointed down the street as if giving directions. "I'll try to get myself hired as a waiter."

"As a waiter?"

"It won't be the first time," he replied grimly. "I'd like to see the situation before you go near Hansel. Now, hurry along to the bank down the street and occupy yourself for a while at one of their writing tables, then walk around home in another direction."

"Did I do right in coming?" she whispered.

"Fine, Callie," he assured her. "You did right. Pretend not to recognize me Saturday night. I suppose that dastardly butler will be there?"

"Yes, of course."

"Then I'll have to use a disguise . . . likely a good-sized walrus mustache," he said half to himself. "What work do you do at a party?"

"Take hats and cloaks, run and fetch things, help with the serving . . . whatever needs filling in."

"I see," he replied. "If I'm hired on, I'll send you a message by post Saturday . . . . something like partridge in a pear tree. Don't do anything further until you have my instructions. Go on now." He called behind her in a louder voice, "Good-day, madam. A pleasure to be of assistance."

She called back. "Thank you, sir."

He gave her a hard look, and she realized that calling him "sir" made her sound less like a young widow with banking business. She glanced around the busy sidewalk behind her. Suddenly she saw a distant man who resembled Mr. Stane disappear into a store. But no . . . she'd only imagined it was the old butler because she was nervous. Surely Mr. Stane wouldn't follow her. Surely he wouldn't go that far.

Still, she felt uneasy. She must be more careful. How full of secrets her life had suddenly become. She only hoped life wouldn't become even more unnerving before she escaped New York and found her family—and the peace for which she so greatly yearned.

When Callie returned home, Mr. Stane was nowhere in sight. Old Molly sat alone at the kitchen table, peeling carrots and potatoes. Since the old woman's feet were swollen with rheumatism, she often helped the cook with sit-down work. Molly's greatest value, however, was in knowing the mansion and its peculiarities, having served in it for most of her life.

"Where's Mr. Stane?" Callie asked.

Molly's voice still held its Irish lilt. "Off to rent chairs an' tables for Saturday night. The usual rental firm got the day wrong for the party, so it's a muddle for Mr. Stane to find everything at the last minute. Mad as an English bull dog, he is."

"I can imagine." She felt a great surge of relief. Surely then, the man she'd seen in town had not been their butler. It had only been her over-active imagination.

Molly chopped a carrot on the cutting board. "He's after havin' things done right, Mr. Stane is. At least, it keeps 'im out o' our hair." She turned a warning look on Callie. "Be careful of 'im, girl. I seen 'im watchin' ye. The other servants been talkin' of it, too."

"Please, Molly, I'd rather not discuss it," Callie said.

"Can't say I blame ye. Yer friend, Becca, told 'em to be mindin' their own business. Threw in plenty of her *donner wetter's* and *ja's* to keep 'em from arguin'. Out shoppin' for silk yard goods for Mrs. Burlington now, Becca is."

Callie felt a rush of gratitude. Becca's English could be precarious when she was upset, but one way or another, she got things said.

Best to change the subject. She'd often been tempted to ask about her father's family and, since Mr. Stane already knew of her connection with them and she was likely leaving the household soon, it seemed there was little to lose. She tried to keep her tone even, to hide the jealousy that assailed her whenever she thought of her half sister growing up here in the mansion and having such a fine life so different from her own.

"When you worked here for the Talbot family, Molly, what . . . what was their daughter like?"

"Abby, you'll be meanin'.'" The old servant took up a new carrot to peel as she spoke. "I knew 'er from the day she was born, and she was as beautiful a colleen as could be. Not uppity, either, like some rich 'uns. Only seventeen when she had to leave for the frontier, but braver 'n most, she was when it counted."

Callie's jealousy faded slightly. She'd never considered her half sister's pain. "It must have been sad for her to leave."

"Sad's not half the word for it, her leavin' the mansion. But by then it was near empty. Most o' the furniture sold 'cause of the bankruptcy. Fierce enough with 'er parents bodies floatin' in the Mediterranean Sea."

"Floating in the Mediterranean?" Callie repeated. All

she'd ever known was that her father had died in Europe, and his wife with him.

Molly nodded her gray head. "Abby didn't carry on much, though. Only when we had to make her mournin' clothes from her dead mother's dresses. She sat pullin' out the seams, an' I did the sewin'. It was hard as could be on both o' us. She was just blossomin' out into womanhood an' had outgrown everythin' but her uniforms from that girls' school."

Callie recalled how wildly her own mother had carried on when she'd heard of Charles Talbot's death. There'd been nothing brave about her, at least not until she'd set out to get as much money as she could from his estate. "Getting her share," as she called it, had consumed her mind as surely as consumption had begun to take her body soon thereafter.

Molly rambled on. "Well, Abby, she wiped her tears, then took her paints an' easel out an' painted Union Square Park an' the rest o' the surroundin's till it was time to leave. Expect she still has the pictures in California to show her babes the New York mansion where she grew up. A good artist, she was. Sold some o' her paintin's from her journey when she lived in Missouri that first year."

"What did Abby look like?" Callie asked.

Molly glanced at her. "Tall like you, but blond hair. Eyes as big an' blue as the Irish Sea off Dublin. Like yers, now that I think on it. Sisters, you could be, 'cept for yer red hair."

Callie gave her a tremulous smile. "Well, I'd . . . better finish the cleaning before Mr. Stane returns."

"Expect ye'd better," Molly agreed. "A stickler for detail, he is, especially with a big dinner party comin' down on us. Plenty to do, even with caterers underfoot."

"Yes. I'd better hang my cloak and bonnet. Please . . . don't mention our discussion to Mr. Stane."

Molly looked up at her curiously, but she said, "I don't

tell 'im anythin' he don't need to know."

After thanking the old woman, Callie rushed up the back staircase to the servants' quarters on the third floor, her mind reeling. It was unsettling to know more about her half sister. To think they could almost pass as sisters—it was a possibility that had never occurred to her.

That evening she was turning down Mrs. Burlington's bed when Mr. Stane stepped into the bedroom.

"Did you get your personal affairs in order-rr, Miss Murray?" he inquired, his gray eyes hooded and his accent more British than ever.

"Yes, thank you," she replied in a voice cool enough to let him know he was unwelcome. Fortunately, she'd already finished with Mrs. Burlington's bathing room and had now only to fluff up the bed pillows.

"Would you have a walk around the park with me this evening?" Mr. Stane asked. "It's stopped raining."

"No, thank you, Mr. Stane," she replied, trying to think of an excuse. "I—I've got letters to write."

"To whom, pray tell?" he inquired. "Has the young man who came calling on you left the city already? I can't imagine his leaving such a beautiful morsel as you behind."

"Why . . . why, the letters are personal, Mr. Stane," she improvised. "Nor does it have anything to do with him."

Mr. Stane stood blocking the doorway. "A great deal of your life is personal nowadays, my dear-rr. I can't help but wonder why."

Her voice shook. "If you'd let me pass, please—"

Mr. Stane gave a low laugh. "I'm sorely tempted not to let you pass, Miss Murray Talbot, but I shall this time."

From the look in his gray eyes, it was clear he was only biding his time. Well, she was biding hers, too! The question was whether Langsdon's plans would come together and she could leave New York before Mr. Stane became even more persistent.

The remainder of the week passed with the household in a tumult of preparations for Saturday night's dinner party. The bustle made it easier for Callie to avoid him.

On Saturday morning the rental company men set up skirted buffet tables in the vast dining room, as well as tables and chairs in the music, drawing, and reception rooms. Mr. Stane kept a sharp watch over them as they laid out white damask tablecloths and napkins, then turned his attention to the florist as he carried in centerpieces of pink and white roses. While Mr. Stane oversaw them, Callie carefully wrote out the place cards in the elegant penmanship to which she'd been trained, and kept an uneasy watch from the library window for the postal delivery. Surely Langsdon would send a message somehow!

At long last the postman arrived, and she rushed to the door to accept the mail. Closing the door, she shuffled through the envelopes. A note for her—and in Langsdon's handwriting! She stuffed it into her apron pocket.

"Pray tell, what are you doing with the mail, Miss Murray?" Mr. Stane asked, appearing suddenly and brushing her hands with his as he took the other letters from her.

"You were so busy—"

"Never too busy to see to my usual duties," he said. "See to it you wear your new uniform tonight and a fresh apron."

She nodded compliantly and hurried back to the library. At the first opportunity, she tore open the envelope and read the scrap of paper. *Partridge in a pear tree. Take no notice.*

Her spirit soared. Langsdon was coming! It could mean one more step toward their journey to California. Oh, how she wished that she'd pressed Langsdon for more details. On the other hand, he'd said it was better for her not to know too much. She ripped the note into tiny pieces and poked them in with the paper and wood laid in the fireplace for the evening fire.

When she returned to lettering the place cards, she came across the names of The Reverend Mr. Charles Loring Brace and The Reverend Mr. Matthew Hansel. She penned each with special care, and noted from Mrs. Burlington's seating chart that Reverend Hansel would sit at one of the tables in the music room. Perhaps she and Langsdon could leave sooner than she'd even dared hope.

Partridge Caterers arrived shortly before the party, but without Langsdon.

"Will there be more of you?" Callie asked a man who carried in a carton of punch cups.

"Two or three extras comin' in just before seven," he answered as he headed for the buffet.

Perhaps Langsdon was already in the kitchen, she thought. She hurried toward it, pretending to check on the spare cloak racks and hangers behind the staircase. She slipped over to the kitchen door and peered in. Already the stove was covered with pots, and the ovens were fired up, turning the huge white room into a cauldron of heat and commotion. Cooks and other caterers' workers were everywhere, but no Langsdon.

Before long, there were last-minute changes to make with the place cards. As she corrected them at the tables, the caterers began to carry in hors d'oeuvres on ice in silver-domed dishes: oysters, lobster, terrapin, partridge, quail, and far more.

It began to rain just before seven o'clock, and Callie found herself stationed in the entry with Mr. Stane, waiting to assist in taking the guests' umbrellas and damp cloaks. Mrs. Burlington, wearing a blue silk frock, and Mr. Burlington, wearing a fine black suit, stood waiting nearby to greet their guests under the great crystal chandelier. In the music room, a harpist played softly.

At seven o'clock the guests began to arrive, their horses clopping along and drawing the carriages to the front door. There was still no sign of Langsdon, and Callie felt frantic. Surely the extra waiters should be here by now, she thought. What had gone wrong?

She was carrying an armful of cloaks and umbrellas to the cloak racks behind the stairway when she saw him. In his black tuxedo and thick walrus mustache, he was almost unrecognizable—nothing like the Langsdon whom Mr. Stane had dismissed from the front door.

Carrying a tray of food to the dining room, he pretended not to notice her, and she tried to be equally circumspect. Mr. Stane, as always, was everywhere, and he turned a suspicious look at them as if he sensed something afoot.

Carriages stopped one behind another by the front door, and it began to rain hard enough for Mr. Stane to fetch guests from outside with the huge black umbrella. Behind the Burlingtons, Callie and Becca took the guests' cloaks.

"You are nervous, *ja?*" Becca asked with surprise.

"*Ja*, I am nervous," Callie admitted.

"Why tonight?"

Callie shrugged, remembering her promise of secrecy. Fortunately there was no more time to talk.

At seven-thirty the rain stopped, and Mr. Stane returned indoors to remove his India rubber cloak. "Who is that walrus-mustached waiter?" he whispered.

Callie felt the blood rush to her face as she took his wet cloak. "How should I know?"

"Indeed," he replied, "I suppose most men do watch you. Only a blind man would miss noticing you."

Callie pressed her lips together, not knowing how to respond. Fortunately the doorbell rang, and the butler had to open the door to let in two gentlemen.

"Ah, The Reverend Mr. Brace, our guest of honor!" Mr. Burlington boomed with pleasure. "And The Reverend Mr. Hansel! A pleasure to have you here, especially since I am certain you have sermons to deliver tomorrow morning."

Callie glanced at Reverend Hansel and saw he was far from a dried up, pinch-lipped prune. He was young, perhaps just over thirty, a dark-haired man who appeared healthy, hearty, and even athletic. As he smiled at the Burlingtons, his brown eyes sparkled under thick brows, and the cleft in his chin broadened. How handsome he was—and, unlike most handsome men, without appearing aware of it.

"Only Reverend Hansel has a sermon to give tomorrow," the other minister was saying. "He's putting in as much time as possible before he escorts the next orphan train west with our Mrs. Lester, then travels on to San Francisco."

The next orphan train west!

Callie tried to take it all in. He was giving a sermon tomorrow, and then he was going to San Francisco! The latter wasn't really so surprising, since more and more ministers were going to California. Instead of making herself inconspicuous, she found herself staring at him as she took their damp cloaks.

Reverend Hansel gave her a warm smile as if he were truly interested in her. "Thank you kindly," he said, his brown eyes shining.

"Yes, sir." She tore her eyes from his and turned abruptly, almost running with their umbrellas and cloaks. Should a minister have such an arresting presence? such an effect on a young woman? Best not to consider it! But she'd have to tell Langsdon what she'd learned without a single ounce of effort.

At the cloak rack behind the staircase, she saw Langsdon

on the way to the kitchen with a tray of punch cups. Hurrying by him, she whispered, "Reverend Hansel is preaching tomorrow, escorting the next orphan train west with a Mrs. Lester, and going on to San Francisco!"

Langsdon darted a glance about and saw that no one seemed to notice them in the bustle. "Find out where he's preachin' and then see to it you're at that church tomorrow mornin'. And find out when the orphan train leaves."

Her lips parted in dismay. "How can I do that . . . and how could I possibly go to his church?

"Pretend you're one of those religious fanatics and ask him yourself."

"You know I've never set foot in a church."

"Do it!" Langsdon ordered. "Do it, Callie."

"I'll try," she agreed reluctantly. "My friend Becca goes to church every Sunday. Maybe she'd go with me."

He nodded and rushed off as Becca came around the corner with her arms full of cloaks. Her frilly apron over the black uniform made her look a bit plumper, but her green eyes danced with excitement.

"Aha!" she said, looking from Callie to the departing Langsdon.

"*No* aha, you romantic," Callie replied, making Becca sigh with disappointment.

"Hurry!" Callie reminded her. "They are coming fast now."

She hung the cloaks as quickly as she could, then rushed behind Becca to the front door just in time to catch a scathing glance from Mr. Stane and another armful of damp cloaks.

At last, most of the guests stood about visiting, their punch cups and small plates of hors d'oeuvres in hand. The harpist was playing stately music—the "Minuet in G" by Beethoven, according to Mr. Stane, who knew such things—and the guests seemed to be having a fine time. Despite the scurry of her work, Callie's mind turned to the question of finding out where Reverend Hansel was preaching. Perhaps Becca could inquire.

But when she asked Becca in passing, her friend shook her head, her eyes sparkling with excitement. "Tomorrow I go to church with Thomas for ze first time—and with his family! He asks me when he made ze delivery today. Isn't that something?" At Callie's forlorn look, Becca added, "Ask ze minister for his card and ze time of service, that's all."

Callie swallowed.

"Ze minister will be happy to tell you," Becca assured her. "He has romantic eyes, *ja?*"

"Romantic? I didn't notice—"

Becca shook her head with hopelessness. "Then look!"

"Not at a minister!" Callie replied.

But as she returned to the entryway, she couldn't help remembering Becca's remark. Romantic eyes? Did her friend refer to the same sense of warmth that Callie had seen in them?

At eight-thirty, Mr. Burlington asked for silence so Reverend Brace could say grace in the parlor. Callie stood behind the stairway, but she was too nervous and too far away to make out much of his prayer.

At last the guests were seated for dinner, and she noticed that Reverend Hansel had taken his seat at one of the tables in the music room. He looked up at her, and his brown eyes held hers for a long and unnerving moment before Mr. Stane called her to help with latecomers at the front door.

"You'll be needed to serve water-rr all around," Mr. Stane informed her before opening the door. "Begin in a few minutes. These straitlaced windbags are great ones for drinking water-rr."

That would be her opportunity to speak to Reverend Hansel—as she refilled his water glass, she decided. It would be then or never.

She filled a silver water pitcher and began to make the rounds in the dining room. Despite Mr. Stane's claim, few guests had emptied their water goblets. Table by table, she worked her way to the music room, saving Reverend Hansel's table for last to get up her nerve.

At his table, everyone seemed to be enjoying themselves, talking and laughing as if it didn't matter that a man of God were present. To Callie's surprise, he even seemed to be leading the lively conversation. She'd expected a minister to be very quiet and holy.

"Excuse me," Callie murmured as she filled the water goblets, beginning across the table from him. She darted a glance at his goblet. Almost full. Just then, however, he took it up and drank it down to halfway, his brown eyes on her. She wasn't certain if they were romantic, but there was something joyous and spellbinding about them.

Her hand began to shake as she neared his place at the table. *I beg your pardon*, she would say, *I'd like to know the name of your church and the time of your service.*

She stepped up behind him now, beginning to fill his goblet. "I beg your pardon," she began, her voice shaking, "I-I would like to go to your church . . . I mean to wherever you are speaking . . . that is, preaching tomorrow."

He held back the silver pitcher an instant before water could overflow his goblet. "We'd be pleased to have you come visit," he said, then smiled and unhanded the pitcher. "We can send someone by to pick you up if you like. The church is some distance from the house."

To pick her up? She hadn't intended that!

Everyone at the table seemed to be listening, and the plump matron beside him said, "We would be most happy to stop by for you, dear. Wouldn't we, Henry? It is right on our way."

Her stout husband looked momentarily astounded, then he nodded. "We'll be here at ten minutes before nine on the dot."

Callie knew it was unseemly for her employers' guests to pick up a housemaid for church, and she wished with all of her heart to back out of the arrangement, but her family's welfare depended on it. Likely Langsdon was watching her too. "If-if you're certain," she murmured.

"We're certain," the woman assured her most kindly. "Ten minutes before nine."

"Thank you." Callie noted that their name cards said Mr. and Mrs. Wharton. "Thank you, then."

"Don't forget," Reverend Hansel called after her.

She nodded nervously at him and hurried on.

If Mr. Stane found out, there'd be trouble. Inappropriate conduct for a servant, he'd call it. Fraternizing with her betters. But wouldn't Langsdon be pleased!

As she crossed the room, she felt as if she were in a dream. At length, she caught Langsdon's eye and gave a nod; she'd been able to accomplish all that he'd asked. It seemed as if a force were setting everything in motion. Maybe fate . . . or maybe God, she thought, uncertain of the difference.

After dinner, the guests retired to the rows of chairs that Callie had helped to set up in the drawing room. When most of the crowd was settled, Reverend Brace stood by the white marble fireplace to speak. Callie busied herself with the chairs on the edges of the room, straining to hear every word.

"Most of you know about the Children's Aid Society, which began with the goal of offering street children educational and trade opportunities," he began. One of our first moves was to establish industrial schools, but attendance was sporadic and only a limited number of children learned a useful trade.

"From the beginning," he continued, "we had Sabbath day lectures to help change the course of their young lives. Alas, we learned that such lectures had little effect. When and if the children came, they were rowdy, profane, and irreverent. Sometimes their salutations to us were showers of stones. Sometimes a general scrimmage occurred over the benches, and sometimes visitors or missionaries were pelted by some opposition gang or bitter enemies of the lads who attended the meeting."

The guests murmured their dismay, and, despite a glimpse of Mr. Stane scowling at her, Callie occupied herself with directing the latecomers to chairs as if it were her assigned duty.

Reverend Brace went on, "I feel a great affection for these children, especially for the newsboys. They have a love of life and a sense of honor that makes them well worth saving from the hardships of the streets. And they do give amazing replies. One minister asked them, 'In this parable, my boys, of Pharisee and the publican, what is meant by the 'publican'?' Came the answer, 'Alderman, sire, wot keeps an ale house!'"

His audience laughed, then quickly quieted.

Reverend Brace added, "Asked about 'the great end of man'—When is he happiest? How would you feel happiest?—a boy replied, 'When we'd plenty of hard cash, sir!' "

The guests laughed again, and Reverend Brace smiled himself before going on. "Still another missionary asked, 'Boys, when your father and mother forsake you, who will take you up?' Their reply was serious and realistic, 'The purlice, sir, the purlice.'"

Callie almost joined in the chorus of laughter.

Reverend Brace smiled again, then sighed. "Yet words that come from the depths of a man's or woman's heart will always touch some hidden chord in these children. I often think hymn singing gives them more religious instruction than anything else. They enter into it with gusto, especially on hymns that seem very personal to them, such as 'There's a Rest for the Weary' and 'There's a Light in the Window.'

"Amazingly, though, they have a rather good time of life in some ways—wandering the streets, living by their wits, free from adult supervision. But I also feel that they need to get out of the slums and into homes before it is too late.

"Now some of you will point to our city's orphan asylums as the solution, but I believe that the best of all asylums for the outcast child is the farmer's home. In every American community—especially a Western one, there are many spare places at the table of life. On the farms of America there is always room for one more pair of hands to help with the chores. And with the prevalence of Christian charity, the addition of another child to a farm home is a blessing."

Callie reflected on Langsdon's experience. Yet, seen from Reverend Brace's viewpoint, it seemed a fine idea. She surely wouldn't have wanted to roam the city's streets with her sisters and brothers. Grayton Orphanage had been as dismal as its name, but life on New York's poorest streets struck her as far worse.

"One of the most serious problems facing our Children's Aid Society," Reverend Brace said, "is the lack of financial support, though it costs as little as ten dollars to take a starving orphan from this city's worst streets and place him or her in a good home in the West. In our first year, 1853, prospective donors seemed to think that the hope of wiping out juvenile delinquency in New York City was a mere enthusiasm. Practical men refused to give their support.

The polite skepticism, the benevolent sympathy, the cold indifference, the distrust and doubt made our work tiring and frequently fruitless. Believe me, my friends, no such disagreeable and self-denying work is ever done as begging money."

Callie's heart went out to him, for this talk was probably an appeal for funds, and she could see that he was highly sensitive. She fervently hoped she would never have to beg, though she would do so for her family, if need be.

Suddenly she grew aware of Mr. Stane's stare. From the entryway, he jerked his head sideways to show her she was to help clear the buffet, but she pretended not to notice.

"Mark my words," Brace said, "some of these orphans, by virtue of being placed in fine homes, will become upstanding citizens. Here's a letter from one transplanted newsboy, who showed his satisfaction in this way."

He took up a letter and read, "I have a first-rate home, ten dollars a month, and my board. I tell you, fellows, this is a great deal more than I could scrape up in my best times in New York. We are all on an equality out here, so long as we keep ourselves respectable."

Now Mr. Stane was clearly motioning her out of the room. As she walked out, Callie felt a chill. What if Glenda, Emelie, and Rolland wished to remain in their new homes in Indiana? What if they preferred their new families to her and Langsdon?

Behind her, Reverend Brace was still speaking. "In 1854, we placed out 207 orphans; in 1855, their numbers grew fourfold to 863; in 1856, it was 936 orphans. Last year, 1857, because of our country's financial conditions, it dipped to 742. . . ."

Maybe her sisters and brothers felt reduced to mere numbers, she reflected. Maybe they weren't as content with their new homes as the newsboy who wrote the letter.

It wasn't until the party was ending and the guests leaving that Langsdon handed her a note in passing. "Put it in yer pocket," he muttered.

During the clean-up there was no chance to speak to him or to read the message. Finally everything was restored to order, and the caterers left. At long last, Callie trudged up to her third-floor room and closed the door behind her. She sat down on her hard cot, exhausted, and read, *Get yourself on the orphan train with Hansel. But don't speak of it until you learn that they need a new woman to see to the orphan girls.*

Get herself on the orphan train with Matthew Hansel? How on earth could Langsdon expect her to do that? The Children's Aid Society had already engaged a woman to escort the girls. And where would Langsdon be if she did somehow manage to get on the train? Would he follow later? It wasn't easy to go forward with so many unanswered questions. She read the note again, then tore it to shreds and pushed the pieces deep under her mattress, where surely no one would find them.

The next morning, Callie made her way down the back stairs, careful not to step on the skirt of her new sky blue cotton frock with the white lacy collar and cuffs. Ordinarily, such a handsome outfit would lift her spirits, but at the moment she felt unsettled at the prospect of attending church. She stepped into the kitchen, tidying a cuff, and realized that the servants' table, usually quiet on Sunday mornings, was in an uproar.

"What's happened?" she asked.

"A pair of small paintings is gone," Becca explained as Callie settled on the oak bench beside her. "Ze Italian oil paintings from the hall near ze entryway. Mr. Stane came in full of *donner*."

"The pastoral scenes," Callie recalled. She'd especially enjoyed dusting them and had often pretended to be in them with a loving husband and children, far away in a new life in the Italian countryside. They were valuable paintings, so Mr. Stane would be "full of thunder" indeed.

When he arrived in the kitchen, he peered at her with his bulgy gray eyes. "Ah, Miss Murray! Judging by the shock on your face, it appears you've heard the news."

"Yes."

"Did you see anything at all amiss near the paintings?

You and Becca were nearby a great deal of the evening, handling the cloaks."

Callie racked her brain, trying to remember, then shook her head. "With a house full of guests and caterers running about, there were many who passed by the paintings."

"Think!" Mr. Stane admonished her angrily. "They're small enough to hide under a cloak. Did you notice anyone suspicious?"

She thought again, but nothing unusual came to mind. "I was so busy I can't even remember seeing the paintings last night."

He didn't appear to believe her, and despite her uneasiness about attending church, she felt relief that she'd at least be out from under Mr. Stane's scrutiny.

He leaned his knuckles on the table and seemed to loom over everyone at the table. "If any of you have those paintings, it would be to your benefit to own up now. I shall search ev'ry one of your rooms this morning, whether you are in them or not."

"*Ach, du lieber!*" Becca exclaimed. "You search our rooms? I did not yet make my bed."

"Better me than the police." He drew an irate breath and shook his head. "A butler's lot is thankless, but in fairness to you, I must tell you that I believe the cat'rers and their helpers are the most likely culprits."

For an appalling moment, Langsdon came to Callie's mind. Surely he hadn't stolen the paintings. Mother—and Father—had often spoken against lying and stealing . . . not that they were so righteous themselves. On the other hand, Langsdon had been in prison, where he could have picked up bad habits from hardened prisoners. Among thieves and murderers, stealing two small paintings during the height of a party might seem like nothing more than an adventure. She hoped not.

"Mark my words, I'll find the culprit," Mr. Stane assured them. "Mark my words!"

There was something frightening, even vengeful, beneath his perfect butler facade, Callie reflected as she helped herself to a bowl of porridge. She poured maple syrup over it and spooned up a mouthful, aware of Mr. Stane's scrutiny. Well, let him watch! She had nothing to hide.

"Maybe one o' them caterers," Molly said. "I saw the one with the big mustache eyein' them very paintings."

"There were several cat'rers with large mustaches," Mr. Stane replied. "If the paintings don't show up here, the police and the insurance agency shall take on the cat'rers."

After a short silence, he turned to Callie. "My, aren't you dressed up? Not deserting us this morning, are you?"

Callie drew an indignant breath. "I am going to church."

"To church? I say, that's a first, isn't it?" he asked. When she continued to eat her porridge without answering, he added, "Let's hope you're not attending church in penance."

She stared him straight in the eyes. "It is my business."

"You have a vast amount of private business lately, young lady," he replied. "Let us hope it has nothing to do with the missing paintings."

Callie shot him her huffiest look. "It does not!" She'd eaten very little and was still hungry, but she rose to her feet. "Excuse me, please!"

"Not so fast, Miss Murray," he said, his gray eyes probing hers. "An envelope arrived through the mail slot for you this morning." He took it from his black jacket and handed it to her. "Under the circumstances, I was sorely tempted, but I refrained from reading it."

"Thank you," she replied coolly. She took the envelope and, noting Langsdon's handwriting, slipped it into her handbag and snapped it shut.

It was only eight-thirty, but she whirled away and hurried

outside into the morning damp, tying on her new blue bonnet. As she rounded the brown sandstone mansion, there was no sign of the Whartons' carriage. Because of her anger with Mr. Stane, she would have to cool off in the morning drizzle. She sat down on the damp stone bench and took the envelope from her handbag, grateful to see the seal had not been broken.

Miss Charlotte Murray, it said.

She tore open the envelope, unfolded the writing paper nervously, and read, *Act immediately if the chance comes for you to go with him. Immediately. LMT*

"Acting immediately" meant accompanying Reverend Hansel on the orphan train. She read the words again, then folded up the writing paper and put it into her handbag. Impossible as his plan was, Langsdon surely seemed determined. She would have to be brave and do her part if she wanted her family together.

As she waited, she began to feel watched. Mr. Stane at a window of the mansion, no doubt. But instead of looking back, Callie glanced out at Union Square Park with as much nonchalance as she could muster. This morning only a few walkers made their way on the gravel paths, some of them bound for church—and doubtless not as troubled about it as she was feeling.

On April 1, just last Thursday, the fountain in the middle of the square had been turned on, and its water sparkled despite the dim light. This afternoon there would be ladies and gentlemen strolling the paths, along with neighborhood children rolling their hoops about under the greening trees. If she did move to the state of California, she would truly miss this sight. From what she'd heard of the west coast, it seemed unlikely that they'd have formal parks with fountains in such an uncivilized place.

At long last, the Whartons' horses and carriage pulled

into the Burlingtons' small circular driveway. Callie stood up nervously to make her presence known. The driver, wearing fine livery, stopped the horses and climbed down from his box to open the carriage door for her.

"Good morning, my dear," Mrs. Wharton said cheerily as Callie climbed up into the carriage.

"Good morning," she replied, growing more apprehensive about her mission. How could she possibly go through with this?

Mr. Wharton gave an amiable nod, and Callie sat down on the black leather seat across from them, resisting the impulse to look back at the windows of the mansion for Mr. Stane. He would surely recognize the Whartons.

"It's kind of you to take me to church this morning," she said, her voice sounding quavery.

"It's our pleasure," Mrs. Wharton assured her, the ostrich feather on her hat shaking with the woman's unconcealed delight.

Mr. Wharton gave Callie another nod.

The driver called out to the horses, urging them on, and the carriage jerked forward, almost unseating Mrs. Wharton.

"Oh dear!" she cried, gripping the seat and the side strap. "We shall have to speak to him again about such perilous starts."

"Now, now, my dear," Mr. Wharton said. "It puts a bit of spice in our lives, doesn't it?"

Mrs. Wharton smiled. "It does at that." She turned to Callie. "Tell me, child, what is your name?"

"Callie, ma'am. Short for Charlotte."

The carriage rattled onto the street. "Is this your first time to attend church, Callie?" Mrs. Wharton inquired.

Callie nodded, then with a jolt remembered that Langsdon had told her to act religious. Honesty might be the best policy, but it could also cause trouble. She clutched the carriage seat, fearing that Mrs. Wharton might probe further, but the carriage was taking a corner precariously, distracting her.

Once they'd regained their balance, Mrs. Wharton said, "We hope you'll like our church as much as we do, especially with that wonderful Reverend Hansel speaking. He's a Princeton Seminary graduate, you know, and most highly recommended from Boston and his own village of Sturbridge." She drew a breath. "I do hope he doesn't preach on abolition, though. I've heard more about the evils of slavery than I can abide."

She rushed on with her mixed views on the keeping of slaves. Callie was grateful that her hostess was so talkative. All she had to do was nod or shake her head and put in an occasional "yes, ma'am" or "no, ma'am." Mr. Wharton leaned his head back against his seat and appeared to sleep.

Finally Mrs. Wharton subsided, and there was nothing but the clopping of the horses' hoofs on the cobbled streets, the swaying of the carriage, the bright spring leaves outside the windows, and the vague, fleeting thoughts of whatever might lie ahead in church.

As the carriage came to a stop, Mrs. Wharton announced, "Well, here we are, and all in good time. Our church is said to be one of the most beautiful in the city."

Callie's heart seemed to spiral up to her throat as she eyed the brownstone Gothic edifice. She'd often admired its stained glass windows and fine carillon tower in passing, but she had never dreamed of entering its carved portals. She knew it was where her father's memorial service had taken place, despite his not being a Christian. Her mother had mockingly mentioned his wife and daughter, Abby, attending its services at Easter and Christmas.

Now churchgoers converged from all directions. As the driver helped her down from the carriage, the carillons began to ring out, their deep tones filling the damp morning air. Moments later, the Whartons escorted Callie up the steps, a flurry of greetings surrounding them and many a curious eye directed at her.

Inside, the nave of the church sloped skyward in a great arc, and soft organ music wafted over the people sitting in the walnut pews. The church was as beautiful inside as it was out, Callie thought.

"After you," Mr. Wharton said, and Callie followed Mrs. Wharton and an usher far up the middle aisle to a second row pew. She felt as if everyone were staring at her—a housemaid attending church with her betters. But when she dared to look up, she saw she was mistaken; no one watched her. There was no sign of Reverend Matthew Hansel, either. What if her visit this morning was for naught?

Mrs. Wharton stood aside for Callie to enter the pew, and suddenly Callie felt dreadful to have come under false pretenses. Her face turned hot. Maybe . . . yes, maybe God would punish her—and right here in the second pew of the church where this great crowd would see it!

She sat down, smoothing her blue frock around her. After a moment, when nothing had happened to her, she summoned up the nerve to scrutinize the magnificent stained glass window nearest them. It depicted Christ, arms widespread with tender welcome. The words below said, "I am the way, the truth, and the life; no man cometh unto the Father but by me."

Despite His tender look, the saying struck Callie as fearsome and exclusive. She regarded His stained-glass eyes, and it seemed that He looked straight into her soul.

She glanced away quickly, down to her program, and read, "Oh, that thou hadst hearkened to my commandments! Then had thy peace been like a river, and thy righteousness like the waves of the sea. . . ."

She didn't know God's commandments! Perhaps that was why she often felt so nervous. Well, she did know about lying and stealing, and she felt terrible about the deception and evasiveness that had become her lot since Langsdon had returned to her life. She looked again at the words: "Then had thy peace been like a river." Becca had once mentioned something like that.

She noticed a message neatly chalked on a piece of slate at the side of what she guessed must be the altar. Likely if she knew what was to take place, she'd be less apt to make a fool of herself. Reading along, she saw the sermon was titled to match the words on her program, "Peace Like a River," and the opening anthem was "Peace."

What she wouldn't do to feel more peaceful!

Now the music changed to a lively marching rhythm, and all around her, hymnal pages rustled. Beside her, the Whartons rose to their feet with the congregation, and Callie stood up belatedly. Mrs. Wharton smiled kindly and handed her an open hymnal, then turned to sing with her husband while Callie eyed the words and tried to sing along:

Lead us, heavenly Father, lead us
O'er the world's tempestuous sea;
Guard us, guide us, keep us, feed us,
For we have no help but Thee;
Yet possessing every blessing,
If our God our Father be.

Her head whirled with confusion, but the music was sprightly, and she went on to the second verse.

Savior, breathe forgiveness o'er us,
All our weakness Thou dost know;
Thou didst tread this earth before us,
Thou didst feel its keenest woe;
Lone and dreary, faint and weary,
Through the desert Thou didst go.

The words seemed clear enough, yet they left her befuddled. Langsdon's suggestion that she feign being a Christian would likely take more than pretending she'd been baptized and uttering "Isn't that a blessing!"

At least she knew the tune now, she thought, as the congregation started the last verse.

Spirit of our God, descending,
Fill our hearts with heavenly joy,
Love with every passion blending,
Pleasure that can never cloy;
Thus provided, pardoned, guided,
Nothing can our peace destroy.

Nothing can our peace destroy? her mind repeated as the others sang the "Amen." How could she lay hold of such peace . . . especially right now, with trying to get on the orphan train?

Suddenly she saw that everyone's head was bowed, and there stood Reverend Matthew Hansel and another minister before them in their black robes. The other minister began to pray about surrender, obedience, and other perplexing matters. Next they read aloud from the front of their hymnals, and Mrs. Wharton gave her another smile.

Likely she's glad I can read, Callie speculated.

After announcements and another hymn, the minister introduced The Reverend Mr. Matthew Hansel.

"As many of you know, he will soon be taking another train of orphans to the state of Indiana, where the people have already given our orphans such an open-hearted reception. For those of you who wish to contribute funds, food, or clothing, we leave in one week."

Callie sat riveted to her seat. One week! There'd be no chance to go on such short notice! Langsdon's secret plans for their family to be reunited would go awry. What would they do? She couldn't bear to spend the rest of her life working in the Burlington mansion.

As Reverend Hansel stepped to the pulpit, his brown eyes stopped on Callie, and she was unable to glance away. He smiled just a trifle, then asked, "Shall we pray?"

Callie swallowed hard as she bowed her head again, but his words about hearts being acceptable in the sight of a Rock and Redeemer barely penetrated her consciousness.

When she opened her eyes, he asked in his nice, deep voice, "Do you have peace? Do you have daily peace, as well as peace about decisions large and small? Do you have peace about your alliances with your fellow man? Peace when the storms of life rage about you?"

He paused for them to consider. "Peace with God brings the peace of God in you. A peace that settles the nerves, fills the mind, floods the spirit, and in the midst of an uproar, gives us peace as a river in our minds and hearts . . . a peace that passes all understanding."

His eyes seemed to fasten upon Callie's, and the words began to whirl around her. She didn't quite understand, but, even so, a mantle of peace descended all about her, and she wondered if it had come to everyone else there, too.

Reverend Hansel read from his Bible, "Be anxious for nothing, but in everything, by prayer and supplication with thanksgiving, let your requests be made known unto God. And the peace of God, which passeth all understanding, shall keep your heart and minds through Christ Jesus."

He turned to them. "Scripture, from the Old Testament to the New, is full of references to peace. In Leviticus, God tells us that if we walk in His statutes and keep His commandments, He will give us peace. Christ told us at the end of His earthly ministry, 'Peace I leave with you, my peace I give unto you, not as the world giveth, give I unto you. Let not your heart be troubled or afraid.'"

Every word seemed to be directed at her.

"With financial calamity falling all about this city, do we turn to the Lord of peace, or do we turn to our own devices?" he asked the congregation. "When we are beset by troubles, do we pray and fully listen?

"In one week, God willing, I set forth on another orphan train for Indiana, and we have just received grievous news. Mrs. Lester, the fine woman who was to accompany the girls on the trip, suffered a terrible accident early this morning. It was still dark when she heard a noise and went to investigate. She is uncertain whether she fell or was pushed down a flight of stairs."

Callie clutched her throat. Langsdon? Surely he wouldn't go to such lengths as pushing a woman down a flight of stairs!

Reverend Hansel went on. "Fortunately Mrs. Lester is not badly hurt, but she will be unable to accompany the orphan train. We asked God whether the trip, which required a great deal of preparation both here and in the various towns, should be postponed. When I arrived at your church this morning, I still awaited God's answer. And this morning, as we sang the anthem about peace, God gave me peace about the entire undertaking. He has it in His mighty hands."

Could it be that God meant her to go? Callie wondered.

She scarcely heard another word of the sermon. Instead, she pondered what to say to Reverend Hansel if an opportunity to go presented itself. Should she say she'd always wanted to see Indiana? That she had kin in Indiana but couldn't afford the fare to go see them? Surely she shouldn't tell him right off that she wished to travel on to Missouri and California.

Finally the service ended and the people rose to their feet and began to greet one another.

Mrs. Wharton turned to Callie. "I do hope that you

enjoyed it, Callie. That Reverend Hansel is so handsome that I can't imagine any young woman not hanging onto his every word. Those brown eyes—"

Mr. Wharton took his wife by the elbow. "Shall we thank the young man for his sermon?"

"Yes . . . yes, of course," Mrs. Wharton replied, abashed. As they moved along in the line of people leading to the front entrance, Callie wondered what to say to him. Her mind spun with the problems of going, of guiding a large group of orphans on a train, of finding Glenda, Emelie, and Rolland in Indiana. Suddenly she stood before Reverend Hansel.

Instead of admiring his sermon as had those before her, she blurted out, "I would like to help with the girls on the orphan train."

His lips parted in surprise, then he beamed at her. "I knew God was sending someone. I only wondered who. Do you have experience with children?"

"Yes, I do. I helped raise four younger sisters and brothers, and I've assisted a governess. I truly enjoy working with children."

"Wonderful. Can you speak with me after everyone has left?"

Callie shook her head nervously. "I'm sorry. I'm leaving with the Whartons."

"Why, I remember you now. You helped serve at the Burlingtons' dinner last night. Shall I call on you at their house?"

"No! Oh, no, they mustn't know . . . yet."

He blinked, then nodded in apparent understanding. "Perhaps you could join me at the Children's Aid Society quarters this afternoon? It would be an opportunity to become acquainted with the children, too."

She was holding up the line of people behind her. "Yes,

certainly," she agreed, scarcely believing her own words.

"Two o'clock?" he asked, handing her a card with the address. "Can you find it?"

"Yes, I'll be there," Callie replied.

"Coming, Callie?" Mrs. Wharton asked, looking back at them with curiosity.

"Yes, I-I had something to tell Reverend Hansel."

Mrs. Wharton gave her another peculiar look and scurried after her impatient husband.

Callie followed along, her mind in a tumult.

Fortunately the Whartons were quiet riding home in the carriage, and Callie stared out the window, oblivious to the places they passed.

When she returned to the Burlington mansion, she made her way toward the kitchen. On Sundays, the Burlingtons dined out after church, but the pantry was open to the servants. She would eat leftovers from last night's dinner, then get ready to visit Reverend Hansel.

What did one discuss with a minister? she wondered. And what exactly should she tell him about herself? Should she mention Langsdon? Probably not. Most worrisome of all, what if Reverend Hansel asked whether she was a Christian? It seemed a proper question for such an undertaking.

She was glad to see Becca already in the kitchen. Dare she tell her friend what was happening? If only Langsdon hadn't insisted upon secrecy!

Becca beamed at her. "I got together a picnic for us from last night's leftovers. We eat outside, *ja?*"

"*Ja,*" Callie answered.

Becca gave a laugh and pressed a basket of food into Callie's arms. "I get a blanket to put on ze stone benches. Ze sun is shining now. *Ach*, it is shining like never before!"

"What are you talking about?" Callie asked.

Becca grinned and put a warning finger to her lips. "I tell you in a minute."

Outside, they headed for the back garden and settled on a stone bench. Callie looked at her friend quizzically. "Becca Schumakker, what are you being so secretive about?"

"*Ach, du lieber!*" Becca exclaimed, then gave her a sheepish smile. "*Ich bin verliebt!* Oh, Callie, I am really fallen in love!"

"Again?"

"Zis time he loves me, too!" Becca announced, her green eyes sparkling with wonder. "Thomas . . . since the first time he saw me, he told me today. And I have been watching him since the beginning, too!"

"Where is he now?"

"Coming! *Donner wetter!* He is here in half an hour! We ride in town in ze delivery wagon to talk. Romantic, *ja?*"

She was bouncing so with excitement that Callie couldn't bear to put a damper on the day with her doubts—or her own problems. Becca would probably say she was *verruckt*—crazy—to take orphans across the country in the company of a minister. And this was no time to tell about Langsdon or her sisters and brother in Indiana, either.

Finally Callie asked, "Do you think Thomas would mind dropping me off at the Children's Aid Society?"

"I think he likes it very much, to meet my best friend," Becca replied happily. "We eat fast now, then get ready to go. But you cannot make eyes at him. You must promise! You look like an angel in your new blue dress and bonnet."

Callie smiled ruefully. "*Ja*, I will not make eyes at him."

Becca laughed. "Zen I help you make more dresses. It is fun, *ja?* Making dresses together?"

"*Ja*, it is fun to sew with a fine seamstress like you," Callie acknowledged. "Otherwise I would not look like an angel in my dress. I would look like a wretch snared by blue cotton and knotted threads."

At one-thirty, the two of them stood outside near the mansion's back door, Callie wearing her sky blue frock and Becca dressed in a pale green dress with a showy, squared-off white collar.

At exactly two o'clock, Thomas drove up in a delivery wagon pulled by a sway-backed gray nag. The tan wagon was enclosed, and on its side letters spelled out, "T. WAR-RICK, GROCER." Two gold-painted cornucopias overflowing with fruits and vegetables curved alongside the smaller letters that said, "Deliveries made anywhere in New York City."

Thomas whoaed the old horse and jumped down, his eyes lighting on Becca with pleasure and Callie with surprise.

"This is my good friend, Callie," Becca said, tugging her forward by the elbow. Her voice turned strangely shy. "We can give her a ride across town, please, *ja*, Thomas?"

Thomas tipped his tan cap. "That we can. Pleased to meet yer, Callie."

"Pleased to meet you, too," she returned, "and thank you."

It was beyond her that Becca thought Thomas Warrick handsome. He was gangly with blue eyes, black hair that stuck out from under the edges of his cap, a great Adam's apple, and what appeared to be a twice-broken nose. He had an endearing smile, though, and looked genuinely pleased to take her along.

He helped them up onto the delivery wagon seat, settling Becca in the middle beside his seat. "Comfortable?" he asked her.

"*Ja*, fine," Becca answered, eyeing him with adoration as

he hurried around the horse and swung up to the driver's seat.

"You comfortable too?" he asked Callie.

"Yes, very comfortable, thank you," she replied. She recalled the old saying about love being blind. Blind or not, she wished she might someday find someone to love her.

Thomas touched the reins to the horse and called out, "Get on, boy. Get on."

They rattled along past the front of the Burlington mansion, and Callie remarked, "At least Mr. Stane isn't home to spy on us. Where do you think he goes on Sunday afternoons?"

"To friends," Becca said. "He claims he has friends. Let's talk about anything but him, *ja?*"

"*Ja,*" Thomas agreed with the same teasing humor that Callie used on her friend. He rubbed the top of his bumpy nose, though, as if with worry.

There was a bit of Don Quixote about his expression, Callie thought. He looked like a modern-day adventurer who tilted with windmills.

Becca ventured, "Your family, Thomas, did they like me?"

"Don't want to talk about that now, either," he answered, his voice flattening.

Becca's eyes widened with dismay, then she clasped her hands in the lap of her green frock without another word.

"What's important is *I* like yer," Thomas stated firmly.

They sat in a shocked silence. Finally he glanced at Callie. "What's the address where yer going?"

She took out Reverend Hansel's card and read the address to him. "The Children's Aid Society," she explained.

"The Children's Aid Society?" Thomas repeated. "Yer don't want to go to that part of town! It's the scummiest section of New York—full of lyin' beggars and the worst kind of street Arabs!"

"That's where I need to go," Callie replied. "If you don't wish to take me. . ."

"Ain't that," he answered, more composed. "Just don't like droppin' yer off there. You heard what our almshouse commissioner said of that section? And about the children?"

Callie nodded. "I know more than I like. I lived in an orphanage on the outskirts of the city myself. And I read the article in the Burlingtons' newspaper."

The almshouse commissioner had written the unvarnished truth about the poverty and utter confusion of immigrants who came to America by ship's steerage, then had no place to go and nothing to do but wander the streets of New York in wretchedness. Even families who began to get a foothold often couldn't support their young, who turned to all kinds of demeaning vices.

"Why do you want to go there, Callie?" Becca asked.

"I have to meet Reverend Hansel," she explained. " I promise to be careful."

"*Ach!* Ze only good I see about it is that Reverend Hansel is very handsome."

"Becca!" Callie objected. "What a thing to say!"

"It's the truth," Becca replied.

"Well, I don't know what yer up to," Thomas put in, "but the first thing to do is hang that handbag strap over yer arm and clutch the handbag under yer armpit."

"I will, then," Callie answered, though the strap was so short it would cut into her shoulder.

Except for the steady clip-clop of the horse's hoofs on the cobblestones, they rode on in silence. Callie guessed that Becca was worried about what Thomas had to say regarding his parents, and Callie worried about what lay ahead for her.

Finally she said, "Isn't it a beautiful day? Look at the trees leafing out everywhere."

Thomas pounced on the subject, and nature remained the topic of conversation as they rode through the worsening neighborhoods. Finally he halted the horse in front of the Children's Aid Society. He eyed the ragged street children and the tough Bowery boys who lurked nearby. "Yer want us to pick you up later?"

"No, but I thank you," Callie said. "I have money to hire a hack to get home." As promised, she inched her handbag strap up to her shoulder and wedged the bag under her armpit.

Thomas eyed an old beggar who shuffled toward them, rattling his tin cup. "We'll pull by on the way back anyhow. Not likely to find a hack down in this section."

"Thank you," she said as he helped her down from the seat.

He waved aside a younger but angry beggar who brandished a cane. "We ain't rich folk," he muttered, then fished in his pocket and tossed a coin into the beggar's cup. He turned to Callie. "We'll be back in two hours. Take care of yerself!"

"I will," she promised, thanking him.

While he hurried around to the street side of the delivery wagon, Callie managed a brave smile at Becca. Turning, she squared her shoulders and headed through a crowd of dirty street urchins wrestling about near the Aid Society door. The soiled hand-lettered sign, which simply said "Come in," hung askew on the door.

As she entered the building, the pungent smell of unwashed bodies and harsh disinfectant assailed her. She choked, then swallowed with determination. Equally disturbing was the sight before her: a roomful of motley children sitting on battered benches in a battered room. These were the kind of children, perhaps even the very children, she would have to care for! Surprisingly, they were listening with such great interest to Reverend Hansel, who stood before them, that they scarcely noticed her.

He glanced over the children and smiled at Callie. "Boys and girls, Mrs. Lester, who as you know was planning to go with us on the train, has had a fall. She'll be unable to join us on our grand adventure next week. This is Miss Murray, who we hope will be accompanying us."

Callie gave a nervous nod and smile as she looked around the room, still not accustomed to the fierce smell. Most of the children turned suspicious glances on her, and even the few who returned her timorous smile appeared distrustful. A good many of them had dull, almost vacant eyes. Troubled children. A room full of troubled children who would be difficult to accompany anywhere, let alone across the country in search of adoptive homes.

Silence fell as they inspected her.

"Ain't she beans!" exclaimed a pointy-nosed boy.

Matthew Hansel grinned. "I'm not so sure about her being beans, Yorker, but she strikes me as a very nice young lady, and I hope you will treat her as such."

To Callie he explained, "Yorker, the young man who has complimented you, is one of our city's fine newsboys."

Yorker asked him, "You goin' ter marry 'er?"

Reverend Hansel's face flushed slightly, and he gave an amazed laugh. "Well, Yorker, I just met her last night. Why do you ask? Are you thinking of proposing to Miss Murray yourself?"

The children roared with laughter.

"A good one, Mr. Hansel!" called out a boy wearing a newsboy cap. "You got old Yorker."

Callie's own face felt red, and she was glad to see the minister busy himself finding a chair for her from the few dilapidated relics that lined the front wall.

"Ah, here's our best chair, Miss Murray," he said, bringing it around so she might sit near the children. The yellow pine chair was no prize, but its legs were unbroken, and he offered it to her with old-fashioned courtliness. "Please be seated. I'm just finishing the parable of the prodigal son for my guests here."

She sat down, the object of the children's scrutiny, still clutching her handbag under her arm. "Please continue," she urged.

"Where were we?" he asked the children.

"The prod'gal son comin' home and scared what they'd do to 'im," piped a girl of about twelve. "Likely thought they'd beat the tar out of 'im, like my old man did 'fore he died."

The girl wore a dress several sizes too small for her, and her dirty brown hair hung in tangles on her narrow shoulders. Yet she was one of the few girls who looked bright-eyed and hopeful.

"Thank you," Reverend Hansel replied. "Yes, the prodigal son saw his father coming out of the house. Jesus tells us when the prodigal son was yet a great way off, his father saw him and ran, and fell on his neck, and kissed him. It's my guess he said, 'How I've missed you, my child! Welcome home! Oh, welcome home!'"

"Sounds too good ter be true," groused Yorker.

"Yeah," another newsboy echoed.

Considering her own father, Callie had to agree with them.

"It does at that," Reverend Hansel said. "But it's an example—a parable—that Jesus told so we'd understand how God feels about us. Who is that father of the prodigal son like?"

"Like God, I'm guessin', from what you told us other times," one boy answered.

"Like God, waitin' ter welcome us home," another added.

Callie was appalled to find tears welling up in her eyes.

"Yes," the minister replied. "God is the perfect father that none of us has here on earth. And we all have some of that stubborn prodigal son in us. God wants to forgive us and welcome us home. Shall we pray now?"

He bowed his head and began to pray, and Callie pulled a handkerchief from her dress pocket to blow her nose. How could she pretend to be a Christian who simply wanted to do her Christian duty? How could she lie to this man?

After the prayer, a woman brought a plate piled high with pork pies, and the children rushed her, scuffling to reach the food. Yorker, smaller than most, pulled off a tattered boot and walloped one of the boys over the head with it.

"Stop it!" yelled his victim, a tall, skinny blond boy with a starved wolfish face.

"Stop hordin' them pies, Franz!" Yorker told him. "Yipes, man, don't they smell good! As good as Franz here smells bad!"

"Boys!" Reverend Hansel interrupted their raucous laughter. "Let's show Miss Murray we have good manners."

"Ha!" Yorker laughed, pulling his boot on again. "We ain't got good manners, and we ain't goin' to get 'em, either."

"Then you'll never have a pleasant life in this world," Reverend Hansel told him. "It's asking for trouble not to exercise some manners."

Yorker stuffed most of a pork pie into his mouth and shot the others an ill-tempered look.

Reverend Hansel walked over to Callie. "The girls are easier to handle. They don't fight as much. But it's not always pleasant, taking a train load of orphans west."

"I guess not," Callie replied. "But I . . . I've always liked children." She glanced at the bedraggled group of girls who looked as if they slept in alleys. Likely they'd think her job as a maid in the Burlington mansion was as fine as being a princess.

"Getting them placed in homes can be most gratifying work," he said, then eyed her carefully. "I'm curious as to why you want to go along."

She froze for an instant, wishing she'd thought out some answers. Best to tell at least half the truth. "I want to go to friends in Missouri, and I don't have the funds. If I can get to Indiana, I could afford the rest of it."

That is, if Langsdon gives me back my money, she thought.

"And the Burlingtons don't yet know?" he asked.

She shook her head. "I don't want to tell them I'm going unless it's certain. It's hard to find new employment in the city now."

His brown eyes filled with assurance. "I'd say with only one week to locate someone to accompany the girls, you can count yourself as almost certain. I would, however, like some recommendation. Family perhaps?"

"I'm an orphan," she told him. No sense in telling about her shirttail family in Missouri and California.

"I'm sorry, that was foolish of me. May I speak to someone on the Burlington household staff? Perhaps the butler?"

"Oh, no!" Callie blurted. "Please, not Mr. Stane!"

Her vehemence took him by surprise, and he asked, "Why not, if I may ask?"

"He-he'd make trouble for me."

"Doesn't he like you?" Reverend Hansel asked.

"Just the opposite," Callie confessed. "He likes me too much. It would be better to talk to my friend Becca, who's coming in a while to pick me up. She knows me best. Or even the Burlingtons, once it's almost sure."

Reverend Hansel gave a nod. "I'll speak with Becca first. I'm impressed by your manners and speech. You are very articulate for having lived in an orphanage."

Callie smiled up at him. "I had a British nanny when I was a girl. And my mother always told us to learn all we can and to be well-spoken, and we'd always be . . . she called it, 'above ourselves.'"

"Was your mother a Christian?"

Callie pressed her lips together and shook her head. She stood waiting for what she knew would be the fatal question. *Was she a Christian herself?*

Just then Yorker yelled, "Stop it, you booger!" and hit another boy, starting a wild scuffle across the room. Fists flew and benches banged over on the floor as the orphans shouted riotously.

Reverend Hansel hurried into their midst, calling out, "Please, boys, no fighting!" and pulled them off each other. It took some doing.

Once the fighting stopped, they righted the benches and sat on them, and Reverend Hansel led them in hymns. They did seem to enjoy "There's a Rest for the Weary," as Reverend Brace had mentioned at last night's dinner. The heartening words filled the shabby room, making a few vacant eyes glimmer.

The poor dears seemed to be weary with life, too, Callie reflected. The hymn singing gave them—and her—more hope.

When Thomas drove up in the delivery wagon, Reverend Hansel escorted her to the door, speaking quietly. "Now that you've seen some of our children, are you certain you'd want to accompany them?"

She had no choice in the matter, she reminded herself. "Yes—I'll do it."

He gave her a thoughtful nod, then looked out at Becca and Thomas sitting on the front seat of the delivery wagon.

"Please," Callie said. "If you ask her for a reference, please don't tell about the orphan train yet. Maybe . . . you could just ask what kind of a person I am?"

Becca and Thomas eyed them with interest, and Callie introduced Reverend Hansel to them the best that she could.

Thomas tipped his tan cap. "Pleased ter meet yer."

Becca beamed. "*Ja*, I am pleased to meet you."

They stared at Callie expectantly, as if waiting for her to get in. She turned to Reverend Hansel, who looked uncertain himself about asking in front of her.

She gave a little laugh. "He wants to ask you what kind of a person I am. You know, like a commendation."

Becca looked taken aback, and Thomas eyes bulged with astonishment. Becca recovered first.

"Callie, she is a good person. Very good, clean and, *ja*, she works hard. *Und* ze Burlingtons, they like her, too."

"Don't know her much meself," Thomas added, "but Becca's a good judge o' character, she is. Can't pull much over on her."

"*Ach!*" Becca said with a laugh. She looked tempted to elbow him in the ribs, but resisted, and Thomas gave a good laugh himself.

"Thank you," Reverend Hansel said, smiling. He lent Callie a hand to climb up to the delivery wagon seat with them. "Exactly what I presumed."

"Why do you ask?" Becca inquired, her green eyes curious.

Callie caught her breath, wondering what he'd say.

"She might be helping me with the children," he replied, to her vast relief. He'd made it sound as though she might just come in to the society's quarters on her day off.

"*Ach, ja*, she has a gift with children," Becca put in. "She took good care of ze Burlington's grandchildren last summer and was very good with them."

A gift with children?

Callie was unsure what that meant, but it was true that

she had been surprised at the enjoyment she had felt in caring for them.

"Thank you," Reverend Hansel said again. Then he turned to her. "I'll let you know as soon as possible. Most likely, I'll send you a letter by courier."

He wants to check more! Callie thought with alarm. She'd need an actual letter of recommendation. "I'll . . . I'll send you references," she told him and quickly climbed up to the wagon seat.

"Fine. I'd appreciate one from your regular minister."

She panicked, but his brown eyes glowed with confidence as she turned to him.

"A pleasure to have met you, Becca and Thomas," he added, sounding as if he meant it. "If you'll excuse me, the children are waiting." He gave a cheerful wave, and Thomas urged on the horse.

As they clip-clopped away down the cobblestone street, Becca asked, "What is happening, Callie? A letter from your minister, when you don't even go to church?"

"Nothing is happening. At least, nothing I can talk about yet," she returned. "Please don't ask . . . and please don't tell anyone."

Becca's eyes searched hers, then she nodded. "*Ja, naturlich. Du bist meine*— You are my friend."

Callie took a grateful breath and, at last, sat back against the hard seat.

Langsdon would know how to get a letter from a minister. And he'd know how to keep Reverend Hansel from speaking to Mr. Stane and the Burlingtons about her. Most important, she had a feeling he'd know how to make her sound very good . . . like a Christian.

4

They had ridden for some time in the delivery wagon, bumping along on the cobblestone streets, before Callie realized how stiffly her best friend sat and that her eyes were slightly red. "What is it, Becca? What's wrong? I've been so addled by my own troubles, I didn't see you were beset by your own."

"*Ja*, I been crying," Becca admitted, honest as ever.

Callie shot a glance at Thomas, ready to spring to her friend's defense if he had wronged her, but he looked heartsick himself. "Whatever has happened? Or dare I ask?"

Becca shook her head in despair. "*Es schrecklich* . . . terrible!" Tears shone in her eyes. "Thomas's family, they don't like that I am German. They want him to marry . . . an English girl!"

The problem wasn't that unusual with so many immigrants flooding into the city, Callie knew, but saying so wouldn't help poor Becca.

"*Und mit Muttie*—my mama, in Germany. . . . I was hoping to have here a mama to love me."

Callie's heart went out to her friend. "I'm sorry, Becca. As sorry as can be."

"Yer can be sorry for me, too," Thomas said, keeping his eyes on the sway-backed gray nag pulling their wagon. "It hurts like a stab in my heart. It's fearful to be in love like this, and I been in love with Becca fer almost a year now. They want me to marry the most awful twit of a girl who's skinny and ugly on top of being light in 'er 'ead."

"Then I'm sorry for you, too, Thomas," Callie told him.

"They say they'll give the grocery business to my younger brother if I don't marry who they want," he added. "You know the English ideas about the older brother inheritin' the family's trade!"

"I've heard of it," Callie answered, "but you're an American now. Is it still so important here in a new land?"

"It is ter them," he answered morosely. "They're makin' a fierce issue of it. And all my life, my 'eart's been dead set on grocerin'."

"I'm truly sorry, Thomas."

She saw only one good point to their heartache. They were so preoccupied with it that they neglected to inquire into her visit with Reverend Hansel.

They dropped her off at the back door of the Burlington mansion. "So we can say our good-byes alone," Thomas explained in a pinched tone, "without that snoop of a butler peering down his nose at us."

"I wouldn't put it past him," Callie answered. "I don't relish seeing him myself."

Once inside, she saw that Thomas had reason to be concerned. Mr. Stane stood in the back hallway, his gray eyes glinting with self-satisfaction.

"I've been following your movements, Miss Murray."

"You've what?"

"Even last night, it was obvious you were a trifle too interested in the Children's Aid Society . . . or, more likely, in The Reverend Hansel himself. You not only went to church to see him this morning, but you spent a good long time with him at the society's headquarters this afternoon."

"How do you know?" she asked in shock.

"I have my sources," he replied, undaunted. "As I've told you before, a good butler knows what transpires in his household.

"I don't see what young women find so romantic about ministers," he added, sounding more British than ever, "but apparently there is some attraction."

Determined to hear no more about it, Callie started for the back stairs.

"One moment, Miss Murray!"

He grabbed her shoulder and swung her toward him. Holding her firmly, a sly smile slowly pulled at his lips. "You don't think you can glide past me quite that easily, do you now?"

Her knees went weak as she pulled away from him. "Please unhand me, Mr. Stane, or I'll be forced to tell!"

"And whom are you going to tell?" he inquired. "You might remember that I am highly regarded in this household and was employed by the Burlingtons even before they moved here. My word stands for far more than that of a young housemaid who has only two years of service here." He paused for effect. "Moreover, we're the only ones present in the mansion at the moment."

"Mr. Stane!"

At that instant, someone pounded on the side window, and Mr. Stane loosened his grip on her.

Callie tore away and, while he hurried to the window, she raced for the back stairs. Her shoes pounded up the wooden steps as she ran, but at the landing she paused and turned.

He was not pursuing her, but was yelling out the back door, "Whoever you are, I'll set the police on you! This is no neighborhood for pranks! Do you hear? I'll set the police on you!"

At that moment Mr. Burlington shouted from the hallway,

"What's the trouble out there, Mr. Stane?"

"Mr. Burlington!" the butler exclaimed. "I-I didn't realize you were home."

"We just arrived and let ourselves in. Who is out there, Mr. Stane? And who is running up the back steps?"

"Miss Murray, sir. She just came home, and then someone pounded on the window. It scared the poor girl half to death, and I was attempting to investigate."

Callie rushed on up to the third floor, not caring to hear more of his lies. Whoever had knocked at the window could not have been more timely for her sake—and to save Mr. Stane's neck. But who could it have been?

Safely in her bedroom, she locked the door behind her and hurried to the window. Pulling the sheer white curtain aside, she peered down at the back garden. No sign of anyone. Well, whoever it was, she felt grateful to be saved from Mr. Stane's clutches. If she could, she'd leave the mansion this very moment just to be done with him.

Growing calmer, she sat down on her narrow bed and eyed her meager wardrobe, which hung on wooden knobs on the wall. The black uniforms had been provided by the Burlingtons and belonged to the household. Beside them hung her faded blue calico frock and a newer one of yellow calico. Best to change into the blue. Old as it was, if and when she did go with the orphan train, she'd have to take it along with her.

In her chest of drawers, she recalled, was a length of fine brown cotton that would make a more suitable frock for accompanying the children and meeting their prospective parents. Perhaps Becca would help her sew it this week, trimming it with a white collar and cuffs.

A pebble hit her window, and Callie leapt to her feet.

Running to the window, she pulled the sheer curtain aside again. Langsdon! She tugged up the window and stuck out her head.

"What is it?" she whispered down to him.

"Come down!" he returned urgently. "In the park . . . other side of the fountain."

Just then, the back door creaked open, and Mr. Stane shouted, "Who's out in the bushes? Who is it? Speak up!"

Callie pulled back from the window and listened.

"Speak up, I say!" Mr. Stane demanded again.

Gathering her courage, Callie called down, "It was me opening my window for air, Mr. Stane. It's warm upstairs this afternoon."

"Ah," he replied, looking up at her. "Well, hurry on down. The Burlingtons have retired to their rooms. We can have supper together. I kept back a bottle of champagne and a tin of caviar for the occasion."

The nerve of the man! she thought. Didn't her rebuffing him just minutes earlier sink it at all? In any case, it was best to appease him. "In a while," she replied.

He'd doubtless helped himself to such delicacies from their employers' provisions, but that wasn't her problem. Right now, she had to slip down the main stairway and escape out the front door. If caught in the family quarters on her day off, she'd have to bluff . . . perhaps say she wondered if Mrs. Burlington needed assistance since Becca wasn't yet home.

She let herself out of her room and tiptoed around to the stairway that led to the family's quarters. No one was in the hallway, and Mrs. Burlington's door was closed.

Callie crept down the front stairs undetected and let herself out the front door. Relieved, she crossed the street to Union Square Park and glanced back to see if Mr. Stane were watching at the windows or door.

No sign of him. Likely he was in the kitchen readying champagne and caviar for the two of them. He'd be furious, but she'd deal with that later. Pretending to be out for a late afternoon stroll, she walked slowly along the gravel path toward the fountain. As usual, children rolled their hoops along the paths, young couples sat courting on the park benches, and the people strolling by seemed most interested in the rhododendron bushes lining the paths.

She headed past the fountain, and there sat Langsdon on a park bench, leaning back in such a leisurely pose that passersby would likely think he owned one of the square's mansions, if not half of New York City.

He patted the bench beside her. "Sit down happily, as if you are meeting your suitor, my dear."

"Langsdon!"

He gave a laugh. "You can act as affronted as you like, but I saved you from old Stane, didn't I?"

"It was you who knocked at the window! Thank goodness!"

Langsdon grinned. "I remembered what you said about him."

"Well, he hasn't improved. Worst of all, he's suspicious of me. There were paintings missing after last night's dinner, and he all but blamed me! Can you imagine! When I protested, he thought it might be the caterers or their helpers. And he knows I went to see Reverend Hansel this afternoon."

"He followed you," Langsdon said. "Rode after you on Burlington's own saddle horse, and I rode along some distance behind him. He's too much of a fool to have even looked back. Thinks he can spy on people without anyone spyin' on him. Thinks everything's always goin' to go his way."

"Why do you say that?"

"I've learned more about your Mr. Stane. More than I plan to tell you."

"Langsdon, do be careful!"

Her brother smiled adoringly at her for the benefit of a

young couple passing by. When they were well past, he asked, "What does the fine Reverend Hansel say about your goin' on the orphan train?"

"Everything was perfect, then he asked for a letter from my minister," Callie said. "You know I don't have one!"

"A letter from 'your minister' is easy to arrange," Langsdon assured her. "I'll see that he has it tomorrow."

"How? Are you going to write it yourself?"

He looked amused at her distress. "Trust me, Callie. Just trust me."

She had to, she decided, and her mind flew on to new problems. "I'll need money for when I leave the orphan train. Enough to get Rolland, Glenda, and Emelie to Missouri with me."

Langsdon glanced about, then removed a fine wallet from inside his frock coat pocket and withdrew several bills. "Hide it well. And don't be in a hurry to spend it. If you're careful, it'll get you to Independence, and I'll take care of the finances from there."

It struck her as odd that he was now giving her money, very likely the same bills that she had given to him. He was dead earnest about it, however, and seemed to know what he was doing.

"I'll be most careful with the money," she told him. She rolled up the bills and hid them in her hand, then peered around past the rhododendrons. No one was near enough to have noticed.

"I handle the finances, and you see to bringin' the family together." He produced a folded paper from his waistcoat's inside pocket. "Here's the names of the families they live with and their addresses in case you have to find them."

"*I* find them?" she repeated with trepidation.

"It's only in case."

Somewhat appeased, she stared at the paper. Glenda,

Emelie, and Rolland all lived around Centerville, Indiana. Just seeing their names and the details of their locations made her feel more hopeful.

"There'll be a message left with the stationmaster for you in Centerville. It's one of the orphan train stops."

She bit her lip and asked, "Why don't you ride along with us?"

"I've got other fish to fry."

Suddenly she wondered if he had really thought out what he was doing. She had a feeling that his plans were in as much of a flux as his life, and that he couldn't even pin himself down yet.

Finally she said, "I can't believe this is happening."

"Like most things, it's possible if you're clever," he assured her. "Now we just play our parts. How did you explain to Reverend Hansel why you wanted to go with them?"

"I said I had family in Missouri and couldn't afford to go all of the way myself."

"Good," Langsdon replied. "A half-truth's always easier to believe. After that, you can muddle it up. Remember that, Callie."

It sounded as though he spoke from experience. She forced herself to ask, "Langsdon, you didn't . . . get the money by selling the missing paintings, did you?"

He grinned, shaking his head. "Your Mr. Stane lifted those paintin's all by himself."

"Mr. Stane stole the paintings?! I can't believe it! Whatever for?"

"Ask him. Not that he'd admit it, but I know for certain he pulled it off. Your fine Mr. Stane has another side to him that's not so revoltingly correct. For one thing, I've seen him actin' big at the horse races on Long Island, bettin' wads of money with his friends. But he's not near as clever as he lets on, especially in his choice of a fence for the paintin's. He's headin' for trouble. Be lucky to get his money without gettin' killed."

Callie stared at her brother, speechless. Then a new thought hit. "You don't gamble on the horses too, Langsdon?"

"That's my affair," he retorted. "It's yours to be on that train Monday morning with the orphans, and to be as good as you can with them and that minister. I'll be watchin' for you in Centerville, sister. You say the isn't-that-a-blessings and the amens, and I'll be workin' the edges."

Suspicion washed over her again. Reverend Hansel had said Mrs. Lester had either fallen or been pushed down a flight of stairs. "Will it be lawful, Langsdon? Not hurting anyone?"

"I'm not goin' to prison again," he shot back, his eyes narrowed with determination.

After a moment, he put on a wry smile. "From now on, if you see me anywhere, pretend you don't know me from Adam. Remember, it's all a part of gettin' our family back together, Callie. It's all a part of the plan. And don't forget to stop for a message at the Centerville station."

Uneasy as she felt, she gave him a grim nod.

When she returned to the mansion, she heard Becca sobbing in her room and knocked softly at the door. "It's me, Becca. Do you want to let me in?"

"*Ja,* just a minute," Becca answered. When she opened the door, her face was swollen from weeping. "*Ach,* it is so awful, Callie!" she sobbed, throwing herself into Callie's arms. "Ve love each other. If you've ever been in love, you know."

Callie held her weeping friend, patting her back and thinking what to say. "If you and Thomas eloped, it would be too late for his parents to change matters."

"Ve talked of it, but I can't bear to have him lose his family's trade. Besides, where could ve go?"

Callie closed the door behind her. "I have an idea."

Secrecy was important to their plan, but this was an exception. "Listen, Becca," she began, "I have a deep, deep secret, but I'm going to tell you because perhaps you and Thomas could come along and it would solve your problems. I'm only going to tell you my part of it, if you promise not to tell."

Becca wiped her tears, then dug into the pocket of her green frock for a handkerchief. "*Ja*, anything is better than nothing, like ve have now."

"You won't tell anyone, except maybe Thomas, if you need to?" Callie asked.

Becca nodded. "*Ja*, I promise."

Callie could scarcely believe the words herself as she spoke them. "It looks as though I'm leaving Monday for California. It just came to me that maybe Thomas would like grocering there. It'd be his own business, and in a new place without his family breathing down his neck—or yours."

Becca's green eyes widened. "California?"

Callie nodded, still overcome by the wonder of it. "It's almost sure. First, I'll be going with Reverend Hansel to help with the girls on the orphan train. Then on to Missouri where I have family, and then to California!"

"And the Burlingtons? Do they know? And Mr. Stane?"

"No one in the household knows except you. I'll tell Mrs. Burlington as soon as it's sure. I just need a final word of acceptance from Reverend Hansel. But I am *not* going to tell Mr. Stane. In fact, I may just tell Mrs. Burlington a thing or two about their fine butler before I leave."

"Well, that is something!" Becca replied, still amazed.

"*Vielleicht* . . . maybe Thomas would go."

"It's something to consider. This is a heartless time to bring it up, but I . . . I was hoping you'd help me make up that brown length of goods into a frock for the trip. I don't have enough clothes, and I want to look presentable when we offer the children to adoptive parents. I'll have to set an example for neatness for the children, as well. Oh, Becca, they look like such ragamuffins!"

"*Ja*, sure I help you. Ve start now! I know it is no sense crying, and California is a wonderful idea. They need grocers there, too, and Thomas has a heart for adventure. Get your brown goods, quick, and ve start the cutting."

Becca put her hands to either side of her forehead, her green eyes widening. "*Ach*, I was praying for help, and maybe this is it. Your Reverend Hansel, do you think he would marry Thomas and me?"

"We can find out."

"Go!" Becca told her, a look of hope on her tear-stained face. "Get the goods while I look for matching thread."

The next morning, Callie set about her housework with renewed vigor. If she had extra time, she'd stitch up more seams on her new brown frock. Becca had insisted on two sets of white collars and cuffs for it—one squared off and showy, the other smaller and more tailored—so it would be suitable, not to mention clean, for more occasions. And best of all, Becca had stopped crying and turned hopeful. When Thomas came with the day's delivery, she planned to discuss the idea of going to California with him.

As for her own situation, Callie felt sure that Langsdon would work out her recommendation for Reverend Hansel. It might not be perfectly honest, but she would more than make up for it by doing her best for him and the orphans, no matter how difficult.

She didn't see Becca until noon at the servants' table. Her

friend's eyes were dry now, but they were full of shock. As she sat down on the bench next to Callie, she whispered, "They sent Thomas's brother with the groceries. Now Thomas serves the other side of the city. But I know he will come tonight to see me, or send word."

The only word that came, however, was a note for Callie. *A fine recommendation delivered. L*, it said.

"Closer! Everything's getting closer," she told Becca with almost unbearable excitement. She felt guilty, but determined to overcome it. "Everything's working out. I should know soon!"

Every spare moment, she stitched up her brown frock, and Becca, despite her tears, was cutting out a navy blue frock for her as a gift. The dresses wouldn't be as fine as those shown in *Godey's Lady's Book*, but they would be suitable for the trip.

"We should be sewing for you, too," she told Becca.

"Thomas comes Sunday," Becca assured Callie, all certitude between her bouts of tears. "When he decides for California, then I make new clothing for me."

Late Wednesday afternoon, the front door bells chimed. From the library where she was waxing the table, Callie saw Mr. Stane invite Reverend Hansel into the mansion.

She touched her hair and smoothed her apron. Moments later, she heard footsteps going into the drawing room, then Mr. Stane leaving to fetch Mr. and Mrs. Burlington.

Surely it was about her going! Callie thought. Why else would Reverend Hansel come today? He would talk to the Burlingtons about it, and she hoped they would recommend her. She made fast work of waxing the library table, then hurried to the kitchen to wash the wax from her hands.

Before long Mr. Stane arrived, amusement dancing around his thin lips. "You are wanted in the drawing room by the Burlingtons, Miss Murray. You are a sly little mouse.

I shall have to tell them about your lack of trustworthiness."

"Then I shall have to tell them that you stole their paintings!" she snapped.

His face turned a deathly gray, and she rushed off before he could reply.

The drawing room was sumptuous with its antique furnishings and fine Italian paintings. As usual, it intimidated Callie. But this afternoon, as she stepped from the white marble floor onto the Brussels carpet, both Mr. Burlington and Reverend Hansel rose to their feet.

"Please be seated, Callie," Mrs. Burlington said most graciously. "We are surprised and delighted to hear that you are interested in missionary work."

Callie drew a breath and sat down on the edge of the fine French empire couch. "Only to escort the orphan train children," she said honestly.

Mrs. Burlington smiled. "I wish you had discussed it with us first, dear, but Reverend Hansel told us about Mrs. Lester's unfortunate accident and how quickly your part in it came up."

Reverend Hansel turned to Callie, giving her such a warm smile that she caught her breath. "I do believe that God has chosen Miss Murray to go along on this trip," he told them, still looking at her. "She has an excellent recommendation, as well."

Langsdon's work, Callie thought, flushing.

"Despite it being at the last minute," Mr. Burlington said, "we are pleased to add our commendation. She has never given our household cause for displeasure."

Reverend Hansel smiled, then turned to Callie. "Do you still wish to go, Miss Murray?"

She swallowed. "Yes, I do."

"Then we leave Monday morning," the minister replied. "If this orphan train is as most of them have been, it will be one of the most memorable experiences of your life. Here is a brochure about it that you might wish to read."

Callie accepted the pamphlet and thanked him without meeting his eyes.

"Oh, Callie!" Mrs. Burlington exclaimed, "it's almost as if we are sending our very own missionary with the Society! We'll donate food and . . . what else do the children need, Reverend Hansel?"

Discussion of food, money, clothing, and blankets bypassed Callie as she perched on the edge of the French empire couch. She was going! She was truly going! Her heart pounded at the thought of being with her brothers and sisters again. As for being a missionary, what a paralyzing conclusion for her employer to have leapt to.

Mr. Burlington furrowed his brow thoughtfully, then spoke. "Reverend Hansel, we can only imagine how heartsick you must be about your fiancée's death, but you should put your mind to the matter of marriage again soon, whether you wish to or not. It behooves a minister to be married."

Callie saw Mrs. Burlington give her husband a silencing glance, but he continued. "Ask the Lord for someone who would happily share the burden, yet someone whom you could wholeheartedly love."

Reverend Hansel answered most solemnly, "I assure you that I've asked Him, sir."

"Then He shall send someone meant just for you," Mrs. Burlington pronounced with confidence.

Talk of a minister falling in love struck Callie as a most inappropriate discussion. After all, ministers . . . even if they were as handsome as Reverend Hansel . . . were to concern themselves with God, not with women. She fervently wished that they would change the subject.

5

On Monday morning Callie stood in trepidation at the New Jersey train station, just across the North River, while the orphans milled about her. The ferry ride across the river had not been threatening; it had seemed a mere festive outing, since they still could see the New York shore. But now the unknown loomed before them, embodied by the great black engine that blasted out a throaty warning as it slowly rumbled and puffed into the station.

"Yikes, it's big!" an orphan yelled. "A black monster!"

"It does have that look about it," Callie agreed.

Staring at the engine, she was reminded of her own monster—an entirely new life before her, starting with the handling of a terrified group of undisciplined orphans.

The locomotive huffed and puffed along the silvery rails and stopped with a blast of steam.

"I don't like no train!" a blond pigtailed girl cried out, her blue eyes wide. "I von't go in det monstar!"

Callie caught her by a thin arm. "It's only metal and smoke, nothing to be afraid of," she assured the girl. "You weren't afraid of the ferry that brought us here."

"I vas on a boat before," the girl declared, her eyes still full of terror. "The boat from *Norge*."

Callie knew she meant Norway. "What's your name?"

"Ingrid Nordgren," the girl answered, still watching the train and tugging away slightly. "You been on von before?" she asked. "You been on a train, Miss Murray?"

"Not yet," Callie admitted, "but I'm going. Thousands of people ride trains all over the world. Just look at how many passengers are waiting to get on this one today."

"Mostly orphans," Ingrid muttered.

"Of course not. Look at the other people, some of them dressed like royalty. It'll be fine, Ingrid. The adventure of a lifetime." She knew she was reassuring herself as well. She slipped her arm around Ingrid's narrow shoulders, which remained stiff and unyielding, and the two of them watched together as the passenger cars stopped before them under the roof of the train platform.

All around, porters flew into motion, carrying suitcases and trunks toward the baggage car. A dozen or so brawny laborers hauled barrels and crates from their wagons, then trundled them toward the freight cars.

"I vouldn't go if it vasn't for my brother Ollie," Ingrid said, almost to herself. She cast a glance toward a tall blond boy amidst the boys with Reverend Hansel. "He says it is only vay ve got of makin' new life and getting avay from New York City."

"What happened to your parents?" Callie dared to ask.

Ingrid looked down at the wooden platform. "Mama die coughin' on boat comin' over, den Papa in New York."

"I'm sorry," Callie told her with heartfelt sympathy. An instant later, she felt panic-stricken—*consumption!* She forced herself to ask, "Do you or Ollie cough?"

Ingrid shook her head. "The doctor, he already look on us. The orphan doctor."

Thank goodness, Callie thought. It hadn't occurred to her that the children might carry deadly diseases. In any event, she would keep an ear out for coughing from Ingrid and her brother, as well as the other children.

The orphans stood wide-eyed in the crowd, some trying not to appear scared. Callie wondered how she could ever care for these poor children when she had no experience with so many and didn't even know what awaited them at the end of their journeys. Had she been a fool to plunge into this, when she might have spent the rest of her life in quiet service at the Burlingtons' mansion?

She could still see the New York shore of the North River, where just a short time ago, she'd called good-bye to her employer before helping the orphans onto the river ferry.

From the edge of the tumult, Mrs. Burlington had called out from the carriage, "God bless you, Callie! God bless you and Reverend Hansel and all of you dear children!"

"Thank you!" Callie had answered over the crowd. "And thank you for the food and blankets and everything else!"

"Our pleasure!" Mrs. Burlington had replied. Then, there being nothing else to say, she'd told old John, the driver, to take her home.

The Burlingtons' cook had baked fruitcakes, small oatmeal-raisin cakes, and chicken pies, and even Mrs. Burlington had helped to fill the hampers with fruit and bread. She'd purchased blankets for everyone on the journey, as well as new clothing to be given to the orphans just before the first stop in Ohio.

"There's nothing like new clothes to make children look more appealing," she'd declared. "All that's left for us at home to do is to pray for your venture, and we will do so every morning. We will pray that those poor children will find loving Christian homes, and that you'll be happy with your family in Missouri."

The lie again, Callie had thought regretfully.

Now on the New Jersey train platform, she saw that the orphans seemed a bit less anxious and were growing more interested in the scene around them.

"Look at the passengers getting off, Ingrid," Callie said. "They appear to be in fine condition, don't they?"

"*Skitten,*" Ingrid said. "Dirty."

"Yes, some are a bit sooty from the smoke," Callie agreed. "But just look at them moving along. They weathered the train journey here just fine."

As soon as all of the passengers had disembarked, the conductor shouted a lusty, "All abboooaarrdd for New Brunswick! Trenton! Philadelphia!"

"All abboooaarrdd!" the street boys echoed, then shouted again with abandon, "All abbboooarddddddddd!"

From the far end of the railroad car, Reverend Hansel spoke to the conductor, then raised a hand over the crowd to catch Callie's eye. "Car number seven! Girls board in front with you! I'll board the boys back here!"

"Yes, number seven!" Callie returned, glad to see he was still there.

The conductors had already put down squatty stools on the platform for stepping up into the coaches, and Callie herded the girls through the crowd. "Hurry, hurry!"

No turning back now! she told herself and saw the same thought reflected in the somber expressions on her girls' faces. *Her* girls! She took a deep breath, then told them, "Please sit in the front benches. Girls in front, boys in back of the coach with Reverend Hansel."

The first two girls clambered on eagerly. The next girl, however, a tall pig-tailed thirteen-year-old named Ruby, hung back. If ever a girl was misnamed, it was Ruby, for she was drab and scrawny under her ragged tan dress.

"What if I don't like it?" she asked, looking back with trepidation at the New York shore. "What if I hate where they place me out? Truly hate it?"

"If you aren't well placed with your adoptive family, the

orphan society will find another home for you," Callie assured her, quoting from the brochure she had been studying. "They check on the families every year to be sure everyone is satisfied with the placements. Most are very pleased."

"But what if . . . what if I'm scared in the country with wild things?" Ruby asked.

"What wild things?"

"Cows 'n pigs 'n chickens."

"Why, cows and pigs and chickens can't run very fast," Callie said, trying not to laugh. "We can out-run and out-think them easily."

"How do you know?" Ruby demanded.

"I just know. Let's get on the train now. It'll be a wonderful adventure," Callie promised between counting the other girls as she hustled them aboard. Ruby still hesitated on the platform, and the conductor shouted another, "All abboooaarrdd!"

Callie eyed the painfully thin girl, and suddenly inspiration hit. "One thing about country living, Ruby, there's almost always plenty of good food to eat. Plates and plates heaped high with meat, potatoes, vegetables, and fruits. Good food."

Ruby drew a brave breath and climbed onto the train. "Guess if I hate it, I'll jest take the train back. Yep, take the very next train right back here, then cross back on the river ferry. It's all free anyhow."

Callie smiled encouragingly, but made no reply. The train fare had been paid by benefactors of the Children's Aid Society, and she had a feeling that it would be next to impossible for her or any of her charges to return to New York. For better or for worse, she, like the children, was leaving her old life behind forever.

"Ain't you lookin' beans?" Yorker asked her as he started

up the steps before her.

Callie laughed. "Thank you, Yorker. Boys at the back of the railroad car, though."

"I like girls better," he objected with a grin.

"Yorker! I do hope you're not going to be a problem."

Undaunted, he continued to mount the steps. "Got a new dress, ain't yer, Miss Murray?"

"I do. My best friend made it for me."

He was already aboard, so she reached out for the next child. Helping the girl on and then the next, Callie's mind flew to poor Becca. Her friend hadn't seen Thomas all week, so she hadn't been able to ask him about going to California. Yet Becca had gallantly sewn half the night on the dark blue cotton frock that Callie wore this moment.

"My friend, Callie, she will look good, *ja*," Becca had declared. "It is good *mit* your blue eyes."

It had been all Callie could do not to pry about Thomas, since Becca had seemed so sure all would go well.

"God gives me peace about it," she'd told Callie. "Peace in my heart like never before. Ve meet you in Independence, Missouri, at ze Talbot farm."

The moment they'd left each other's arms, though, Callie had turned to hide a tumult of emotions. What if she never in her life saw Becca again?

The locomotive blasted a warning, emitting a cloud of dark steam, and the conductor called what sounded like a final "All abbooooaarrdd!"

The train huffed louder than ever, and Callie hurried the rest of her charges aboard, counting, "Eleven . . . twelve . . . thirteen! That's all of the girls!" she called out to the conductor.

She climbed on and joined the girls in the railroad coach, looking for a place on one of the hard benches. The front bench was taken up with the pile of gray blankets the

Burlingtons had donated, and Ruby sat alone on the opposite front bench. Behind them, the girls had paired off on the other forward benches.

In the back of the coach, she saw Reverend Hansel had all of his boys seated. He raised a hand toward her. "All the girls on, Miss Murray?"

"Yes, we're all on."

The conductor looked about for more passengers and, seeing none, he scooped up the stool and hopped into the train. Leaning out, he clung to the handrail and waved the engineer on.

The train blasted another warning before the doors slammed shut and the cars jerked into motion.

Callie almost fell into the front bench next to Ruby as the train's wheels clanked over the rails. Gripping the armrest, she peered out across the river at the New York shore for what would most likely be the last time.

"Good-by, New York!" the children called out through the open windows. "Good-by and good riddance!"

Good riddance was right, Callie tried to tell herself as smoke billowed all about them. *New York City, you've brought nothing but shame to me and my family!* Not that it was the city's fault; it was Father's and Mother's fault for "flouting convention." Likely Reverend Hansel would put it more bluntly: for living in sin and visiting their sin on the entire family.

Staring at the railroad car's wooden ceiling, she remembered that her half sister Abby had also left New York in anguish. At least they had that in common—that and an immoral father whom Abby might also resent. No, she must forget about him and Mother, Callie reminded herself. She could finally be done with that part of her life if she erased the memories and concentrated on being together with Glenda, Emelie, and Rolland again.

"This yer first time, too?" Ruby asked.

"Yes, my first train ride, too," Callie answered. She must stop worrying about herself and think of the children. She gave Ruby a heartening pat on her thin arm. "We're off on a grand adventure!"

"I sure do hope so," Ruby answered.

Smoke billowed all around them, and Callie glanced out the window as the train chugged out of the station. Her lips parted with shock as she saw him through the smoke. Langsdon!

He wore his walrus mustache and a black suit, and strode along the platform as if he were a disembarking passenger. She felt an instant's resentfulness, thinking that he didn't trust her; then she realized he'd come in their best interests. He'd done a good job of it, too, for she hadn't even seen him on the North River ferry. She just wished that he wasn't so preoccupied with what appeared to be other matters and that he didn't seem quite so sinister.

As discussed at their last meeting, he'd take a train to Chicago and arrive in Indiana before them, since their train made so many stops. She closed her eyes and felt the movement of the train beneath her as they chugged out of the station. Brother Langsdon, as promised, would be around the edges, always taking care of everything—except this railroad car full of children!

They were no more than underway when Reverend Hansel strolled up from the back with two baskets full of small oatmeal-raisin cakes. It seemed odd, a minister in a black suit and white clerical collar carrying baskets of food. When he arrived by Callie's bench, he glanced back at the girls on either side of the aisle.

"All's quieter than usual," he remarked to Callie. "Even a bit solemn."

"Yes, but they can't seem to get enough of looking out

the windows," she replied. "Neither can I, for that matter."

He smiled. "I expect most of them will soon return to their more exuberant natures. And you, do you have an exuberant nature, Miss Murray?"

She shook her head. "I've grown quiet as I've grown up."

"Full of responsibility, I presume," he replied. "I often regret that we allow so much of the childlikeness in us to be pummeled out by the cares of living."

She was unsure how to answer. All of her life she had been admonished to be grown up, responsible. Moreover, the brown eyes that met hers were entirely disconcerting. She suspected there was a great deal more to him than the preacher she'd heard in church, or seen at the Burlingtons' or the Children's Aid Society headquarters.

"Let's have a prayer, then pass out breakfast," he suggested, handing her a basket. He stood at the front of the railroad car, bracing himself firmly as the train bumped and jolted along the tracks.

"Boys and girls," he called out in his deep voice over the clickety-clack of the train, "we are embarking on the journey of a lifetime. Let's speak to God about it and thank Him for our breakfast, which will follow."

Beside her, Ruby had already closed her eyes and folded her hands for prayer, and Callie hastened to do so herself.

"Heavenly Father," Reverend Hansel began, "we come to Thee with praise and thanksgiving for the opportunities Thou hast set before us as we embark on this journey to new lives and new homes. We ask for Thy wisdom and favor as the hours and days pass. We thank Thee for sending Jesus Christ to be our Redeemer and Lord, and that Thou hast sent Him to be our model for life here on earth."

A model for our lives here on earth? Callie wondered, clasping the basket on her lap.

"And now we ask Thee to bless this food," he continued,

"that it may sustain us on our journey. We pray in the precious and powerful name of our Lord Jesus Christ. Amen."

"Amen!" Yorker and some of the other boys yelled from the back of the railroad car. "Amen, and let's pass the cakes! Reverend Hansel says two each."

Callie rose to her feet with the basket, pausing to offer it first to Ruby, who snatched up her two cakes greedily. The railroad cars jerked, and Reverend Hansel caught Callie's elbow with his strong hand to steady her. He held her elbow firmly, long enough for her to catch her balance.

"I . . . thank you," she managed, pulling away as her gaze met his for a perplexing moment. Something stirring passed between them, something she had never before experienced. As her wits returned, she quickly started down the aisle with the basket of cakes.

Behind her, Reverend Hansel spoke kindly to each child as if nothing peculiar had taken place. After a while, Callie decided she was making too much of it. Likely it was just that she was unaccustomed to being touched by a man—particularly by a handsome young minister.

As she moved along, she heard him continuing to reassure the girls, and it occurred to her that his kindness ran as deep as his voice, and that his hand on her elbow had been very strong. He might be a gentle man, but in a physical sense, there was nothing soft about him. What's more, she was glad of it, for it made her feel secure.

At the back of the train, Yorker was making his way among the boys with the other basket of cakes on his arm. "Oat cakes fer the poor!" he called out in an alms-for-the-poor tone. "Oat cakes fer the poor!"

"Why, Yorker!" Callie admonished him. "Even the very rich enjoy oatmeal-raisin cakes for breakfast. Mrs. Burlington had her cook bake them for us very early this morning."

"Well, ain't that beans!" he returned. Then he called out,

grinning, "Oat cakes fer the rich! Oat cakes fer the high 'n mighty! Oat cakes fer the king 'n queen o' England their-selves!" Making his way toward her up the aisle, he scraped and bowed to the boys as he offered the basket, nearly losing his balance, but not spilling a crumb.

When they met halfway through the jolting railroad car, Callie was glad to see that there were still plenty of the small cakes left. With the fresh air from the countryside beginning to waft in through the windows, she suddenly felt starved herself.

She turned to find Reverend Hansel behind her. "Do you care for an oatmeal cake?" she offered.

"Thank you, Miss Murray, indeed I do," he replied, taking one from the basket. "You serve with uncommon grace."

She returned an uncertain smile and was saved from having to reply by the children's shouts.

"Look outside! Look outside! It's wild animals!"

Callie peered out the window at a pastoral scene that reminded her of some of the Burlingtons' oil paintings.

"Sheep," Reverend Hansel told them. "It's just sheep grazing out in a meadow. Look there, at the little spring lambs, the newborn ones."

Callie edged past him to her seat in the front.

Behind her in the aisle, he was saying, "Now you can see what the Lord Jesus Christ meant when He spoke of sheep. In His day, the lands about were full of sheep and shepherds tending them most carefully. Jesus was called the Good Shepherd, and those who believe in Him, follow Him and know His voice."

Callie bit into her oatmeal cake. Mr. Burlington had spoken of that too. But what God had to do with shepherds and sheep was beyond her. Reverend Hansel spoke on about Christ giving His life for His sheep and about the door of the sheepfold, but he might as well have been speaking another language. She only wished that she didn't find him so appealing. Surely it was wrong to feel that way about a minister.

As time passed, Callie, like the children, grew more accustomed to the sights of the New Jersey countryside and its "wild animals" and "trees that grew apples!" But it unfailingly interested them to look out at the towns and speculate about the lives of the people who lived there.

In New Brunswick, Reverend Hansel directed them to disembark and get some exercise while the train took on more wood and water. On the platform, a daguerreotype man met them to take their picture for the Society's records.

Callie snapped a mental picture of them herself as they posed before the railroad car. They ranged in ages from eight to fourteen and were a motley group. The newsboys, as everyone called the boys, were bullet-headed, short-haired, bright-eyed, shirt-sleeved, go-ahead boys. Boys who knew too much for their ages; boys who could cheat you out of your eyeteeth, whose minds were as fast as rat traps. They stood heads-up, eyes on the daguerreotype man, mouths closed, legs stretched out, wide-awake for signs of trouble around them.

The girls posed unhappily for the picture in dresses too small or too large or too ragged or too thin, and Callie felt chagrined in her new navy blue frock with its neat white collar and cuffs. Instead of being sharp like the boys, the girls seemed suspicious—of each other and everyone else—and had a look of desperation about them.

It was, however, a perfect opportunity to learn all of the girls' names, which were lettered on the papers pinned to their dresses. Alice, eight, blonde with slightly crossed blue eyes. Camille, ten, dark and likely French, thin as a nail and frightened. Dora, eight, a curly dark-haired Irish colleen with great green eyes. Tillie, nine, dark pigtails and boyish.

Suzannah, thirteen, a red-haired mingler, with motherly instincts toward the younger girls. Manda and Marcia, eleven, dark-haired twins who stuck together. Frieda and Gretchen, fourteen and eight, blond German sisters who had two brothers, Horst and Gunther, along on the train. Ivy, eight, a violet-eyed enchantress with an unfortunate limp that she tried to hide. Lavina, nine, with blondish-red curls. And Ingrid and Ruby, of course.

After the daguerreotype man finished with their picture, they found the townspeople and train passengers staring at them. Yorker immediately stepped onto the conductor's step stool and announced, "Bummers, snoozers, and citizens! Me 'n my friends have come here to this fine town ter see how yer gettin' along and to give yer free advice."

The boys laughed, and the girls smiled a little. "Citizens," Yorker continued as loud as a politician, "don't spend yer money on penny ice-creams 'n bad cigars—"

Here and there in the crowd, people laughed with the orphans.

"Well, folks, let me tell you a story. My dad was a hard 'un. One day he went on a spree, and he came home and axed 'Where's yer mother?" and I told him I didn't know, and he clipt me over the head with an iron pot, and knocked me down. Just then, me mother drapped in on him, and at it they went. Ye should o' seen 'em. And whist they were fightin', I slipped meself out the back door, ran like a scairt dog, and lived on New York's streets fer a long time 'til finally I found the Orphan Society. When they raised up the notion to go West, I was the first bummer to put me hand up."

The onlookers no longer smiled but listened with interest, as did Callie. Yorker wasn't too different from most of the boys, except he was more vocal and had a sense of the comical. She couldn't help wondering if her brother Rolland, who'd been a quiet and serious boy, had turned into a Yorker. As for her sisters . . .

"Maybe ye'd like to hear summit about the West," Yorker went on, "the great West, where so many folks are settled down and growin' up to be great men, maybe the greatest men in the great Republic. Now that's the place for growing congressmen and governors and presidents. Out there you don't have to be newsboys and shoe-blacks and match sellers. That's why we're headin' west o' New York instead o' bein' snoozers, rummeys, and policy-players. Citizens, we aim to be great men . . . and women! And now let me give you some free advice—"

The train's warning bell rang out. "Come along, Yorker," Reverend Hansel said, "before you give too much free advice."

"Wasn't goin' ter be anythin' free about it," Yorker returned. "I aimed to hold a collection fer vittles next."

"We're financially set for now," Reverend Hansel said, trying to hide a grin. But his words didn't stop several bystanders from tucking bills and coins into his hands.

"For the orphans," they said. "Get 'em something good."

A woman handed him a box of fine strawberries.

He thanked them and hustled the children onto the train. "No begging," he warned Yorker. "I know some of you have reduced it to a fine art, but you'll have to unlearn it. Begging isn't appreciated, and I can almost guarantee you, your new parents won't like it. We're going to rely on God for help."

"On God!" some of them echoed with disbelief. They clambered aboard the train, arguing the whys and why nots of begging versus depending on God.

"We have food for now," Callie told them. She feared, though, that they might grow too accustomed to the Burlingtons' fine food as they rode along, and that such largess wouldn't continue all the way to Missouri no matter what Reverend Hansel told them.

As they stopped in other towns along the route, she was surprised to see church people, who'd been told ahead of their coming, waiting to meet the train. They offered the children lemonade and baked goods, and cheered them on. Callie didn't quite know what to make of it; she only hoped she could cheer the children as well when they stopped in Ohio for their first meeting with prospective parents.

Benjamin Talbot sat down in the parlor, letters in hand. The first came from the investigator in New York, the second from an old New York friend in the ministry. He tore open the investigator's letter first and read,

> *Dear Mr. Talbot:*
>
> *I am in receipt of your letter and thank you for your confidence. I have begun to investigate Miss Charlotte (Callie) Murray Talbot. To date, there is no evidence of her having worked for a New York Stafford in the banking industry. I suspect the letter of recommendation is fraudulent.*
>
> *I am, at this point, in receipt of information about a younger brother, Langsdon, who was imprisoned for theft in Albany, and shall check further.*
>
> *In the meantime, please be assured that I shall investigate the matter to your entire satisfaction. Again, thank you for your confidence.*

Benjamin reread the letter, then shook his head. Just as he'd suspected. It occurred to him that the girl, Callie, might already be underway. What if the brother and other children were with her? *Lord,* he prayed, *what part dost Thou have in this? Give us Thy wisdom.*

Drawing a deep breath, he opened the letter from his friend in the ministry and smiled to see that it looked far more promising.

Dear Benjamin,

I bear tidings of great joy about the great awakening in New York which goes on unabated. You asked for the details, and details you shall have, my dear friend.

As you might know, North Church was suffering from a loss of membership, and last July they appointed a quiet but zealous businessman named Jeremiah Lanphier as City Missionary. He had been converted in 1842 in the Broadway Tabernacle built by Charles G. Finney in the '30s. A local newspaperman describes Lanphier as "tall, with a pleasant face, an affectionate manner, and indomitable energy and perseverance; a good speaker, gifted in prayer and exhortation, a welcome guest to any house, shrewd and endowed with much tact and common sense."

Lanphier decided to invite others to join him in a noonday prayer meeting to be held on Wednesdays. He distributed a handbill titled, "How Often Shall I Pray?" and answers: "As often as the language of prayer is in my heart; as often as I see my need of help; as often as I feel the power of temptation; as often as I am made sensible of any spiritual declension, or feel the aggression of a worldly, earthly spirit. In prayer we leave the business of time for that of eternity, and intercourse with men for intercourse with God."

His invitation read, "A Prayer Meeting is held every Wednesday from 12 to 1 o'clock in the Consistory building in the rear of the North Dutch Church, corner of Fulton and William Streets.

"This meeting is intended to give merchants, mechanics, clerks, strangers, and businessmen generally, an opportunity to stop and call upon God amid the

perplexities incident to their respective avocations. It will continue for one hour, but it is also designed for those who may find it inconvenient to remain more than five or ten minutes, as well as for those who can spare the whole hour. The necessary interruption will be slight, because anticipated; and those who are in haste can often expedite their business engagements by halting to lift up their voices to the throne of grace in humble, grateful prayer.

"All are cordially invited to attend."

Well, my friend Benjamin, at noon on September 23, the door was opened, and Lanphier took his seat to await the response to his invitation. Five minutes passed. No one appeared. Lanphier paced the room in a battle of fear versus faith. Ten minutes elapsed. Fifteen. Lanphier was yet alone. Twenty minutes, twenty-five, thirty, and then at 12:30, a step was heard on the stairs. The first person appeared, then another and another and another, until six men were present and the prayer-meeting began. On the following Wednesday, there were twenty in attendance, and on the third Wednesday, forty.

In the first week of October, they began to meet daily. That week, extraordinary revival swept the city of Hamilton in faraway Canada. The next week, the New York financial panic reached a crisis and prostrated business everywhere. One must connect the three events, for in them was manifested the need of religious revival, the means to attain it, and the provision of Divine grace to meet the situation.

Within six months, ten thousand businessmen were gathering for prayer daily in New York, and we expect a million converts to be added to the American churches in a year, a heartening percentage in a popu-

lation of thirty million! The greatest number of conversions have taken place in Massachusetts, New York, Pennsylvania, Ohio, and Illinois. May God extend this great awakening of faith to California.

My brother and friend, may God use you to His glory!

Benjamin's heart leapt. This then was the exact news of what had been taking place on the eastern seaboard—far beyond what he'd read in the newspapers. Not that it should surprise him. No matter how objective the newspapers claimed to be, they all had their own philosophical positions, which were not always Christian.

He looked at both of the letters before him and began to ponder the possibilities that God might be placing in his hands at this very moment.

Suddenly he came under great conviction.

He must petition God for salvation for Callie and her family, and he must repent for his lack of enthusiasm in receiving them. Why, oh why was it that he'd felt such apathy and even dragged his feet when God began to lay these possibilities of Callie and her family before him? The reason, of course, was that Satan, the great discourager, had blinded him with the shame he felt over his brother's illegitimate children and had entangled him in resentment and anger.

Forgive me, Lord, forgive me! he prayed. *I pray for salvation for Callie and her family . . . give me Thy love for them! And I beseech Thee to spread Thy great awakening to California!* It occurred to him that God always began with one man, be it Adam or Moses or Abraham or Jeremiah Lanphier.

Lord, Benjamin prayed, *here am I, Thy inept and unworthy but willing servant. Use me . . . use me!*

6

Despite Callie's qualms about carrying out her work with the girls, the train's steady clickety-clack through the moonlit night finally put her to sleep. She must have slept for hours before the train's plaintive wail for a Pennsylvania station roused her.

"You awake, Miss Murray?" Ruby whispered.

Callie pushed away her gray blanket and sat up, slowly easing the stiffness from her back. "Yes, I think so, Ruby," she whispered back. "Haven't you slept yet?"

"No. I got to . . . I got to ask you somethin'." Ruby's voice trembled. "It ain't just cows 'n chickens 'n pigs I'm scared of, Miss Murray. It's . . . well, it's men."

"Men?" Callie echoed a bit too loudly. She cast a glance back at the rest of the car's occupants in the dim light. Most were snuggled under their blankets, fast asleep. A few had risen up to look out the window at the lighted depot where the train had stopped for passengers to disembark. She whispered, "What do you mean, you're scared of men, Ruby?"

The girl shook her head with an almost frenzied motion. "I ain't no . . . innocent little girl, Miss Murray," she whispered back. "But it's not my fault, I swear. My stepfather, he hurt me in a bad way. And now I'm scared o' what's ahead with another family. Maybe . . . maybe it'll be the same or worse."

Callie swallowed. She wouldn't have believed such a horror if the poor girl weren't so shaken. She didn't know anything about such matters herself, nor did she care to. It certainly wasn't something one discussed.

"Ruby, I'm so . . . so terribly sorry."

"I can't talk to Reverend Hansel about it," Ruby whispered. "But I thought you, bein' grown 'n a Christian, would maybe know the answer to my question."

Callie hesitated. "Perhaps." Her reservation didn't stop Ruby.

"What I want to know is, does . . . does God love me anyhow?"

Tears rose to Callie's eyes. A Christian companion for the girls would likely know the answer to such a question. This is what came of going on the journey under false pretenses.

She recalled the stained-glass window in the church where Reverend Hansel had preached; Christ's arms had been outstretched as if in welcome to all. "I . . . think He does, Ruby."

"Oh, Miss Murray," Ruby whimpered like a stabbed kitten and threw herself into Callie's arms, "I want to know for sure once 'n for all. I don't like all this goin' back 'n forth in my head about it. Does God love me anyhow, or not?"

Callie held her close. "Reverend Hansel said in church last Sunday that we're to be anxious for nothing, but to pray—and the peace of God will come to us."

Ruby wept silently against her, her frail body trembling. "But will God forgive me?"

"Ruby, it wasn't your fault!"

Ruby wept even harder. "Maybe it was. Maybe if . . . if I'd told my ma, she would have stopped it. But my stepfather said she wouldn't believe me . . . and he'd leave us, and then we wouldn't have no money again. I never told the orphan train folks. When the chance came for me to take the train away, I lied. I told 'em I didn't have any family . . .'n I know lyin's bad."

The whole story was so appalling that all Callie could say was, "Oh, Ruby! Oh, my poor dear!"

The next moment, Reverend Hansel's hand touched her shoulder. "Night problems?" he asked softly. His clerical collar seemed particularly bright in the moonlight, and his face was full of compassion.

Callie held Ruby closer, patting the girl's frail back as she wept silently. Callie didn't dare look up at him again, partly because she couldn't possibly pose the problem to him, and partly because she knew what a poor replacement she was for Mrs. Lester, who surely would have known how to handle such questions.

"Problems always seem worse at night," he went on in his kindly voice. "During the day, we look out at the interesting sights and joke and laugh. At night, there's not as much to see or do, and we always seem to examine our heartaches. Night problems, I call them. The children understand them all too well."

Callie tried to think how to tell him about Ruby. Finally she whispered, "Ruby has endured something . . . unspeakable."

"Perhaps I might sit with her for a few minutes to talk and pray, and you can sit on the next bench, where the blankets were," he answered. "I've heard most of the world's problems. Nothing surprises me much, and it surely doesn't surprise the Lord, for He knows what each of us has endured."

Callie whispered to Ruby, "What do you think?"

Ruby nodded her assent against her shoulder. "Only if you promise to sit right nearby."

"I promise," Callie answered with relief. She dug in her cloak pocket. "Let me give you a handkerchief."

Ruby accepted the handkerchief and blew her nose.

As Callie moved to the adjoining bench, the train sounded its mournful warning through the darkness, then the cars jerked forward. They rode out of the station, gathering speed, and Callie heard only the wheels' endless clickety-clack and the hushed sounds of conversation across the aisle. Reverend Hansel's broad back was to her, and Ruby sat stiffly against her seat as she listened to him.

After a time, Callie saw they were praying, then the minister gave Ruby a kindly pat on the shoulder and rose to his feet. He turned to Callie.

"Sleep well, Miss Murray. As we go on, it's likely there will be other night problems from the girls, and some day problems, too. If they're spiritual questions, feel free to call on me. I've been trained to handle such matters. It seems that when their lives are in transition, even long buried problems come to the fore."

She nodded, and after he'd departed, she sat down uneasily beside Ruby, feeling as if she'd let her down.

To her surprise, Ruby looked at her hopefully in the dim light. "Reverend Hansel says God loves me," she whispered, "that's part of why He sent Jesus Christ . . . to make us new and clean . . . in our souls."

"Did you tell him what took place?"

Ruby shook her head. "He just seemed to know without me tellin'. He said I wasn't to take on others' sins. And . . . and no matter what lies I'd told or hateful things I'd done on my own, I only had to repent and ask Jesus Christ into my heart, and if I meant it, He'd give me the peace I been hopin' for."

"Reverend Hansel knew without your telling?"

"I guess it's like he said—he knows about most problems."

Callie nodded. "I guess he must."

"Anyhow, I said the prayer with him," Ruby told her, "and I feel better . . . lots better."

"I'm glad to hear it," Callie replied softly, though she didn't know what particular prayer she meant.

"I'm goin' to trust in God," Ruby announced, as if marveling at the idea of it herself. With that, she curled up with her blanket on the bench and looked out at the moonlit night pensively.

Callie's thoughts went to Reverend Hansel, and she wondered if somehow he knew all about her, as well . . . about her coming with the orphan train under false pretenses . . . about Langsdon and their plan to abduct Glenda, Emelie, and Rolland . . . and, worst of all, about her finding him—a minister—far more appealing than she should.

Of course he couldn't know, she decided, appalled at such a ridiculous notion. His being a minister might grant him experience in dealing with people's problems, but it didn't give him secret knowledge of what was in people's minds or hearts. After all, she had given him a broad hint by saying that Ruby had endured something unspeakable.

But even as she decided against the Reverend Hansel's omniscience, it occurred to Callie that it might be helpful if she could confide her own difficulties to him.

The next morning for breakfast, they ate the last of the bread and cheese Mrs. Burlington had sent. At mid-day, Reverend Hansel bought chicken pies and milk from the vendors who hawked their wares from the railroad station platform. In addition to buying food at the stop, it was a relief and a diversion for the travelers to get out and stretch their legs, even if twenty-seven children accompanied by two adults presented a curious spectacle to the townsfolk.

At a later stop, as they took a walk alongside the railroad tracks, a group of town boys began to taunt them. "Orphan train riders, ain't ye?" they yelled. "We had other trains through here, 'n no one in town wanted any of the orphans!"

"Yer lyin'!" Yorker yelled back.

"Ain't either!" a town boy returned, and he and the others began to throw stones at them.

Since Reverend Hansel had stepped into the station, Callie had to take charge. "Stop it, boys!" she called out to the locals. "Stop it right now!"

"Says who?" a particularly nasty boy shouted. He aimed a stone at her, and she barely dodged it.

"Well, if it ain't snoozers and bummers!" Yorker yelled at them. "Can't ye see she's a lady?! Looks like we got to teach you yokels some manners!"

"Orphan scum!" the town boys countered.

"Country yokels . . . bumpkins!" the orphan boys replied as they gathered up stones themselves.

Moments later, stones were flying from both directions while Callie cried out to halt the fight. Finally she threatened, "I'll have to call the town authorities out on you if you don't stop this right now!"

They laughed at her, and another volley of rocks filled the air.

"Stop it, boys, please stop it!" she implored.

Reverend Hansel and the stationmaster ran out to halt the fight, but not before Yorker and one of the bigger boys, Samuel Bruder, had been bloodied.

Yorker marched back to the train, proudly wiping the blood from his forehead. "Guess we showed 'em what's what."

"Guess we did!" Samuel agreed.

"The other boys are probably saying the same thing this very minute," Callie told them as they all climbed back into their coach.

"Naw, we taught 'em a lesson," Yorker replied. "They won't pick on other orphan trains goin' through here."

Reverend Hansel drew a breath and shook his head. "Don't be too sure. You know the proverb, 'Pride goeth before destruction, and a haughty spirit before a fall.'"

"What's that mean?" Samuel asked.

"Ain't supposed to brag or yer go down," Yorker answered ruefully.

Reverend Hansel's brown eyes met Callie's with amusement. He spoke just loud enough for all of them to hear clearly. "Sounds as though Yorker's a born preacher."

The boys roared with laughter, while Yorker blinked with astonishment. "Me a preacher!" he finally repeated, then laughed hardest of all.

Settling back into their coach benches, their talk turned from the battle of stones with the town boys to the amusing notion of Yorker as a minister.

The train traveled on into the vast state of Ohio, where the countryside grew more wooded and fewer farms were cleared. Farmers out planting corn returned their waves, and the children marveled at the sight of immense plowed fields.

As time wore on, the boys became more obstreperous— arm wrestling, bending back fingers, and punching each other. Reverend Hansel tried to reason with them, but finally he stood up in the aisle and shouted, "Quit it! Quit your fighting, or I'll give you all a good thrashing!"

The boys settled down immediately.

After a moment, he said, "Forgive me for losing my temper. It's just that, with our first placing-out stop coming up tomorrow, it's important that you not act like ruffians. Adoptive parents will not want troublesome children."

They all settled into their seats, and he said again, "I do ask your forgiveness for my . . . outburst."

It amazed Callie that a minister could lose his temper, but she had to admire him for admitting it and asking their forgiveness.

That evening, while Callie passed around the cracker basket and the train clickety-clacked toward their first placing-out destination, she noticed that the children were growing restive again.

After a while, Matthew stood in the middle of the aisle and talked to them about Christ, then led them in hymns, including "There's a Rest for the Weary," which Callie had heard them sing in New York. The words not only made the orphans more hopeful, but made Callie feel less beset by fretfulness. They finished the evening with a final hymn.

Just as I am, without one plea,
But that Thy blood was shed for me,
And that Thou bidd'st me come to Thee,
O Lamb of God, I come, I come!

The idea of Christ's blood shed for her left a sickly taste in Callie's mouth, yet she felt that somehow she must be missing something about Christianity.

The next morning, she felt as nervous as the children. "Time to bring out your new clothes so you'll look clean and neat. If you look good, you'll even feel better."

"Huh!" Samuel Bruder protested. "Won't do much good fer a big ugly fellow like me."

"You're not ugly," Callie told him in all honesty. "In a year or two, when you've outgrown your gangliness, you'll be a handsome young man."

Samuel shot her a look of disbelief.

"I think so, even if you don't," she added. "I wouldn't be at all surprised if the girls won't be after you."

The boys teased him, and Samuel ducked his head to hide a pleased grin.

Grinning himself, Reverend Hansel gave the boys new

white shirts and dark trousers as Callie distributed bright cotton dresses to the girls.

The boys managed to change clothes in their seats, but the girls took turns using the coach's tiny lavatory. They emerged with satisfaction in their new store-bought dresses, and were eager to receive their matching hair ribbons.

After Ruby had put on her new pink dress, she made her way back, far too serious, to sit beside Callie. "How do I look?"

"More like a Ruby should," Callie answered. The color brought out the soft pink tones in Ruby's thin face, and the flared skirt hid her gauntness.

"Come on!" Ruby objected. "I ain't even sure I like pink."

It had been the only dress long enough for Ruby, but Callie insisted, "You look very nice in it. Let's take out those braids and brush your hair."

Ruby twisted away. "No. It'll seem like I'm . . . lookin' fer trouble!"

"Let's try it," Callie said, getting her own hair brush. "If it makes you appear the least bit brazen, believe me, I'll be the first one to tell you."

Ruby grabbed a hopeful breath and turned around on their train bench. "Will you braid it back up if it looks wrong?"

"I will," Callie promised, removing the India-rubber bands from around the girl's braids.

"They got rid o' the lice for me in New York at the Orphan Society. I hope they ain't back."

Callie brushed out Ruby's hair, glad to see no sign of the vermin. "They did a good job of it, Ruby. And it looks as if you've a natural wave in your hair. It's going to be very pretty . . . soft and girlish. Let's just tuck it behind your ears and tie a pink ribbon on top."

Pleased when she'd finished it, she handed her mirror to

Ruby. "See how nice you look . . . like a proper young lady. It's a shame to have to pin the name tags on your new dresses."

Ruby took the mirror and stared into it with amazement. "I look different, all right. Now I'm prayin' the right family will take me. The *right* family. Will you stand with me?"

"I will," Callie assured her. Most of the other girls had gathered around to watch Ruby's transformation, and they wanted Miss Murray to do the same for them.

"And stand by me, please," Ingrid requested, perched beside the blankets piled against the next bench.

"I'll stand between the two of you."

"They promised that Ollie and I vould be placed in ze same home," Ingrid reminded her anxiously.

"Then you shall be," Callie said.

Frieda and Gretchen, the German sisters, put in a quick, "*Ja*, zey promise it from the beginning. All four of us sisters *und* brothers together."

Callie nodded. It would be difficult to place four children together. "I'm sure Reverend Hansel stands by that promise. Here, let me brush your hair too."

Her own brother and sisters had endured this very anguish just a few years ago, she thought, her heart going out to them again.

Busy as she was brushing the girls' hair and tying on ribbons, it seemed to Callie that it took forever for the train to pull into the small rural depot. She stuck her head out the window and saw that the station was surrounded by buggies and wagons. A young woman ran across the tracks ahead of the slow moving train, pulling her three young children after her, and a crowd was gathering at the edge of the platform. Most had gathered, Callie realized, to look over the orphans.

The train puffed to a halt, and Callie rose to her feet, taking a last look at the twenty-seven strangely quiet children behind her in the coach. They looked as neat and clean as she had ever seen them, but half excited and half frightened.

Standing at the back door, Reverend Hansel said, "Let's have a last prayer." With that, he bowed his head, "Heavenly Father, Thou knowest how these children yearn for a good home, and how our hearts yearn with theirs for exactly that. We ask for Thy perfect wisdom in matching the children with new parents and for a useful future for them in good Christian homes. In Christ's powerful name, we pray. Amen."

The conductor pulled open the door and, from the platform, an older minister introduced himself to Callie. "I'm Reverend Gresham, here on behalf of the parents who wish to take children into their homes."

Callie swallowed. "I'm Charlotte Murray, the girls' escort. Reverend Hansel is at the back door. We only stop here for half an hour."

The minister nodded and called out a thank-you, then rushed off toward the back door.

Callie stepped down to the platform, turning to help Ingrid, then Ruby and the other girls.

The crowd of would-be parents spilled onto the platform, most of the men in overalls and the women in calico dresses. They eyed the children with great interest.

"Smile and be friendly," Callie whispered to her charges. "Don't look so frightened."

The girls pasted on uncertain smiles, and she wished with all of her heart that she could be more helpful.

Looking at them as they lined up in front of the coach, it seemed to her that the younger children would be most in demand, and this turned out to be true for the girls. The first to be chosen were eight-year-old Alice, with the slightly crossed eyes, and Dora, the small Irish colleen. They were claimed by farm families, and Reverend Gresham began to fill out their orphan society contracts. The grocer's wife took an interest in Ivy, then noticed her limp and moved on to nine-year-old Lavina.

The choosing of boys was a different matter. The farmers headed straight for the biggest like Ollie, Samuel, and the German boys, Horst and Gunther, and asked to feel their muscles.

"I go only with my sister, Ingrid," Ollie told them, jerking a thumb at her. "They promised in New York, no families separated."

"*Ja,*" the Jung brothers agreed. "We are four of us . . . two sisters over zere."

A blond farmer stepped back from Ollie with regret. "Don't need a girl. Need strong boys for a farm."

His pregnant wife took a long look at Ingrid, then approached her husband shyly. "A girl would be a good help for me in the house now, and I think they are Norwegian like us. See, the name papers they wear say Nordberg."

"From *Norge* . . . Norway," Ingrid put in hopefully, joining her brother. "Our mama and papa died on ze boat to New York."

"*Kara mig!*" the woman said with an oh-dear! tone. Her blue eyes shone with compassion as she turned to her husband. "*Gud* meant them for us, Sven. If ever a family vas made for each other." She turned to explain to Ingrid and Ollie, "Our son, he died from fever last year."

Ingrid glanced from the couple to Callie, who gave her an encouraging nod. She whispered, "She seems nice, and you and Ollie could be together."

The man said, "*Ja,* we take both and give them a good home. They should be together."

Reverend Hansel stood up on a train stool and explained, "For those of you who don't already know, the contract calls for boys fifteen years and older to work for their board and clothes until they are eighteen, when they can make their own arrangements. Children under twelve are expected to remain in the household until they are eighteen, and are to be treated as one of the family in schooling, clothing, and training."

Beside Callie, a couple had approached Ruby, who in turn eyed the man with trepidation.

"Spindly," he said, scrutinizing her as if she were a horse at an auction. "Spindly, like you," he told his wife with more than a hint of disapproval. "But if you want her, I guess she'll do."

Dark circles lay under his wife's eyes, and she darted a frightened glance at him. "You sure? I don't want no blame from you later."

Uncertain, Callie asked, "Do you live on a farm?"

The man answered begrudgingly, "We got a small place on the edge of town."

"He's the undertaker," his wife explained nervously. "Silas Stillman, Undertaking."

His gray eyes shot her a silencing look. "Ain't a thing wrong with the work! Somebody's got to do it if folks won't bury their own."

"I'm sure that's so," Callie agreed.

He added, "We do some farmin' besides."

Callie disliked the glints of rage she saw flickering in his eyes and of fear in his wife's. "This is a very important decision for Ruby," she told them, gathering her courage. "Likely the most important decision of her life."

The wife nodded, and her husband's jaw hardened.

"It's our decision, though," he muttered. "Our decision."

"And Ruby's," Callie told them. "Would you expect her to help you with your work?"

"I would," he answered, almost indignantly.

"If you'll please excuse us, I'd like a word with her."

Ruby hurried a short distance away with her. Peering back, she whispered, "It's not just his work, Miss Murray. I plain don't like him. I-I don't like the fierce look about him. He reminds me of . . . my stepfather."

Callie drew a deep breath. "Get back in the coach, Ruby. I'll manage this somehow."

When she returned to the couple, the man appeared angrier yet and his wife more terrified. Callie clenched her fists. "I'm sorry, but Ruby has other plans."

"Other plans?" the man repeated. "What other plans?"

"Just other plans, sir," Callie replied and walked on, amazed at her own nerve. Heading for the coach, she caught the Reverend Gresham's eye, and he gave her a small nod. Encouraged by his approval, she spoke to him in a low voice. "I had to do it for Ruby. If I did right, I hope you'll explain to Reverend Hansel."

"I will," Reverend Gresham replied. "Don't worry."

Callie was glad that, for a change, she had made a difficult stand.

By the time the train whistled its last warning, eight of the orphans had been placed with local families. They climbed into the wagons and buggies, and turned to wave emotional farewells to the rest of them back by the train. "Good-bye!" they shouted. "Good-bye and good luck at the next placing-out stop!"

Callie stepped up into their coach and smiled at Ruby, who sat huddled with her back against the window, her face pinched with misery.

"I promised you'd go with a good family," Callie said as she sat down beside her, "and I plan to keep my promise." For an instant she was tempted to say, *If I have to take you myself!* No—best not to get too caught up in the children's lives. Soon she would have two younger sisters and a brother to see to. Likely Langsdon was gathering them up now.

As the train began to huff and puff past the station, they all waved again to the children riding off with new families. Ingrid and Ollie sat among grain sacks in a farm wagon, their blond hair shining. Like the others, they waved back wistfully.

"Looks like they made it," Yorker said, sounding rejected.

"It looks to me like the rest of you just haven't been paired with the right families yet," Reverend Hansel answered. He made his way down the aisle toward them as the train gathered speed. "Some things in life take longer than others."

"*Ja*," Gretchen agreed. "It vill take longer to find a family that wants four of us."

After talking to the children, Reverend Hansel said, "Miss Murray, we need to have a discussion. Would you sit with me in the middle of the coach for a while?"

She hoped she wasn't in for trouble. "Yes, of course."

He had removed his black frock coat, and she noticed that his shoulders were even broader than she had imagined. She rose from her seat, and just then, their coach swayed over the train track. She grabbed the back of her bench for balance, and caught it. For an unsteady instant, she had half-wished he'd catch hold of her again, but he'd been busy keeping his own balance. Or perhaps he was angry with her.

"After you," he said, standing aside carefully.

Despite the train's swaying, she staggered onward into the middle of the coach, where five rows of wooden benches now separated the girls from the boys. "Here?"

"Fine," he replied with an encouraging smile.

She slipped into the window seat, wondering what he wished to discuss. He sat down beside her, and she touched her hair anxiously, finding it still well tucked into the French twist she'd done up tightly this morning.

"You look very nice, as usual, Miss Murray," he said,

noticing her gesture.

"I . . . thank you." His brown eyes shone warmly, and she found herself giving him a small smile in return.

"Reverend Gresham told me about Ruby's encounter with the undertaker and your decision in her behalf."

"I can explain—"

"No need to look so worried, Miss Murray, and no need to explain. We prayed for wisdom, and God gave it to you and Ruby when you turned the man down for her. I understand he has a poor reputation. Reverend Gresham didn't realize they were there until it was too late. Thank you for your courage on Ruby's behalf."

A tumult of emotions shook her. "I'm glad you think it was the right thing to do. I was afraid of over-stepping my authority."

"Not at all. You've been doing a fine job with the girls," he added, "not that it should be so surprising. You're a sensitive and caring young woman."

It was the kind of praise she'd seldom heard. "Thank you. Thank you, Reverend Hansel. You. . .make my job easier for me."

"Prayer has a way of doing that."

"You've been praying for me?" she asked, darting another glance at him.

He nodded, his broad smile making his eyes sparkle. Romantic eyes, as Becca had said. In fact, everything about him was romantic. Everything except his white clerical collar.

"I've been praying for everyone in this coach, not to mention the prospective parents, the conductor, and the engineer. Wouldn't you expect that of a minister?"

"Yes, I guess so."

"There are a great many things that people expect of a minister, aren't there?" he asked.

"I suppose so."

"What do you expect of one, Miss Murray?"

She drew an uncertain breath. "Why, I've never thought about it. I suppose that he's a good man and prays a lot."

He gave a little laugh at her answer. "Then why are you so wary of me?"

Every nerve in her body went on alert. "I don't know."

"You failed to mention one thing about ministers . . . that they are human . . . that they are men who are prone to human feelings like anyone else."

Callie swallowed, wondering where this conversation might lead.

After a long moment, he smiled. "Would calling me Matthew be hard for you?"

"I . . . don't know." Instead of thinking of his name, she was noticing his sensuous lips and a fine angular chin with its intriguing cleft.

"Try it," he said.

"Matthew," she pronounced softly into the clickety-clack of the train.

"And may I call you Callie?"

She nodded." Yes."

His brown eyes twinkled. "Best to be Miss Murray and Reverend Hansel in front of the children. What do you think?"

She nodded again. "It's probably wisest."

He hesitated, then inquired, "What is the most important thing for me to know about you, Callie?"

It struck her as a peculiar question, but an answer came readily. "I've been an orphan since I was eleven years old. Ten years now. I lived in Grayton Orphanage, north of the city, until I was sixteen."

"Your minister mentioned that in his letter of recommendation. He said it had strengthen your faith."

She swallowed, knowing that Langsdon had somehow obtained that letter. She grasped the first thought that came to mind. "They often spoke of God at the orphanage, and we always had prayers." She didn't tell him, however, that the prayers at Grayton had seemed empty and made little difference in their bleak lives. She hoped he wouldn't pursue the matter and quickly posed the same question he had put to her. "What is important about you?"

"The most important aspect of my life is that I love the Lord God and my calling as a minister. But the reason I wanted this discussion is to tell you how pleased I am with the way you are managing the girls. Mrs. Lester, whom you replaced, is a fine lady, but she's considerably older than you and was rather stern. Your friend Becca is right; you do seem to have a gift for tending to children."

Callie's lips parted with surprise. Perhaps that was why she yearned so for her own brothers and sisters to be together—and to have a family of her own. She saw Matthew waiting for a reply, so she said, "I truly do care for the children. I can't seem to help it."

He smiled at her. "I'm not sure whether I should say it, but I am growing more and more fond of you, Callie."

She stared at him with disbelief, then suddenly recalled what Mr. Burlington had said—that a minister should be married. Perhaps he was determined to achieve that status before he reached California.

"Does that shock you?" he asked.

"I don't know. I-I've never thought . . ."

"Never thought that way about a minister?" he prompted.

"No . . . I haven't." She was glad to be sitting down. If she had been standing, surely her knees would have buckled.

He looked as if he wanted to hold her hands in his, and she placed hers carefully toward the window.

"In Centerville, we may have a short time to ourselves

once the children are placed," Matthew continued. "Would you spend it with me?"

Centerville was the very town where they'd pick up Glenda, Emelie, and Rolland! Callie didn't know what to say. Best to let him hear what he—and yes, she!—wished to hear. "That would be fine."

When he learned her motive for coming, she reflected, he wouldn't spend another minute with her, nor would he look at her again with such interest. She spoke into the silence, "Won't you tell me more about yourself?"

He straightened in their seat. "I grew up in Massachusetts . . . Sturbridge Village, where my father and brother run the printing shop. My mother worked hard for the church before she went to be with the Lord. My sister is married to the minister there, and they have four children."

He smiled at Callie. "I can't think of anything remarkable to tell you except that I was called to become a minister of the gospel when I was fifteen years old. Later I attended Princeton and its seminary. The Lord has kept my life on the straight and narrow path, so there is nothing outrageous or very interesting to relate. Actually, last year's orphan train excursion was one of the more interesting times of my life. Of course, Mrs. Lester, the girls' escort, was experienced and guided me in what to do."

Callie wondered about his late fiancee, but was reluctant to inquire.

"Well, ain't this beans?!" Yorker said, grinning at them from the aisle. "Just what I expected! Be careful, Miss Murray, or he'll be after you fer a 'holy kiss'!"

Matthew's color deepened, but he replied with a chuckle. "Now, Yorker, you mustn't let that imagination of yours run away with you. I suppose I am wanted by you boys."

"You ain't wanted back there t'all," Yorker objected.

"Well, I am coming nevertheless," Reverend Hansel

replied. "Miss Murray and I just needed to discuss some matters."

Callie managed a bright smile, though she feared she must look embarrassed. As she rose up beside him in the aisle, he smiled so warmly at her that her knees began to weaken again.

That evening as the train rolled ever westward through Ohio, she hoped he would come by for another discussion. They had exchanged arresting glances as they'd passed out sandwiches and apples to the children for dinner, but, surrounded with extremely curious children, they'd had no opportunity for further conversation of note.

After the spirited eventide hymn singing, Matthew's eyes met hers with eagerness. It didn't surprise her when he came calling on her after darkness fell.

"Miss Murray, I wonder if we might discuss some matters of importance again."

"Of course, Reverend Hansel," she replied, blushing in the dimly lit coach. She rose so hastily that she nearly tripped over her skirts.

Ruby gave her a knowing smile, and Callie blinked hard to make a show of innocence.

Tonight clouds obscured the moonlight, but the lantern swinging from a ceiling hook in the aisle gave enough light to see that most of the children were already asleep. As Callie slid into the window seat, she darted a glance up at him. Surely he was the most appealing man she had ever met— kindly, intelligent, and very manly. It felt fitting and proper to be sitting with him.

At first they spoke of the fine weather and the day's events, then they fell into silence.

At length Matthew said, "I am hesitant to confess it, Callie, but I've looked forward to being with you again."

And I with you, she thought. Though she didn't say the words aloud, she suspected that he could read her feelings in her expression, even in the dim light.

"Tell me more about yourself," he urged quietly, so they wouldn't awaken the children.

"What shall I tell you?"

"About working at the Burlingtons' home, perhaps."

"I was only there two years," she began, "but it was wonderfully interesting, and the Burlingtons were most kind—especially after they became such enthusiasts about religion."

"Yes," Matthew said, "they found the Lord in the Great Awakening going on in New York. Reverend Gresham tells me it has spread into Ohio, and they are praying that it travels far beyond into the west."

She nodded. "The Burlingtons often spoke of it."

He looked at her, waiting, and she managed, "It—it is very interesting."

"Only interesting?" he asked.

"And . . . amazing, of course, especially their using the theaters for prayer meetings."

At a loss for further comment, she felt certain her ignorance would be her undoing. On the other hand, there was the letter of commendation Langsdon had arranged to come from "her minister." Matthew had told the Burlingtons that it was excellent, and she hoped it would help to allay any suspicions on his part.

She turned back to their original topic. "My best friend in the Burlington household was Becca, Mrs. Burlington's personal maid and seamstress. And, of course, there were Molly and Joseph, who have worked in the mansion forever. Joseph is the one who drove Mrs. Burlington and me down to the wharf in New York. Then there was the butler . . . Mr. Stane, who greeted you at the door."

"Ah, yes, the very proper and interesting British butler," Matthew remarked. "Tell me about him."

She felt relieved to have diverted his attention. "Mr. Stane was a fine butler, but he was also . . . forward."

She could see the flicker of interest in Matthew's eyes, even in the dimly lit coach.

"Forward?" he asked.

"Yes." She glanced around the coach and spoke quietly. "Forward . . . with young women." Having piqued his curiosity, she decided to go on. "Becca once loosed a volley of German on him and kicked him in the shins."

Matthew gave a chuckle. "And you? Did you kick him too?"

Callie bit back a smile. "I am ashamed to admit it, but I hit him over the head with the duster."

Matthew put a hand over his mouth to muffle his laughter. When he recovered, he asked with seriousness, "Would you hit . . . another man over the head with a duster if he tried to kiss you, Callie?"

His intimate tone made her feel strangely shy, but honesty rose to the fore. "I don't know. No man has ever truly . . . that is . . . no man has ever kissed me."

He spoke softly. "I'm glad to hear it."

He stared at her, and she felt miffed at herself for having told too much, not to mention having brought up an unsuitable subject. Not knowing what to say next, she blurted, "You were engaged. I would think you'd know a lot about it."

Matthew hesitated, then said, "She was chosen for me, a fine and intelligent woman, but the fact is, we scarcely knew each other. When I did get her out for a walk, she was rather . . . unfriendly."

Callie's heart swelled with gratefulness and then with another burst of daring. She whispered the very words he'd said to her, "I am glad to hear it."

He hesitated, then a slow smile spread across his face and he reached for her hand. "Callie . . .?"

Entirely unnerved, she forced herself to stand. "Excuse me. I'd better see to the girls."

He rose to his feet and stepped back into the aisle most courteously to let her pass. "It appears that you have better sense than I. I'm sorry if I've offended you."

She shook her head, then quickly made her way up the aisle of the swaying coach. She hadn't felt in the least bit offended; the truth was, she hadn't felt like leaving his side.

7

April 18, 1858
On the train in western Ohio
Dear Becca,

What an adventure my life has become since I last saw you, my friend. But first of all, I hope that matters were righted between you and Thomas, and that you might meet me in Independence in early May. And I fervently hope the Missouri Talbots will welcome me. If not, I shall have to make other arrangements before I go on to California.

Oh, Becca, I finally understand why people in love act as if they are living on clouds. You will never believe it, but Matthew Hansel, the minister, has told me that he is fond of me, and I am equally fond of him, if not more so! I can scarcely concentrate on the matter at hand, which is placing the orphans in homes here in the Midwest, because I can't keep my mind from him—a minister! Remember your saying that he has romantic eyes? He does, oh my dear friend, he does. He is romantic through and through. He was engaged once, by arrangement of others, but his fiancee died. I am grateful that he did not originate their engagement, or I fear I would feel like second *choice. He has made it very clear that I am not.*

We are trying to be circumspect around the children. We are rarely together without them—not that I haven't become very fond of them, too. Matthew and I steal time together every night in the middle of the coach when the children are asleep.

In Centerville, Indiana, a town that took many orphans in the past, they are planning festivities as they did last year when an orphan train came through. We hope to have some time together there after the children are placed, since our railroad coach will be parked at the station siding, waiting to join up with the evening train.

At our first scheduled placing stop in Ohio, eight of our orphans found homes, and at the next stop, three were placed. At the third, no one came to the station for children because of fevers in the countryside. Yesterday, four children found homes. Unfortunately, the twelve remaining children are more difficult to place. For example, we have four German children whom we hope to put in the same home, and it is hard enough to get a family to take even two from one family. We also have a perfectly beautiful enchantress, Ivy, who has a severe limp. My seat mate, twelve-year-old Ruby, is terrified of men, and for a good reason. I hope we'll find a good home for her.

Among the boys, we have characters like Yorker, who is far too ready with his mouth to please some of the prospective parents, although I must admit he can be most comical. As we travel along and these children are not chosen, it grows more difficult for them to have hope, so we have to do a mighty job of cheering them.

I will say that being—dare I say it?—in love with Matthew lifts my spirits so high that I have been able to encourage the children. Never in my wildest expectations did I think I might fall in love with a minister, and I still feel uneasy about that aspect. I often think that a churchgoer like you would be more suitable for him. In any event, the bright moments are tempered by dark worryings and wonderings about whether I am truly good enough for him.

Please excuse the jiggling script, my dear friend, but the railroad tracks are imperfectly laid, and the coach sways wildly at times instead of gliding straight along. And that may be the perfect way to describe the romance: our suitability seems imperfectly laid in places, and for me, at least, the alliance sways wildly at times. On the other hand, I think of the trials you and Thomas have endured, and I know that the course of true love never did run smooth, as Mr. Shakespeare said. I hope with all of my heart that yours does now!

I hope to see you in Independence, Missouri, and, if not, to receive a letter from you telling me what is happening with you and Thomas. If I am unable to find you, I shall inquire after a letter at the post office. One can only hope that they have regular postal offices on the frontier!

Your loving friend,
Callie

P.S. Matthew sends his regards to you. I have told him a bit about you, and he already cares about you very much. He also admires the frocks that you helped me sew.

Reverend Daniels, the interim minister, spoke from the pulpit. "Benjamin Talbot, I believe you have an announcement."

Benjamin rose from the front pew of the small white country church and made his way up the steps to the altar.

Daughter Martha sat smiling at him from her bench behind the small pump organ, and he returned her smile before turning to face the congregation. In the first few rows, he saw encouragement on the faces of the rest of his family: Abby and Daniel with their children; Martha's husband, Luke, and their children; Jennie and Jeremy and their children. His sister, Jessica, gave a nod of her gray head, likely to remind him that she was praying for him while he spoke.

For an instant, he wished he still led the Sunday services in his own parlor, back when Jessica played the organ and one never knew what God had in store for them. Exciting as those days had been, they were over, he reminded himself, and usually it was better to have a real minister and a church building that belonged to the entire congregation.

"Reverend Daniels," he began, "my friends . . ."

Some smiled, but a few regarded him with suspicion as if they were thinking, *What now, Benjamin Talbot?*

"I have further news of the great revival taking place in New York City," he told them. "It is already being referred to by many as America's Second Great Awakening and also as the Fulton Street Prayer Meeting, that being where it was begun by one layman."

"One lone layman," he repeated to prepare their thinking. "As you may know, hundreds of thousands of believers have already been added to the church's rolls, not only in New York but in other northeast states, and the spirit of revival moves now through the Midwest. It is expected that a million will be converted, a mighty awakening in a nation of thirty million inhabitants. One million among thirty million."

He paused to let the numbers sink in. "I am certain you are all as pleased as I am about this good news. I hope you'll agree that, since we are part of the United States, albeit on the Pacific slope, the Lord would want us to pray for revival where we are, as well."

Several eyed him with skepticism, which was nothing new for him. There had been doubt and apprehension in Missouri when he'd suggested the journey by covered wagon in 1846 . . . . appalled faces in the California Territory when he'd proposed the first brush arbor meetings at the beginning of the gold rush . . . outright opposition when he'd fought for statehood, and, in 1855, fierce disagreement when he'd encouraged the churches of San Francisco to join together in an all-out battle against lawlessness.

"I am not going to propose anything outrageous, as some of you seem to suspect," he assured them. "Instead, I am going to suggest that we begin as they did in New York with Wednesday noon meetings for prayer. Nothing formal, nothing dramatic . . . only that those of us who can manage would meet here in this church to pray for spiritual revival for our great land."

Already a murmuring grew, and he quickly said, "We know that not everyone can leave work to come on Wednesdays at noon, and that some of you can only come for five minutes, which is fine and would be greatly appreciated. We will arrive and depart as required. My proposal is merely that those of us who are able to attend, join in prayer that the revival spreading across our great land might come in great strength to California."

He added, "From 1800 to 1850, the population of our country grew over four times as large, but the churches did even better, their membership increasing twelve times over. Let us stand up and be counted for the Lord!"

Reverend Daniels was adverse to long announcements, and he rose to his feet behind the pulpit.

"Thank you, my friends and Reverend Daniels," Benjamin finished quickly. "I hope to see you here Wednesday at the noon hour. I hope you'll be one of those who will say with Isaiah, that great prophet of old, 'Here am I, Lord, send me!'"

On Wednesday, just before noon, Benjamin drove the buggy slowly down the dusty driveway past the four gravestones and to the church's hitching post. "Well," he said to Jessica, "it appears we're the first arrivals."

"And perhaps the only ones," his sister answered as the horses halted. "But God hears our prayers and has often answered them far beyond our expectations. I don't need to tell you that, Benjamin."

He nodded as he climbed down from the buggy. In her old age, Jessica had begun to repeat herself, but likely he did himself. "Thank you for reminding me, my dear sister. It would be nice, though, if just this one time Reverend Daniels might veer from his custom of writing his sermon on Wednesday. Perhaps attending our prayer meeting would even give him grist for the mill."

Taking the reins, he tied the two horses to the hitching post under the straggly oak trees. Daniel was busy in town at the shipping and chandlery warehouse, and Luke and Jeremy had their chores at the ranch. He knew it would be difficult for them to come. And the women, as always, were inundated with work, with so many young children.

"Perhaps the others might still come," Jessica said, reading his thoughts. Stiff with age, she waited for him to help her down from the buggy. "In any event," she added, "we're commencing our prayer meeting with one more person than Jeremy Lanphier did in New York. The Lord tells us that where two or three are gathered together in His name, He will be in the midst of them."

Benjamin grinned as he helped her down from the buggy seat. "No need to preach to me on it, Jessica."

She laughed and straightened the skirt of her dark blue frock. "I remember Father preaching on that verse from his pulpit in Boston as if it were yesterday. 'If two of you shall agree on earth as touching anything that they shall ask, it shall be done for them of my Father which is in Heaven.'"

"I remember too," he admitted. "I might have acted the rebel, but I remember Father's sermons all too well."

He turned, scarcely aware of the occasional buggies and horseback riders passing by on the road up above the small graveyard. An odd compulsion overcame him, and he raised his arms heavenward like a prophet of old.

"Our Heavenly Father, Jessica and I stand on that scripture," he prayed with fervor. "The two of us stand in agreement here on earth that Thou wouldst move upon the people's hearts for ongoing revival across this vast land and, in particular, for this still ungodly state of California. Lord, stir the hearts of lukewarm Christians and touch the souls of unbelievers!"

He paused and, just as amazingly, Jessica raised her arms in petition with him. "We beseech Thee for this, Heavenly Father," she called out, "in the blessed and powerful name of our Redeemer and Lord, Jesus Christ."

"Well," Benjamin said as he lowered his arms, "I didn't quite expect to be praying out here, arms to the heavens. Especially not with an audience above on the road."

Jessica chuckled. "Perhaps it will give them something to reflect upon." She glanced back to the sprawling oak trees. "I don't believe you could have stopped that prayer any more than those birds could stop singing."

He nodded. "Mayhap not." He heard horses and a buggy coming along the road, then turning down the churchyard driveway. "Ah, it's Abby and Daniel in the old buggy!"

Jessica beamed at him. "And where four of us are gathered. . . ."

"Yes. Four of us to start."

"As always, there will be opposition," she warned.

"I know it," he answered. "Let it come. And let it be

known that we revere the Lord more than we fear the opposition."

"Centerville!" the conductor called out, sticking his head into their railroad car. "Next stop, Centerville!"

Callie peered out the window at the countryside where Glenda, Emelie, and Rolland lived. The land was heavily wooded, and she wouldn't have been surprised to see bears and other wild animals coming from the forest. She remembered a man at the last train stop telling about life in Indiana.

"We live the same as Injuns 'ceptin' we take an interest in politics and religion," he had said. When the talk had touched on art, he'd added, "I know a fellow down in Terry Haute 'at kin spit clear over a box car!"

What would this rustic life have done to Glenda, Emelie, and Rolland? Between the New York orphanage and living in the wilderness, they'd surely have forgotten all of the niceties of life they had learned from their British nanny.

As the train slowly huffed into the station, Callie was glad to see that Centerville was a small town. The usual sight of wagons and buggies at the hitching post near the train platform was reassuring. She half-expected to see Langsdon standing there with Glenda, Emelie, and Rolland at his side. Instead, a man wearing a dark suit and a clerical collar stood on the depot's platform. Likely the local minister in charge of placing out orphans.

Once they were off the train and organized, she'd have to stop in the station to see if Langsdon had left a message. If only she dared tell Matthew about her sisters and brothers. If only she and Langsdon could get them back without being so secretive about it!

"Where's all the placing-out families?" Ruby asked.

Reverend Hansel had just joined them at the front door of the coach. "Probably over at the church, getting together a fine mid-day meal for us, as they did last year. Wait until you see the pies these Centerville ladies bake."

"Can't wait to get my teeth in a pork pie," Yorker said.

"These are more apt to be fruit and lemon meringue pies," Reverend Hansel told him.

"Fruit 'n lemon pies?!" Yorker repeated. "Ain't there no meat in this town? Don't tell me yer bringin' us to a place poorer than the streets of New York City!"

Reverend Hansel laughed. "You'll find plenty of roast beef and fried chicken, as I recall. And I dare say you'll like fruit and meringue pies better than what you've had."

Yorker stared out the window. "Don't look anythin' like New York City," he remarked, unconvinced.

"Thank goodness, for your sakes," Matthew replied. He glanced at Callie. "Pray tell, Miss Murray, why are you looking so concerned?"

She spoke quietly. "I'm hoping we'll find families to take the rest."

"We'll leave that in God's hands," Matthew replied with a smile. "No need for you to worry." He glanced at the children, who gazed anxiously out the windows, then added to her, "You haven't forgotten our walk after our duties are over, I hope?"

She blushed. "I haven't." She wondered if there would be time for a walk, between placing the children and finding her own family.

"Centerville!" the conductor called out, banging open the front door of their coach.

"Before we go, let's have a prayer," Matthew said to the children.

Their faces were white with strain, and Callie bowed her head with them.

"Our Heavenly Father," Matthew prayed, "we come in praise and thanksgiving for our many blessings, unworthy though we are, and also with a special petition for these children. We ask for Thy guidance and wisdom for placing them with the right families, the ones Thou hast already chosen for them, and we ask for Thy special blessing on them and their new families. In Christ's holy name we pray."

"Amen," several of the children said in firm agreement.

Callie scrutinized her charges. They'd dressed in their new clothing again for the occasion and looked fine, but instead of growing accustomed to the placing-out stops, they appeared more agitated.

"You all look wonderful," she assured them. "Here, Ruby, let me fix your ribbon."

Yorker piped up, trying to be funny, "Say, that's exactly what I need—a pink ribbon in me hair."

"Oh, Yorker!" Callie put in when the children didn't laugh. "We're going to miss your humor when you leave us. We're going to miss you fiercely."

His eyes darted up to hers. "You jokin', Miss Murray?"

"I'm being perfectly honest."

"I hoped so." He quickly looked out the window again, jutting out his chin.

"All off for Centerville!" Reverend Hansel called out. "I'll go first to speak with Reverend Klingman."

Callie stood at the door, adjusting the girls' ribbons and smoothing the boys' cowlicks as they filed past her. "You look good," she told them, "much healthier than when we left New York."

They had devoured a huge amount of food on the train and, though they were still thin, they no longer appeared emaciated. Best of all, their eyes were no longer dull.

"You think ve find a family here?" Gretchen asked.

"If it's meant to be," Callie answered.

"Maybe zey take too many orphans here last year," her brother Horst remarked, his brow furrowed. "Or maybe zey don't want German children."

"Reverend Hansel says God will take care of it."

Horst looked straight at her. "What do you think?"

"I . . . I hope so," Callie answered, then quickly realized she had undermined Matthew's firm assurances.

She followed the children off the coach and onto the railroad platform. The other minister was already gathering up the orphans, and Matthew told her, "We'll walk to the churchyard from here. The church is just down this main street, beyond the schoolhouse."

"I'll be along in a moment," Callie replied. "I need to stop at the depot first." Doubtless he would think she wanted to use the depot's lavatory. "I'm sure I can find the church."

He smiled. "Not apt to get lost in a town this size."

Inside the clapboard depot, she headed for the ticket window. "Do you have a letter for me, Miss Callie Murray?"

"Yes, indeed," the clerk said, eyeing her with interest. He got it for her from his desk. "Handsome young fellow left it an hour ago. Figured you'd be on the orphan coach."

An hour ago! Langsdon was here then!

The clerk waited as if she might explain, but she merely took the letter and said a hurried, "Thank you. Good-day."

Hastening outside, she tore open the envelope and read, *Will find you for next message. L.*

Had something gone wrong that he wanted to talk to her in person? she fretted. Had his plan failed?

No, he'd only written that he would find her for the next message. Perhaps the plan was just now underway. Surely that was it. He wouldn't take the children from their homes until just before the train left. She must not read more into his words than what was written on the paper.

Up ahead the children had apparently seen something they liked, for they were shouting, "Hip, hip, hurray for Centerville!"

She tucked the message into her handbag and looked about. The town had a mercantile, a two-story brick hotel, a feed store, and other small buildings. Ahead, there were houses, a log schoolhouse, and a white-steepled church. Behind the depot stood the town blacksmith shop and a lumber mill. Since it was such a small town, it seemed likely that Glenda, Emelie, and Rolland lived out in the country.

Callie noticed that a goodly number of people had gathered in the churchyard. Saddle horses and draft horses, their wagons still behind them, were tied to the church hitching post. Now the horses dozed, occasionally swishing their tails and stamping off the flies.

"Miss Murray!" Reverend Hansel called to her.

"Yes?" She wished again that she weren't so concerned about Langsdon. How would she ever explain to Matthew?

"Thought I'd wait for you," he said, coming out to the road to meet her. "They're having a mid-day meal for us in the churchyard, as they did last year. If I weren't led by God to go on to California, I'd think seriously of settling down in a friendly town like this."

The way his brown eyes sparkled as he helped her up the churchyard steps, she knew what he was considering: settling down and having a family. Her mind flew on to reality. What would he think when he realized *why* she'd come on the train? Worse, that Langsdon meant to abduct orphans who'd been placed here a few years ago!

"Is something disturbing you, Callie?"

She thought fast. "The wonderful smells of roasting corn and fried chicken. You'd think I hadn't eaten in days."

"You've been so preoccupied lately, I was beginning to think it might have to do with your family in Missouri," he replied. "You don't happen to have a hopeful young man waiting for you there?"

"No, not at all!"

He looked relieved. "I've been thinking about your traveling to Missouri once we've placed all of the orphans. I hope you'll travel on with me."

Exactly what Langsdon wanted! Callie thought gratefully. But the way Matthew Hansel was looking at her made her heart stop for an instant, and he was definitely not part of the plan.

"Well, Reverend Hansel," a strange voice intruded from behind her shoulder. "Sorry to interrupt what appears to be an intriguing discussion. Who are you hiding away from us here?"

Callie felt blood rush to her cheeks and noticed that Matthew flushed, too.

"This is Miss Murray, our escort for the girls," he explained. "Miss Murray, may I introduce you to Reverend Klingman, who is the society's agent for this region."

She extended her hand most properly, hoping to quell any suspicions on his part. "How do you do, Reverend Klingman?"

He nodded genially. "A pleasure to meet you, Miss Murray. Won't you come along for a drink of cold cider before we have dinner? We find it's far better for the children as well as the prospective parents to have some hours together, eating and visiting, before final commitments are made."

"Yes, a fine idea." She darted a glance at Matthew, who clearly approved too, then joined their host as they walked to the side of the white clapboard church.

Immediately she saw why the orphans had raised a cheer for Centerville. The scene was as colorful as a country painting. Plank tables had been set up at the side of the church, and the women, in bright calico frocks and snowy white aprons, were covering the tables with white tablecloths and fussing with the food at the buffet tables. The men, in their shirtsleeves, carried over wooden benches for seating. Small children played under the watchful eye of the older girls, and many of the other children ran about, playing spirited games.

This, she thought, was where her sisters and brother had been living. After enduring the grayness of an orphanage, it seemed a fine place.

Seeing her interest, Reverend Klingman said, "It's a good town for children to grow up in."

"I'm sure it is," she replied, then searched for something to change the subject. "I'm concerned about the four Jung children. They expect to be placed with the same family."

"Ah, yes, the German children," Reverend Klingman replied. "We have plenty of German families here, but placing four children in one family is a lot to ask. Still, God works miracles, wouldn't you say?"

Never having witnessed any, Callie only nodded.

Most of the orphans, she noticed, were drinking cider and visiting with families. Even Ruby was talking with a young couple who had twins and another babe in arms. Yorker was holding forth with the town boys, boasting rather loudly of his life as a "streeter" in New York City.

Reverend Klingman introduced her to a Mrs. Preskitt who served her a tin mug of cold cider.

"A pleasure to have you here," the woman said with enthusiasm. "My daughter came here by orphan train two years ago, and it's been a wonderful match. We couldn't be happier, having her in our family. Ah, here she is now."

Callie turned and almost gasped.

Emelie . . . her very own sister, Emelie!

She'd been eight years old when Callie had last seen her before leaving the orphanage, and five years made a great difference, but with the girl's blue eyes and thick red braid, it had to be Emelie.

"How old are you?" Callie asked.

The girl eyed her uneasily. "Just thirteen this week."

It was exactly her sister's age, and even her voice sounded familiar. "What's your name?"

"Emelie Preskitt."

"She's our only child," Mrs. Preskitt explained, then added with pride, "and she wished to take our name. My husband and I have formally adopted Emelie."

Callie swallowed, trying to appear unperturbed. A thousand questions flew to mind: *Did Emelie recognize her, too? Had Langsdon approached her? Was she going to California?*

"A pleasure to meet both of you and . . . to see that you're so happy together," she said, the words coming too quickly. "It makes my job seem all the more worthwhile to see such a success story. If you'll excuse me now, I'd better make my way around to see to the children we brought with us. Thank you for the very good cider."

She nearly tripped over her skirts in her haste to leave them behind, then saw that Matthew had been taking it all in from not too far away.

"What transpired there?" he asked.

"Almost spilling cider," she replied, forcing a smile. "I'm afraid I haven't got my land bearings yet."

"Allow me to take you to your table," he suggested. "They want us to sit at separate tables so prospective parents can ask questions, but I've managed to put you at the table next to mine. Reverend Klingman has offered to take charge for a while to give us some time off, as he did last year."

"Time for you and Mrs. Lester?" Callie asked.

"Why, Callie! Mrs. Lester is an older woman, a fine Christian lady."

"I'm sorry. I should have known better."

He grinned slightly. "Did I detect a bit of jealousy?"

She gazed up at him. It was true. For the first time in her life, a man had made her jealous.

"Don't look at me like that, Miss Murray," he said. "You quite take a man's breath away."

You take a woman's breath away too, she thought.

Someone rang the church bell, and Reverend Klingman stood on the church steps. Once the crowd had quieted, he said, "I welcome all of you on behalf of the people of Centerville, Indiana. It's our pleasure to meet you, and to invite you to sing 'Old Hundredth' with us before we go to the buffet to get our food."

He led out with an entirely different version from the hymn Callie had heard at the Burlingtons'.

Praise God, from whom all blessings flow,
Praise Him all people, here below;
Praise Him above, ye Heavenly Host,
Praise Father, Son, and Holy Ghost.

Embarrassed, she struggled with the unfamiliar words, turning from Matthew so he wouldn't notice. Surely he'd see through her pretense soon.

At the buffet tables, they busied themselves with taking roasted beef and pork, chicken, ham, and sausages, green beans and peas, salads, and pickled beets. Yorker was just in front of her, and she pointed out, "Those are the fruit pies for dessert . . . for later, after we've eaten the rest of dinner."

He grinned. His plate was heaped high, and he no longer seemed concerned that Centerville might be a poorer place than New York City.

Matthew seated her at the table next to his, and Ruby sat across from her, looking like a fish out of water with the young couple and their twins. It was clear that they were interested in her as a potential housemaid. While they ate, Callie tried to carry the conversation for the girl, since there was nothing to do about Emelie, who sat several tables away.

Later, when dinner was over and the tables were being

cleared, Emelie came to her. "Excuse me, Miss Murray," she said nervously. "I'd like to talk with you."

"Yes, of course," Callie answered.

"Over by the road?" she suggested, and Callie nodded.

They walked toward the road, talking about the horses at the hitching post and a robin chirping nearby. When they stopped under a tree, Callie scarcely knew how to begin. In the orphanage, they had been separated by age groups and had rarely seen each other. What did she have to offer this girl who was her sister?

"I know who you are," Emelie said warily.

"I thought perhaps you had guessed," Callie answered with a hopeful smile.

Emelie gulped before she spoke. "Langsdon was here. He wants me to go along to California with the rest of you."

"I do hope you're coming," Callie said. Concerned at the girl's silence, she rushed on, "I've dreamed of us all being together again, and it's Langsdon's hope, too."

Emelie shook her head. "I won't go. I won't leave the Preskitts. They're my family now."

"Emelie, please consider how we feel."

"I barely know you," the girl continued. "They couldn't find a family willing to keep all three of us. We thought we'd at least be near each other, but we've hardly seen each other since the orphan train. Glenda lives on a farm way out in the country, and Rolland even further away. I'd like to be with all of you, but I can't bear to be . . . all pulled apart again. The Preskitts are my family now!"

Callie reached for Emelie's arm, but her sister stood resolutely away. In the face of such determination, Callie could only think to say, "Mrs. Preskitt seems to be a fine, loving woman, but—"

"She's wonderful!" Emelie interrupted, her blue eyes narrow with determination. "And Mr. Preskitt, too. I won't leave them. I won't go!" She stood with her fists clenched. "If Langsdon tries to kidnap me like he said, I'll only run away and come back here. I already wrote a letter about him saying it, and I told all about your plans to go to Missouri and then California. I hid it where the Preskitts will find it right away if I disappear."

Callie stared at her. At last she said, "I'm glad you're happy with them, Emelie, but I had hoped we could all be together."

"Please don't make me go!" Emelie pleaded.

Callie hesitated. Then, hard as it was, she knew what she must say. "I won't force you to come with us."

Emelie sighed with relief. "Langsdon and I had a dreadful row. He finally said I should talk to you today."

Callie's heart hurt for all of them. "I see."

"I hope you'll tell the others good-bye for me," Emelie added, looking sad but still determined. "Tell them I'm sorry, but I want to stay here with my new family. I'll tear up the letter when I get home."

Callie could make no reply. Another difficult decision, but this time she wasn't feeling so uncertain. "Shall I tell the others you're too happy here to go?"

Emelie nodded, her thick braid moving against her back. "And that I'll miss them despite it."

Callie pressed her lips together.

Emelie glanced behind Callie. "Here comes the orphan train minister. We have to go."

"I'll write to you, Emelie, if you want me to."

Tears shone in the girl's eyes. "Oh, yes. And I'll write back, I promise. Mrs. Preskitt used to be a teacher, and I go to school, too, so it's easy for me."

Matthew had stopped, standing a discreet distance away.

Emelie spoke loudly enough for him to hear. "It was very nice to meet you, Miss Murray. Thank you for talking with me. We have to leave early, so I won't be seeing you again." And with that, she gave Callie a tremulous smile and started away.

Callie watched her thirteen-year-old sister as she hurried to Mrs. Preskitt, who awaited her with a curious but loving expression on her face. What a different woman from the one who'd given birth to Emelie and the rest of them. How different their lives might be if they'd all had a Mrs. Preskitt for their mother.

"A very secure young lady," Matthew remarked as Callie started toward him.

"Yes, she appears to be."

She wondered what he was thinking, but he didn't say. Instead, he changed the subject.

"Let's take a walk behind the church, down by Turkey Creek. They tell me we might even catch a turkey if we're fast on our feet."

She stared down at the grass as they walked. "I don't feel very fast on my feet right now."

"Good," he replied. "After such a big dinner, I don't feel much like running, either." They fell into step, heading around the side of the church and past the gravestones, then down through the maples, willows, and sycamores near the creek. "After so many days on the train with the children, it's pleasant to have some peace and quiet with you."

She darted a sidelong look at him, and he smiled lovingly.

He'd taken off his black jacket, and his broad shoulders filled his white shirt more than seemed suitable for a man who wore a clerical collar.

How she loved him! she thought as they walked alongside the creek. She loved him beyond anything she'd ever guessed love could be. That collar, however, was a frightening reminder of her unsuitability. Nothing had truly changed since the beginning. She wasn't a believer. She'd been conspiring with Langsdon to take Emelie, Glenda, and Rolland from their homes.

Her roiling thoughts narrowed to a hard determination: she would have to be as courageous as Emelie had been in her situation. No matter how much it might hurt, and no matter how much it upset Langsdon's plan, it would be best to break off with Matthew Hansel as soon as possible.

His voice held a hint of concern. "I should like to know what you are thinking, Callie."

She shook her head, then glanced around in the silence. "A deer," she whispered.

"So it is," Matthew said, and they admired the doe in silence until it disappeared in the underbrush. Nearby, a squirrel scampered from tree to tree, and red-winged blackbirds flitted from a willow to a maple up above.

Suddenly Callie felt watched—and not by the animals, either. She glanced around, but there was no one else to be seen.

His voice was as soft as the burble of the creek. "Look at me, Callie."

For an instant she thought to refuse, then she knew that for the rest of her life she wanted to remember how he looked at this moment. She turned to memorize his every feature—the deep cleft in his chin, the thick dark hair blowing slightly in the breeze, the brown eyes overflowing with love. Then slowly she began to harden herself against him.

He must have noticed, for he said, "I wish you would tell me what makes loving me so difficult for you."

"It's *not* loving you that's difficult," she replied, her voice trembling. "It's *not* loving you that's so impossible."

His expression filled with hope. "Then it can be worked out. If you love me half as much as I love you, anything can be worked out. Please don't look so unapproachable. Come, let me at least hold your hand."

His voice was so compelling that she reached a hand to him. Instead of simply holding it, he pressed it to his lips.

Meadowlarks sang in the distance, and the place seemed so beautiful and enchanted that suddenly she was moving into his arms.

"I love you, Callie," he whispered against her hair. "I love you. Nothing can ever change that or come between us."

He moved his head back, and his face was so filled with love that what little remained of her fine intentions fled. "Oh, Matthew!" she whispered. "I do love you!"

His lips met hers with such joy that she hoped their kiss would never end. He was right—nothing or no one could ever come between them. She was scarcely aware that he'd lifted her from her feet, only that she was being loved as never before. *I love you, I love you*, she thought. *I shall love you forever.*

When the kiss ended, he whirled her around, then gazed at her, half joyous and half guilty. "I'm sorry, Callie. I lose all reason just being near you. . ."

A loud "Harrruummm" sounded from just above them.

Reverend Klingman!

He was smiling, however. "Shall I post the banns?" he asked with amusement.

Matthew set Callie down, and heat raced to her face.

The minister smiled. "I'm sorry to interrupt, but I can't hold the children off much longer. Now that they've eaten twice their fill, several are determined to examine Turkey Creek before the square dancing begins."

Matthew nodded. "Let our little friends come."

"Six of the children are spoken for by families," Reverend Klingman continued, recounting their names. "The papers are already filled out. It's the others who need to get away."

Ruby, Yorker, and the Jung children were left to go on to

Illinois. Callie's heart went out to them when she saw them running down the hill toward them.

"Well, ain't you two beans?" Yorker said to her and Matthew again.

"I'm not sure what 'being beans' means," Matthew replied with a grin, "but I am certain as certain can be that Miss Murray isn't one."

They all laughed except Ruby, and Callie put her arm around the girl's angular shoulders. She wanted to ask what had happened to the young couple with the children, but decided it best to wait.

As they walked along on the rocks by the creek, Ruby warned under her breath, "Bein' in love ain't at all what it's claimed to be."

"How do you know?" Callie inquired.

"It's what my mum always said. Love will do you in."

"I suppose it depends on the people involved."

Ruby shook her head. "It ain't fer me."

"Maybe when you're older."

Ruby shook her head again. "Ain't fer me."

Callie didn't know how to answer. Her own feelings were in such turmoil; and her resolve to give up Matthew Hansel had vanished in his embrace.

She threw herself into exploring Turkey Creek with the children. Birds sang and flew about, but there were no wild turkeys to be found.

Later, when they returned to the churchyard, a scrawny man had taken his place on a caller's box. As the fiddlers began to play, the caller shouted in a peculiar rhythm, "All right, folks, let's make those sets. Find your honey, find your sweet, get that gal out on 'er feet."

Couples began to step forward, one at a time, blushing and peering about at their friends and neighbors. After three sets of dancers had been formed, the caller leaned into the fiddlers, tapping his toe until they had a rousing rhythm going between them.

"Swing her, boys, and do it right, swing the gals till the middle of the night!" the caller shouted, and the dancers flew into motion.

Callie and Matthew stood side by side watching them. The dancers whirled and turned, swinging from arm to arm, following the caller's rhymes, while around them folks clapped with the music and tapped their feet.

After the first dance, Matthew asked, "Shall we try it?"

"I don't know how," Callie confessed.

"It's simple. Even I caught on last year."

She let him lead her out to a new set and was pleased to see that Yorker had invited Ivy to dance, despite her limp.

"Miss Murray, I got placed with a family," Ivy told her joyously as they got ready. "The smithy's family in town. Their girl died last winter and they like me! See, there they are, dancing."

Callie saw the couple, who waved at her. "I'm so glad, Ivy. They look like fine people. I'm so glad!"

When the fiddlers and caller began, Callie was entirely unprepared. Before she knew what was happening, Matthew swung her around one way and then another, laughing as she tried to follow the "allemanding" and "sashaying." Out of breath, she ducked with him through the tunnel of hands.

"Atta way, Miss Murray!" Yorker called out as he swung her. "You're doin' real good!"

"You too, Yorker! You too, Ivy!"

The townsfolk joined in with their encouragement.

When the dance ended, Callie stood out of breath and laughing with the others. Her face flushed, she pinned back loose curls where her combs had come loose.

"I should like to see your hair entirely loose about your shoulders," Matthew said under his breath.

"What talk from a minister!" she protested.

"From a man," he reminded her. "A man who loves you."

She looked up at him with joy, but a moment later, her eyes were caught by a figure who stood at the edge of the afternoon shadows.

Langsdon!

Nervously she suggested to Matthew, "Why don't you ask Ruby to dance? She looks so unhappy."

"You're right, of course," he answered, "and here I've been enjoying myself most selfishly." With a grin and a bow, he left and went to Ruby.

Callie watched him coax the girl out to dance. Ruby darted a look at her, and Callie gave a nod of encouragement. She made herself stand and watch the dancers walk to their places. Yorker had found a pretty town girl as short as he, and the Jung sisters had their brothers as partners.

When they began to dance, Callie headed for the table where the cold cider was kept. Smiling and nodding at the townsfolk as she passed, she arrived at the cider table and filled a mug for herself. She took a sip of the cider, glancing to where Langsaon had been.

No sign of him now!

She strolled along with her cider, almost wondering if she'd imagined it. A second later, she saw him disappear around the back of the church building.

Glancing around to be sure no one was watching her, she went around the corner behind the church and saw him waiting for her. "Langsdon!"

He raised a sensuous brow at her. "Doesn't appear that you're hittin' the good reverend over the head with a duster."

She smiled guiltily. "I guess not."

"You talk to Emelie?"

Callie nodded. "She's happy here, Langsdon. She doesn't

want to leave. She told me she'd run back to her new family if we made her come with us."

Langsdon eyed her silently, so she finally added, "I-I told her she could stay, since that's what she wished."

"Wondered if you would. Maybe best. We don't need her makin' trouble wherever we go. Four of us is enough family."

Callie hoped so. "Where are Glenda and Rolland?"

"They'll be in the railroad coach ahead of yours."

"I hope they wanted to come!"

He nodded. "No arguin' there. They don't know where you'll be, only that you're on the train. Just ride on like nothin's changed. Stay with the orphans till you're rid of them, then ride on to the Mississippi River with Reverend Hansel. Once you're across the river, you'll have to spring Glenda and Rolland on him. Unless I miss my guess, you can coax him to accompany you to Independence. I have other fish to fry."

"How shall I do it?" she asked.

"I saw him kissin' you down by the creek. Appears to me you know just fine how to keep a man followin' you. Seems you're your mother's daughter after all."

She glared at him. "I am not!"

He laughed. "Somethin' else of interest. Your Mr. Stane was in town."

"Mr. Stane! Whatever was he doing here?"

Langsdon smiled. "Seems he's smitten with you too."

"I don't believe that for a minute, Langsdon, and neither do you!"

"At least you're that smart," he replied. "The Burlingtons fired him, and there's a New York warrant out for his arrest." Langsdon's blue-gray eyes glinted with mirth. "Appears someone reported that he stole their paintings. He figures it was you."

"Me!" she exclaimed incredulously. "Where is he?"

"I ran him out of town on the train ahead of yours."

"Mr. Stane is on the train ahead of mine?"

Langsdon grinned. "That's what I said."

It took a moment for Callie to assimilate everything. Then suddenly she knew the truth. "You told them, didn't you? You told the Burlingtons that Mr. Stane stole the paintings!"

"No. I never in my life spoke to the Burlingtons."

"But you let them know somehow . . . and he thinks it was me. What did you do? Sign my name to a letter to them?"

A new thought hit, and it was just as unpleasant. "Langsdon, when we were in New York, you said you wrote to the Talbots in California. Did you sign my name to their letter too?"

He raised his chin. "I do not forge female script."

"Then you had someone write the letters and sign my name to them." The words were no more than out than she saw they were true. She clenched her fists. "One of your lady friends wrote the letters for you."

He laughed. "Best you don't know too much. Best to be innocent, Callie, except to know your name will turn into Charlotte Murray Talbot in Independence. And don't tell the reverend you're married until you're on the Missouri riverboat."

"Tell him I'm married?!" she echoed. "Married to whom?"

Grinning, he answered, "Married to me."

While she stood shocked and speechless, staring at him, he added, "Now get yourself to the churchyard and keep blinkin' those blue eyes at him."

"And . . . and if I won't say I'm married to you?"

"They don't allow single women on wagon trains, sister, because single women cause trouble." He paused so the words would sink in. "I'm figurin' you want to go to California with us, to be with your family. You do want to go?"

Callie tried to swallow her indignation. "Yes," she replied. "I don't like what you're asking me to do one bit, and I don't like the way you always want to be in control . . . but I do want to go."

"Then tell him just before you get to Independence. Make sure of it."

8

With Centerville behind them, the coach had many empty seats. Callie sat across the aisle from Ruby, too preoccupied to hear more than the train's continual clicking and clanking over the rails, or to see more than fleeting glimpses of the flat Indiana countryside.

Her mind returned endlessly to Langsdon. From his initial appearance at the Burlingtons' front door, he'd led her along into his scheming. First to befriend Matthew, then to work her way into this job on the orphan train, next to help gather their family in secret. . . and now she was to keep Matthew in her company until they reached Independence, and tell him she was married!

Why was so much scheming and deception necessary? Was the presence of a minister Langsdon's way of insuring their safety on the frontier? And Callie had to wonder, why was the presence of his family so important to him? Did he truly want to bring them all together for a new life in California—or were they a kind of disguise for him?

Her thoughts raced on to Mr. Stane. How had Langsdon run him off? It couldn't have been easy in the face of Mr. Stane's usual persistence. As if that weren't worry enough, did Mr. Stane really think *she* had turned him in for the theft of the Burlingtons' paintings? Worst of all, was he following her to seek revenge?

Trying to set her worries aside, she fixed her mind on seeing Glenda and Rolland soon. After the upcoming station, she planned to walk through the next coach to observe them, perhaps even talk to them if it seemed safe.

"You're quiet, Miss Murray," Ruby said from across the aisle.

"You are too, Ruby."

"I been tryin' to see things the way Reverend Hansel told us when we got back on the train in Centerville. Yorker and the Jungs and I were feeling awful bad about not bein' taken by a family. The reverend told us that all things come out for good to them that love God and are called for His purposes. He says we should leave the matter of our new families in God's hands."

Callie wished it were that easy to comfort herself. "What happened to the young couple with children who seemed so taken with you?"

Ruby shook her head. "Ain't no secret. The wife decided she'd make do without a helper. But I think they just didn't want a stranger in their house."

"I'm sorry, Ruby. I truly am."

Ruby shrugged. "I thought maybe they didn't trust me. I wouldn't of hurt their children or stolen a thing from 'em."

"I know that, and you do too," Callie told her, then added, as much to herself as to Ruby, "No matter what happens, we have to go on."

Ruby sat back in her seat with resignation and squinted out the window as the train sped through the flat countryside. "We're goin' on now. The reverend says it's like a wonderful mystery, ridin' into our futures."

"You think a lot of him, don't you, Ruby?"

"He's the nicest man I ever met," the girl acknowledged, "but it ain't like bein' in love with him, like you."

Blood rushed to Callie's cheeks. "Who said such a thing?"

"Anybody who ain't blind could see it, and see that he fancies you, too. Like I said before, that kind of love ain't for me. I'm for the Christian love that the reverend and I have between us. It's kindly 'n caring, 'n it don't hurt yer heart half so much."

Callie replied with an unintended harshness. "You might change your mind when you get older. I once thought it wasn't for me, either, and now I wish—"

Ruby put a hand to her mouth. "I shouldn't of spoken."

"I'm sorry, Ruby. I didn't mean to sound so . . . peevish. I'm tired."

"It's all right, Miss Murray."

Callie darted a glance to the back of their almost empty coach. "The reverend," as Ruby called him, was in deep conversation with Yorker and the Jung children. Otherwise, their car now seemed sadly quiet.

Before she could turn away, Matthew looked up and beamed at her. She couldn't help smiling back. He certainly would not feel so well disposed to her when she had to tell him she was married to Langsdon.

After a long time, the train slowed for the next town. "I'm glad there's no families here to look us over," Ruby remarked. "It ain't easy bein' lined up in front of the coach for 'em."

"I guess not," Callie replied. She felt a pang of guilt for being less sympathetic because of her own difficulties.

Suddenly a new thought hit. What if Mr. Stane had gotten off at the next station to watch for them? He was so clever and everlastingly persistent, it seemed exactly the kind of maneuver he would choose.

As the train slowed near the town's station, she peered out the window for him. But there was only a portly man waiting to board. Even with a great deal of padding, he couldn't possibly be Mr. Stane.

When the train blew its warning whistle to leave, Callie rose to her feet. "I'm going for a stroll to the next cars," she told Ruby. "If Reverend Hansel asks for me, please tell him I'll be back in our coach after the next stop. Much as I care for all of you, I need some time to myself. I'm sure he'll be kind enough to honor my request."

Ruby sat up straight in the seat. "You ain't thinkin' o' gettin' off here, Miss Murray?"

"Of course not. Why would you ask?"

"You're awfully quiet . . . 'n lookin' peaked."

Callie made herself smile. "I suppose I'm more tired than I know."

"I guess we all are," Ruby answered uneasily, then sat back again.

"All aboooaaaard!" the conductor called out from the platform. "All aboooaaaard!"

"Please remember to tell Reverend Hansel I'll be back at the next stop."

Ruby nodded apprehensively.

Callie hurried through their coach door, then balanced on the narrow platform to the next coach. The walkway, from which she saw the rails rushing by below, seemed like the unnerving path of life she now trod. Still, she had to welcome Glenda and Rolland, who must be feeling unsettled too. She was the older sister, the one who'd allowed their family to be scattered. Even if she disliked Langsdon's methods, his plan must go on.

Callie entered the next coach. Just as the door closed behind her, the train gave its usual throaty blast and set off, jolting the cars forward. Callie stood at the back of the half-filled car, reminding herself that Glenda would be fourteen now, a young woman, and Rolland would be fifteen, almost a man. Nonetheless, she looked for Glenda's childish mop of curls.

Suddenly her heart pounded wildly. There! A young woman and man with reddish brown hair, though the young woman's was subdued in a single long braid that hung down her back.

Her heart pounded even harder as she made her way forward. The coach swayed over the rails, giving her an excuse to grab hold of the bench back in front of theirs to catch her balance. Yes! It had to be them!

"Glenda?" she asked quietly. "Rolland?"

"Callie?" they asked, almost in unison.

She nodded, tears pressing against her eyes. "It's really me. We'll have to speak softly."

"You look so grown up," Glenda marveled when she finally spoke. Her cornflower blue eyes—even bluer than Callie's—shone with sudden tears too.

"So do both of you, but I still recognize you. I'd have known you anywhere." Remembering their need for secrecy, she put a hand to her mouth. "We have to speak softly."

With every fiber of her being, she yearned to hold them and to never again let go, but already passengers were taking notice. Callie sat down in the empty bench in front of theirs and turned to them. "Best we seem mere acquaintances. I have to go back to my coach at the next station, but I wanted to assure you that I'm truly on the train . . . that we're almost together and will be soon."

She gazed at them, savoring the moment that for years had seemed impossible. "It's so amazing to see you again. I wish I could shout my happiness to the heavens!"

Glenda bounced with excitement in her seat. She was no longer a little curly locks, but she still had her sweet smile. "Oh, Callie," she whispered, "we thought we'd never see you or Langsdon again."

"We did," Rolland agreed, his hazel eyes shining and a crack in his voice betraying his emotions. After a moment he asked, "Where's Emelie?"

Callie shook her head. "Not here. She wanted to stay with her family in Indiana. She loves them and couldn't bear to be dislodged again. She promised to write to us in California, though, and sends you her love."

Neither spoke until at long last Glenda said, "A month ago I might have chosen to stay in Centerville. I loved my family too . . . but they died when the house burned down . . . and two of their children. Some neighbors said I musta done it, when all the time I was out in the barn milkin' cows. I didn't burn the house, Callie . . . I promise, I didn't!"

"I'm sure you wouldn't do such a thing," Callie told her, indignant but keeping her voice low. "Sometimes people just like to blame others . . . especially if they're outsiders."

Glenda drew a deep breath. "Only good thing about 'em dying is they were believers, so I know they're in heaven."

Callie hesitated. "Are you a believer?"

Glenda's blue eyes flashed with excitement. "I am. My family, the Palmers, they led me to Christ and taught me about praying. I always went to church with 'em."

"I see," Callie replied, noticing that Rolland looked uneasy too. Best to change the subject. "Where have you lived since their house burned down?"

"An aunt took the rest of their children, and Reverend Klingman worked it out for me to move in with Rolland's family for a while."

Callie looked at her brother, who'd seemed somewhat shy and had said very little. "Did you want to leave, Rolland? To go to California with us?"

He gave a solemn nod. "I did. When Langsdon came and told us about goin' to California, I was more'n ready—but not for gold. I aim to find me some rich farmin' land. They say you can get two or three crops a year there." He had an earnest face and a kindliness about his hazel eyes; his nose was straight and slightly pointed, although not as pointy as Yorker's. Callie felt a great relief that Rolland didn't in any way resemble their father or Langsdon.

"I'm thankful to hear you wanted to go," she said. "I was afraid you'd feel like Emelie. Did you like your place?"

"At first, it was fine," Rolland said. "Workin' with horses, bein' outside all day long, growin' crops. . . . I like farmin'."

"What didn't you like?"

He stated quietly, "I'm only talkin' about this once . . . only this one time. The fact is they wanted me to marry their daughter Phoebe when I got to be sixteen."

"This next year?"

He gave a nod. "They said it'd be an honor for an orphan like me, and that I'd inherit their place since their boy died. Well, Phoebe was a lot older and couldn't get herself a husband, probably because she was so coarse and loutish. Called me a street-rat, among things I'm not mentionin' in polite company."

He set his angular chin so firmly that Callie could see it would indeed be the end of the subject as far as he was concerned. "I can't blame you one bit," she told him. "We won't discuss it again, Rolland."

"Tell us about you, Callie," Glenda put in quickly. "Langsdon told us you'd worked in"—she hesitated, then plunged on—"in our father's New York mansion."

Callie still felt mixed emotions about it herself. "Yes, I worked there for two years."

Her sister's eyes brimmed with interest. "What was it like, being there where he'd lived?"

"A bad mistake on my part," Callie replied. "I didn't belong there. Being where he and his real family once lived made me miserable. It's better to forget."

Rolland lifted his brows. "It won't be easy, bein' with his real family in California."

"We'll have to *forgive* and forget," Glenda said earnestly. "The Palmers always told me it's best to forgive, even if you have to do it over and over until you finally forget."

"I guess so," Callie said. "It's what Reverend Hansel tells the orphans too."

"I can't wait to meet him," her sister said, brightening. "Langsdon says Reverend Hansel's in love with you."

Callie swallowed, unsure of how to reply.

"Shouldn't have meddled," Glenda said. "Let me ask a different question. Is he a good minister?"

"People in New York thought so, and the orphans like him, too," Callie answered, feeling on safer ground.

The train gave its warning blast for the next stop.

"The next station already?" Glenda asked. "Or are we stopping for wood and water again?"

She and Rolland looked out the window.

The train was already slowing, and Callie peered out with them at the edge of another small town. "Maybe both," she answered. "We won't see each other again for a while."

Glenda turned to her with concern. "Langsdon said we're to pretend not to know you until you beckon us on the other side of the Mississippi River."

"Yes, I'll let you know, don't worry."

"We'll be fine," Rolland stated firmly, narrowing his eyes with determination.

"I'll pray for it to work out," Glenda added. "The Lord can take care of anything."

Callie hoped so. "Just watch for me to beckon you when we get off the ferryboat in St. Louis."

The train chuffed slowly into the small town as Callie made her way to the back of the coach. When it came to a stop, she glanced out the window and nearly recoiled.

Mr. Stane!

His arm in a sling, he still resembled a black thunder-cloud as he stood on the platform waiting to board this very coach that held her sister and brother. Standing on the plat-form, he glanced in her direction, and she pressed herself flat against the door. His eyes stopped on her, then seemed to slide past in the shadows of the coach. For an instant, Callie felt sure he had seen her, then in the next, was uncer-tain.

She yanked open the back door and let herself out onto the narrow walkway between the coaches and hurried across, grateful now for the sign on the orphan coach door that said, "Private car. No entry." She tugged open the door and eased it shut behind her.

She knew that Mr. Stane, a man particular about appear-ances, would be furious and perhaps even vengeful at having his reputation sullied by an accusation of grand theft, no matter how true it was. If he had seen her, what might he do?

"Miss Murray!" Ruby said. "You look like you seen a ghost!"

Matthew was walking to the front of the car and stared at her, too. "What's wrong, Miss Murray? What is it?"

Callie inhaled deeply. "I'm just a bit breathless. I wanted to be back here before the train started off again."

"We missed you," he said, his brown eyes holding hers. "But you didn't have a long rest."

"Long enough," she told him. "I'm glad to be back with all of you again."

He must have assumed that a man had been rude to her, for he said, "Now that we're coming closer to the frontier, it's probably best for you to stay under my protection."

"Yes," she agreed. "Perhaps it is."

The train sped on into central Illinois, the black locomotive huffing and puffing before them like a great monster and, behind it, the coaches clanking and swaying on the silvery rails. The flatness of the land was broken only by occasional stands of oak, hickory, and maple, and here and there, fields of newly planted soil.

Callie peered out at the long green grass that bent as the train streaked by, then rose up after it had passed. If only Mr. Stane had passed through her life that quickly and easily!

Matthew came to sit beside her. "Flat country, isn't it?" he asked, glancing past her out the window.

"Yes, it is," she answered, gazing out the window with him. "Flatter than flat."

He smiled. "There used to be a saying, 'corn won't grow where trees don't.' Between that and the danger of prairie fires and the lack of wood, early settlers shunned the prairies in favor of forested river bottoms."

"What made them change their thinking?" she asked, still looking out the window and trying to put Mr. Stane out of mind.

"In '26, a Virginian came out to Missouri to start what he named Experiment Farm. In no time, he exploded the myth about prairie land being infertile. That's what started the rush to prairie farming, now said to be the best in the world."

"You're a regular encyclopedia," she said, turning to him and feeling somewhat better..

He chuckled. "Exactly what my mother claimed. She was known to call me Encyclopedia Hansel, and blamed it on my father's being a printer. She feared I'd ruin my eyes, always reading."

Callie had to smile a little. "Was she a good mother?"

Matthew nodded. "As fine a mother as a boy could ever

wish. It didn't occur to me as a boy, but in later years, after her death, my father often said I resembled her."

"Brown eyes, dark hair, bookish, and a kind nature?"

"True about the brown eyes and dark hair. The love for books comes from my father. And any kindness in my nature comes from the Lord."

She was tempted to ask more of how he came to be a minister, but decided against it.

At length, he asked, "What do you know of encyclopedias?"

"Not a great deal," she admitted. "But I did have free rein of the Burlingtons' library, and I read a journal or a book nearly every evening. But not an encyclopedia. I wasn't given to such ponderous reading."

He laughed.

After a moment, she added, "It was hard to find a friend who shared my interest in reading or learning. I suppose that would be one of the best points about going to a university. Others would share the same interests."

"Yes. I imagine it would be difficult for a woman who was bent on learning and had little encouragement. They must have thought you peculiar in the Burlington household."

"A bit—but usually the others were so occupied with their work or their own affairs that they didn't bother much about a bookish housemaid."

"Were you happy?"

She gave a small shrug. "Not entirely, though it was likely my own fault." The truth, she reflected, was that she had felt out of place—an orphan out of an orphanage and into the mansion once owned by her father. What had driven her so resolutely to get employment there, only to have it end in bitterness?

"Did you have friends in the mansion?"

"Becca." She turned to the window. "Let's not speak of it anymore."

"Let's have a walk at the next water stop. I can tell you all about the new hemp and tobacco plantations along the Missouri River . . . unless there's something less encyclopedic you'd rather discuss."

"Hemp and tobacco plantations would be most interesting," she answered. "You must tell the children about them too. They seem so uneducated." Suddenly she remembered Mr. Stane again. "But I'd rather not get out for a while."

"If you think it best."

She nodded. "I think it best."

Thus began the educational talks as they rode along. The orphans seemed glad enough for a reason to hold together, even if they only half-listened. The talks gave them a feeling of family. Yorker, however, took an interest in everything. And, best of all, Mr. Stane was not to be seen. Callie began to hope that she had only imagined him.

Evenings, while the train rolled along through the darkness, Matthew still came to sit with her. Something about him had changed, though. He seemed to be battling back his passion for her. Once when he appeared tempted to touch her arm, he pulled back and murmured to himself, "It is good for a man not to touch a woman."

What did that mean? Was he quoting Scripture?

She drew further from him.

They sat silent for a long time, then he seemed to arrive at a decision. "I can't abide leaving you in Independence, Callie. I've thought and thought about this. I want you to marry me."

She stared at him with astonishment. "Please don't speak of it, Matthew. I would far rather hear about the prairie soil or hemp plantations."

He caught her hands in his. "Why won't you speak of it?"

"I can't marry you, Matthew . . . I can't!"

At his heartbroken expression, she added, "It isn't that I don't want to."

"Then why can't you, if you truly want to?"

"Don't ask . . . please don't ask." She dropped her head against the seat before them and, thinking of the complications in her life, wept.

He placed a comforting hand on her shoulder. "I'd do anything to help you."

"It's not just me," she sobbed, remembering she couldn't let her family down again. In the coach in front of theirs, Glenda and Rolland were dependent upon her. And Langsdon was probably in St. Louis or Independence making plans for them to live as a family again. This might be their last chance. And besides, there was always the matter of her not being a believer.

Matthew repeated, "I'd do anything—"

"I know," she replied and sobbed against the seat again. "I'd do anything, too, if I could make things different. Please go back. Go back to your seat."

She woke the next morning feeling sick at heart, wishing that she felt for Matthew only what Ruby had mentioned— a kindly Christian love.

Shortly after the sign proclaimed "Stephensburg, Illinois," a new conductor stuck his head into their coach, though he must have known this wasn't one of their stops. "Stephensburg!" he called out. "Stephensburg!"

Likely he expected them to be buying sandwiches or fruit if there were vendors hawking food at the station, Callie thought as he left. Or perhaps Mr. Stane, who was good at such things, had slipped the conductor some money to see if she were there. Frightened, she told Ruby, "I'm going back to the middle of the coach to lie down a while."

"You sick?" the girl asked.

Callie shook her head. "Still tired."

She hurried down the aisle to an empty bench and curled

up on it. If only Mr. Stane hadn't taken a liking to her in the mansion! And if only she might have known better how to handle it!

After a while, the train came to a halt with its usual grating clash of steel against steel. A moment later, someone must have stuck his head in their coach, for Matthew said, "This is a private coach, sir."

"Begging your pardon, I'm sure," a voice said with a distinctly British accent.

Mr. Stane! Callie thought, curling up tightly on the seat. *Please, please, Matthew send him off!*

She heard the coach door close, then the usual flurry of activity on the platform. Slowly she peered over the seat in front of her, and was glad to see no one was there. Outside the window, however, she heard Matthew buying sandwiches from a food vendor, and Mr. Stane nearby.

"I say, sir," the butler said, "is this one of those orphan trains from New York?"

"Yes, it is," Matthew answered.

"Most int'resting concept," Mr. Stane replied. "Does it actually work?"

"We've placed thousands of orphans in the past four years," Matthew told him, "and we hear of a great many more successes than failures."

"Int'resting indeed."

Callie stayed down on the seat so he wouldn't see her through the window. What could she do during the two-hour stopover in Vandalia, just down the line? She'd have no way to hide from him.

Yorker came into the coach and headed down the aisle with a basket of sandwiches. "Ye hidin' down here, Miss Murray?"

"What makes you think that?"

He grinned at her. "I wasn't a streeter fer nothin'."

"Can you . . . ah . . . do something for me?" she asked.

"Me pleasure, Miss Murray!"

She felt as guilty as could be, but something had to be done before Mr. Stane caused trouble. "You know that British man, with his arm in a sling . . . the one who was speaking to Reverend Hansel?"

"Yep, the one nosin' around. He went in the station to use the washroom. Probably too hard to use the train terlet with his arm all slung up."

Callie peered out the window. Nearly all of the passengers had detrained or boarded, and the train stood chuffing on the track. "Could you do something dreadful in secret for me, Yorker?"

He grinned. "Bet I could. What ye got in mind?"

"I need you to lock that British man in the depot washroom until the train leaves. I know it sounds terrible. . . ."

Yorker grinned and handed her the sandwich basket. "That's right down my alley, Miss Murray. No need to explain. I'll be back in a minute."

She peered out the window as he dashed across the platform to the depot. It didn't seem long before he sauntered back out—and just in time, too, for the conductor shouted, "All aboooaaaard! All aboooaaaard!"

Yorker swung into their coach, grinning more broadly than ever. "Job done," he told her under his breath, before he sat down on the bench across the aisle. He asked more loudly, "Didn't ye pass out them sandwiches?"

"I forgot entirely. How did you . . . accomplish your mission?"

"Easy with a jackknife," he answered. "I loosened the screws. Britisher or not, I expect he'll yell fiercely when the washroom doorknob falls off in 'is hand!"

The train's warning bell rang, and Reverend Hansel climbed aboard. "I wondered where you were, Miss Murray.

Yorker says you were taking a nap."

She gave him a nervous smile and felt guilty as the conductor shouted a final, "All aboooaaaard!"

The train chugged slowly out of the Stephensburg station, then gathered speed. As usual, the children stuck their heads out the windows, yelling and shouting as they watched the train's shortened shadow rush alongside the tracks, urging on the shadow to win the race. They were some distance from the station when Mr. Stane ran onto the platform, wildly waving his good arm and shouting, but they were already too far away.

"Looks like the British fellow who was trying to get into our coach a while ago," Matthew remarked. "You know, Miss Murray, if it weren't for the man's sunburned nose and his rumpled appearance, I'd say he could have been your butler at the Burlingtons' mansion."

Callie didn't say a word, but Yorker replied in a half-serious voice, "Didn't know them butlers could run so fast, Reverend Hansel. Didn't think they had it in 'em."

Ruby and the Jung children laughed, and Matthew tousled Yorker's hair. "We'll miss you and your humor when you're placed out in Westville, Yorker. It won't be long now."

"Not if no one wants me," Yorker answered, staring out the window again. "I ain't big muscled like Horst and Gunther fer farmin' 'n such, 'n I don't know a thing on milkin' cows."

"Ve don't know milking cows, either," Horst Jung objected.

Gretchen Jung added, "But ve learn how."

Yorker lifted his scrawny shoulders. "I figure I'd do better at somethin' that takes talkin'."

Matthew gave a laugh. "You'd make a good salesman, that's certain. But the Westville people will want you. We had so many letters from them asking for children, we won't have nearly enough to suit them."

Yorker drew a deep breath. "You know how you're always talkin' about God, Reverend Hansel?"

Matthew smiled. "Yes, I suppose I do."

"Well, I was thinkin'," Yorker continued, "maybe God has it in mind fer me to go to California with yer. I figure I'd be beans at findin' gold."

"What makes you think so?" Matthew asked.

"My bein' short. It's just right in gold country, havin' yer nose close to the ground."

Callie laughed with them, half in relief. Mr. Stane and the Stephensburg station were long out of sight.

Westville was beautifully situated on the west bank of the river, and when the train chugged into the station, the scene on the platform was equally picturesque. Half the town seemed to be cheering, and a great white banner hung from the station roof saying, "WELCOME ORPHANS!" What lifted Callie's heart most, though, was there was no sign of either Mr. Stane or Langsdon.

As she and Reverend Hansel stepped down onto the platform with Ruby, Yorker, and the Jung children, two fiddlers struck up "Old Dan Tucker," and a clergyman stepped forward.

"Welcome," he said. "We'd hoped for a crowd of you, but we've just had a letter from the society saying more children are coming. This way, we can have another welcoming party this summer."

Surprisingly, the townspeople applauded.

Reverend Hansel stepped forward to thank them, then introduced the orphans, who had lined up alongside their railroad coach. "Here we have the four Jung sisters and brothers, who hope to be in one home together. May I introduce Frieda and Gretchen, and Horst and Gunther. And this is Ruby, who is experienced with children and most conscientious, and Yorker, a very bright fellow."

The town minister welcomed them again. "If you'll follow me over to those benches, there's enough apple cider and raisin cakes for all."

Ruby gave Callie a hopeful look, and Callie nodded. "I have a feeling they'll be fighting for you in this town. What you want to look for is the kindest people."

Ruby smiled with expectancy. "Reverend Hansel said I should look for real believers."

Catching her breath, Callie simply nodded. There was something decidedly different about Ruby since she'd become a Christian, something more trusting and hopeful and sometimes almost joyous.

As the children and Matthew followed the fiddlers and the crowd to the church, Callie walked along behind them. Before they left, she'd have to hurry into the depot on the chance that Langsdon had left her another message.

A table had been set up in the churchyard under the trees, and while the fiddlers played lively music, the church ladies handed around cider and raisin cakes. Callie visited with the ladies, observing the scene.

The train stood not far away at the station, a constant reminder that time was fleeting, that decisions would have to be made quickly. The four Jung children met with the minister, who in turn discussed them with two sets of parents. It didn't appear hopeful. Ruby spoke with a young woman, who seemed alone with three children. On the other side of the trees, Yorker had been discussing his fate with a shopkeeper. Matthew hovered about with the home placement contracts.

At long last, the town minister came over to Matthew. "A placement for the Jung children! They will live on neighboring farms owned by the Schmidt brothers—almost the same as being in one family."

Callie was glad to see Frieda and Gretchen smiling happily, and Horst and Gunther looking most pleased. As the papers were signed, Horst called over to Callie, "Ve vill all be together on Sundays! It is good, *ja?*"

"*Ja*, it is good," she replied, reminded of Becca. "It is good indeed!"

As Matthew finished the papers, the local minister went on to speak with Ruby. Before long, he brought her with him, as well as the woman with the three small children. Beaming, the minister said, "My wife has found us an older daughter. We have asked Ruby to become a part of our family."

Ruby beamed, and Callie caught her in her arms.

"I prayed like anythin', 'n then found 'em at the same time they found me," Ruby whispered against Callie's shoulder.

"Well, what do you know?!" Callie answered, holding her tight. "Westville looks like a fine town, too."

Yorker came along with the shopkeeper's family, looking uneasy but determined.

"Reverend, we would like to sign papers for this young man," the shopkeeper told Matthew Hansel. "We think he shows a lot of promise for working in our store."

Or for loosening washroom doorknobs, Callie thought. She exchanged a knowing smile with Yorker, and knew he'd get along just fine.

The fiddlers struck up "Yankee Doodle," and all in all, it was a most joyous scene. Every orphan had been placed out with what appeared to be a good family, and another train would soon bring more orphans to Westville.

At long last, the train rang its warning bell, and Callie's worries assailed her again. Was Mr. Stane following on the next train? Where was Langsdon? And how was she to explain Glenda and Rolland to Matthew in St. Louis while still keeping him interested in accompanying her?

She tried to forget her predicament while she and Matthew hugged each of the children and called out their final good-byes.

Making their departure, Matthew said, "It's a relief to see them placed with good families, but I'll miss them."

"I will too, especially Ruby and Yorker," she said.

The moment she looked toward the train, though, her sadness fled. Glenda and Rolland stood on the platform, pretending very hard not to know her, and she pretended not to recognize them.

"I'll run into the depot for a moment," she told Matthew.

"Hurry!" he replied. "I'll be here waiting."

In the depot, she asked the clerk, "Do you have a message for a Miss Murray?"

"One moment," he said, eyeing her over his spectacles.

"I'm in a bit of a hurry!"

He nodded and searched through all of his cubbyholes, but found nothing with her name on it.

She would have to try again at the St. Louis station, she decided. How she'd hoped there would be word from Langsdon saying she no longer had to tell Matthew she was married . . . and that there would never again be any deceptions.

9

The spirit of the Lord filled the small sanctuary as the twelve sang, "Amazing grace, how sweet the sound. . . "

Benjamin Talbot sang out the familiar words in their small white country church where they'd gathered again for the Wednesday noon prayer meeting. Jessica sat at the pump organ, playing with reverence.

Although Benjamin loved the hymn mightily, it was a difficult one for him to sing. It reminded him all too clearly of his daughter Rena, whose soaring faith and soprano voice had transformed it into her hymn . . . and of the shallow desert grave where they'd buried her in '46, when she'd died during their covered wagon trek to California. As they sang the final verse, he remembered speaking the words with a trembling voice but firm conviction at Rena's brief memorial service under the blazing desert sun.

When we've been there ten thousand years,
Bright shining as the sun,
We've no less days to sing God's praise
Than when we've first begun.

What a wonder it was, the timelessness of eternity, he reflected, and that God gave grace and eternal life to those who loved Him.

They sang "A Mighty Fortress is Our God" and "Fairest

Lord Jesus," then sat down in the pews and waited in silence for those who wished to lead out in prayer.

At length, Benjamin rose again to his feet and bowed his head. "Our Father, Who Art in Heaven," he began, "we gather to praise and thank Thee for Thy many blessings, particularly the blessing of increasing our numbers at these weekly prayer meetings, and for the two new believers in our body. We pray that Thou wouldst guide them clearly in their new lives, that Thou wouldst deliver them and the rest of us from all evil. . ."

When he'd finished, Jessica stood and gripped the organ for balance. "Heavenly Father," she began, "Thou hast said in Scripture that if Thy people, who are called by Thy name, will humble themselves and pray, and seek Thy face, and turn from their wicked ways, then Thou wouldst hear from heaven and forgive them their sins and heal their land. Father, we do repent of our pride and greed and endless other sins. . ."

When she sat, Daniel rose to his feet. "Heavenly Father, we come in the blessed name of Thy son and our Redeemer, Jesus Christ, and ask for revival in each of our hearts, and revival in and beyond our community. . . in San Francisco, Sacramento, in all of California, and beyond to the uttermost parts of the earth! Revive the hearts of believers, and open the hearts of unbelievers, so that they might find faith, followed by joy and peace and eternal life."

"Amen," the believers agreed after each prayer.

The prayer meeting had gone on for some time when, to everyone's amazement, Abby stood and spoke out from the pew in a majestic voice, "Thou art my people, the apple of my eye."

The startling message seemed to hover in the small sanctuary, and Benjamin felt the words penetrate his heart: *Thou art my people, the apple of my eye.*

To have a message thus spoken in their church—moreover by a woman—was unheard of. Tears filled Benjamin's eyes. Around him, others began to sob and then to do something equally unheard of—confess their sins.

"Pride."

"Greed."

"Lusting in my heart."

"An untruth told last week."

"Anger in my heart at others' lack of perfection, when I am so imperfect myself," said Benjamin.

When the curious confessing of sins ended, an awesome stillness filled the white sanctuary. At long last, people began to gather up their Bibles and file silently out the front door.

Outside mockingbirds sang with uncommon beauty, and a great eagle wheeled high in the blue sky. Even the native grasses and trees around them seemed to take on a special radiance. Below, by the church hitching post, the plainest of horses seemed transformed by a singular splendor, as if God were showing His people how He saw the common things of their lives.

Not a word was spoken as the band of twelve made their way down to where their horses, buggies, and wagons stood. But, finally, at the hitching post, Benjamin asked Abby the question that everyone must be wondering.

"How did it come about, Abby? How is it that the words came to you in such a manner?"

She shook her head, her blue eyes wide. "I don't know. The words simply came to me. I heard them first, and then I couldn't have stopped speaking them if my life had depended upon it."

He hesitated. "And now . . . how do you feel about having spoken them?"

"Peaceful . . . entirely peaceful," she replied. "And what

might best be called a sense of obedience."

"I see," he said, though he didn't. Not quite.

One of the elders, Thomas Oglevy, pulled him aside. "The message that your daughter-in-law spoke, is it scriptural?"

"The words themselves are often found in Scripture," Benjamin replied, still somewhat bewildered himself. "As for the method of delivery, it's my observation that God speaks to us in any way He wishes."

"I don't know," Oglevy said skeptically. "In my opinion, it is best to hold with the old traditions."

"That's what many told me before we held the first brush arbor meeting in '48," Benjamin replied. "The man who objected the most strenuously saw his own sister find salvation at that very meeting."

"Ach, I'm an old Scotsman who holds strongly to the old ways," Oglevy said gruffly. "Yet I confess that my heart was penetrated as never before when your daughter-in-law spoke."

"Mine as well, friend. Each generation is somewhat different, and perhaps might be reached differently. What's of importance is that we hold tightly to Scripture."

"Agreed," Oglevy answered. "I just wonder what the pastor will make of it."

When they arrived at Casa Contenta, a letter from the New York investigator awaited him. Benjamin tore it open with apprehension, then scanned the page for words of importance.

Until recently, Charlotte Murray was employed in a Union Square mansion belonging to Weston Burlington, and formerly to your own brother, Charles Talbot. She left her employment to serve as an escort for girls on an orphan train to the Middle West, under the auspices of the Children's Aid Society of New York City.

Shredded paper found under her mattress was pieced together; it contained instructions for her to get herself onto the orphan train with Matthew Hansel. It was unknown to the Burlingtons that her stepfather had once owned the mansion. They found her a fine worker and of good character.

The more disagreeable news concerns her brother, Langsdon Murray, who has apparently assumed the last name of Talbot. The State of New York has a warrant outstanding for his arrest for bank theft from the New York Trust and Savings, where he recently worked as a guard. There is also a warrant out for him in Chicago, Illinois, for bank theft. In addition, he and the Burlingtons' former butler, a Mr. Ian Stane, are under suspicion for the theft of extremely valuable paintings from the Burlington mansion. From all indications, Langsdon Murray has advanced from petty theft to grand theft, and is a confidence man who sometimes resorts to forged letters. He is also known to be extremely attractive to women.

Our investigation shows that on April 12, Langsdon Murray left New York City by train and held a ticket for Chicago. His sister will pass through central Illinois with the orphan train, but we have no evidence of their meeting. A rumor in the Burlington household leads us to believe that they are both bound for Independence, Missouri.

Benjamin needed to read no further. Like many fugitives, Callie and Langsdon Murray were fleeing to California. He felt certain of it. He must warn his son Adam in Independence about them immediately in the event they stopped there. The last thing he and his wife Inga and their eleven children needed was lawless relatives in their midst.

Benjamin clenched his fists. Jessica had predicted that if they prayed for revival, the adversary would come at them. Apparently the enemy meant to use his late brother Charles again. Only this time, instead of using the rebellious brother who'd caused his parents heartache unto death, the foe meant to use Charles's illegitimate offspring.

Lord, Benjamin forced himself to pray, *give me Thy love and forgiveness for them. I beseech Thee, don't allow me to give in to anger towards Charles or to his children!*

As the week went on, word spread about Abby's speaking out in such an odd manner at the weekly prayer meeting. The next week, there were eighteen in attendance; the following week, thirty. Nothing else peculiar took place, but Benjamin, like the others, found his faith lifted and enjoyed the fellowship. Moreover, Sunday church attendance began to grow, added to by several surprising conversions. Not in years had their small congregation seen such an increase in faith and new believers. And Benjamin proclaimed to all who would hear, "The Second Great Awakening is now spreading to California!"

* * *

Callie and Matthew crossed the Mississippi River from Illinois to St. Louis, Missouri, on a crowded ferryboat. Despite her worries about Glenda and Rolland—and the jam of carts, farm wagons, and smelly livestock on the ferry—Callie found the broad Mississippi a most impressive sight. Ahead at St. Louis where it joined the muddy Missouri River, a conglomeration of vessels tootled, blasted horns and whistles, and maneuvered about.

In addition to ferryboats on the two rivers, there were rafts, skiffs, canoes, barges, pirogues, flatboats, broadhorns, keelboats, steamboats, and great white paddle boats. Each craft, no matter how fine or dilapidated, seemed bent on its own course. Heart in her throat as she held onto the ferry boat's railing, Callie envisioned collisions at every turn and was glad when they neared shore.

Matthew stood beside her at the railing as they docked, and Callie thought he seemed exceedingly pleased at the sight of the shoreline. As they'd made their way to the frontier, he'd become increasingly interested in what lay ahead, while she'd become increasingly nervous about what lay in store for her.

Accepting his hand for balance, she hurried off the ferry-boat onto the St. Louis landing. Not daring to look back for her sister and brother, she had to agree that St. Louis looked like an interesting frontier river city.

From the wharf, she could see a tannery, a foundry, a brewery, an ironworks, and a repair yard full of enormous steamboats. Around them, black roustabouts sang and called out over the tootling and shrill whistles of the boats; horses and mules shied in the thick mud, and drivers cursed, fighting for control as they steered their teams up from the wharf to the street. The nearby street bustled with drays, hacks, buggies, carriages, ox carts, and covered wagons.

Finally gathering her courage, Callie turned back at the edge of the wharf and was grateful to see that Glenda and Rolland were not far behind in the crowd of disembarking passengers. Despite their rumpled, outgrown clothing, they were appealing children. As she looked back, their eyes met hers for an instant, then shifted away as if they didn't know her. They'd been good about following instructions—that under no circumstances were they to approach until she beckoned them forward. Moreover, their color was good, so they must have weathered the ferryboat crossing without seasickness. Oh, she did hope that Matthew wouldn't mind them too much!

"Did you forget something?" Matthew asked her, glancing back himself.

"It's not that I forgot anything . . . it's something I haven't told you, Matthew. I've deliberately withheld something from you for fear . . . for fear that you'd be angry."

He eyed her carefully. "Let's get a porter and a hack before we're trampled to death." He signaled a black porter to help them. Once the man had their baggage on his cart, Matthew said, "Now, what is this secret you've been keeping from me?"

"You won't hate me?"

"I promise I will not hate you. Callie, is this the secret that has been keeping you at arm's length?"

"In part," she replied, more and more nervous as she followed with him behind the porter.

"What is it?" Matthew asked.

She hesitated, then made herself say it. "I'm not alone."

"Of course, you're not alone," he answered. "I'm here with you, and we are surrounded by this great raucous crowd disembarking."

She shook her head. "It was despicable of me not to tell you sooner, but I thought you . . . oh, I don't know what I thought you might think or even do."

The porter had called for a hack, and the horses were nearing them when Callie said, "I don't believe that's large enough to hold all of us."

"All of us?" Matthew repeated.

She nodded, swallowed hard, and then turned to wave Glenda and Rolland forward. They must have seen her anxiety, for their expressions were most worrisome.

"Matthew," she said in a quivery voice, "this is my sister Glenda and my brother Rolland. They rode in the railroad coach in front of ours all the way from Indiana."

His lips parted with surprise, then his usual courtesy came to the fore and he extended his hand. "How do you do?" he said in a slightly incredulous tone.

He recovered quickly and kissed Glenda's fingertips, making her blink up at him and then smile with amazement. Next he shook Rolland's hand firmly. "Yes, with that auburn hair, you both surely look like Callie's family. How did this come about?"

"You want a bigguh hack, suh?" the porter interrupted.

"Yes, it appears there are more of us than I anticipated, and a bit more luggage, too."

The porter signaled for a nearby carriage that had just let out passengers, and Callie pressed her lips together as Matthew cast a peculiar glance at her.

"I hope you'll explain once we're inside," he said, his voice somewhat strained.

"It's a very complicated tale, Matthew," she replied, grateful he didn't appear furious. "It's better to tell in private. In any event, I shall pay for the carriage as well as the hotel room I mean to share with Glenda and Rolland. I promise, you'll have no additional expense."

"The expense of it hadn't even occurred to me," he began, his voice still strained, but there was no time for further discussion. The carriage was now before them, and the porter was opening the door.

Callie dug in her handbag for a tip for the porter, but Matthew was faster and quickly took care of it. He called out to the driver, "City Hotel, if you please."

In the carriage, Glenda and Rolland took the backwards-facing seat, and Callie was glad not to be forced to confront Matthew directly. She handed a silver coin to him. "For our part of the gratuity."

He waved it off. "I won't have a woman pay my way . . . not that I don't appreciate your thoughtfulness."

"It's not fair that you pay for all of us," she objected, avoiding his gaze. As it was, she'd spent very little money on the trip, although the real expenses would now begin.

When she glanced at him, he was serious, and a faint light of anger filled his eyes. It was as if the entire import of the matter had finally fallen upon him.

He spoke in a low voice, almost more to himself than to her. "We'll leave this in the Lord's hands."

The horses started down the street, jolting the carriage forward, and Callie sat with the others in an awkward silence. After a while, the carriage turned away from the river and rattled along into the heart of the city.

"I told you that you'd hate me," Callie said to him, her voice quivery again.

"I don't hate anyone, particularly not you," he replied evenly. "I am only wondering what other surprises you might spring on me. You have been rather secretive, but you had such fine recommendations. . . ."

She drew a deep breath, unable to stop herself. "If you don't wish to accompany us to Independence—"

He closed his eyes, and it appeared that he might at last lose his patience. Either that, or he was praying. When he opened his eyes, he said, "Of course I wish to accompany you to Independence, Callie, and I hoped by now that you would know it. I've even considered staying in Independence myself, since it's your final destination."

Her eyes met Glenda's and Rolland's across the carriage, and they looked at her with astonishment and ill-concealed disappointment, knowing she had deceived him.

She'd have to explain to them when they were alone, she decided, and she would tell Matthew about California later. But under no circumstances would she tell him she was married until Langsdon arrived on the scene in Independence.

"Do look out the windows," she told Glenda and Rolland with a show of enthusiasm. "I had no idea that St. Louis would be such a big city, did you?"

They shook their heads as if they were mutes, then peered silently out the carriage windows as the horses clip-clopped along through the streets of the city.

Aware that Matthew was watching her, she didn't risk looking his way. Oh, why did she have to be doing this? she agonized, staring blindly at the city. Why couldn't circumstances have been different? And why did she have to care so much for The Reverend Mr. Matthew Hansel?

Once the three of them were in their comfortable room in the brick City Hotel, Callie told Glenda and Rolland, "It would be best not to tell Reverend Hansel about your coming by orphan train to Indiana two years ago."

"Why not, Callie?" her sister inquired.

"Because I asked it."

"We didn't do wrong, except for Rolland running off from his family, and that couldn't be helped with them wanting him to marry their daughter. I promise you, she was awful."

"Then trust what I say, too," Callie replied, feeling more nervous about their situation than ever. "It's better not to discuss your orphan train circumstances." She tried to harden her heart as she continued. "As it is, it's unlikely that we'll be seeing Reverend Hansel after we arrive in Independence. Everyone knows that a great many wagon trains set out from Independence."

She glanced at her reflection in the hotel room mirror. She'd changed into her good blue frock this morning on the train, and fortunately it still looked fresh. But she was appalled to see that her auburn hair was even brighter and her face had turned brown from sometimes being out in the sunshine during the journey. Well, no sense in worrying about it. What she could do was tuck up the strands of her upswept hair that had slipped loose from her tortoise shell combs. Tidying her hair, she noticed that at least her brown skin made her eyes appear bluer.

"He loves you, doesn't he?" Glenda asked. "He's surprised about us, but he loves you anyhow. I can see it by the way he looks at you."

"We won't discuss it," Callie returned, finally satisfied that her hair looked tidy.

"Oh, how I should like to marry a minister!" Glenda said.

"Please, no more!" Callie told her. "We will simply be traveling on to Independence with Reverend Hansel, though I'm not sure why Langsdon was insistent about it. I suppose he didn't realize you'd be so grown up, Rolland, and wanted him along for our protection here and on the way to Independence."

Rolland grinned at the compliment. "I can hardly wait to see Langsdon again."

"You'll have plenty of time to get to know him on the way to California," she said. "I wouldn't be surprised if he isn't in Independence now, outfitting a covered wagon and making all of the arrangements for us."

"Suppose we'll use mules or oxen?" Rolland asked.

"I've no idea," she replied as she looked through the things in her carpetbag. She decided to put the showy white collar on her blue frock, changing its appearance.

Glenda watched her every move. "I wish we could be in the same wagon train as Reverend Hansel on the way to California."

"Let's hope not!" Callie answered sharply, then saw her sister's face droop.

Callie sighed with regret. This was her family, the very family she had hoped to bring together. "I'm sorry for sounding abrupt, Glenda. I'm so tired from traveling, and my nerves are on edge. Let's wash up and change into clean clothing now. There's a bathing room on the first floor. When I arranged for our room, I reserved the bath for the three of us late this afternoon, before supper."

"Do you have enough money?" Rolland asked with concern. "I know that you've worked—"

"Yes, I have enough."

No need to explain about the money coming from Langsdon by way of her own savings, when she didn't understand it herself. In fact, there was no need to explain anything more to them, or to Matthew, for that matter.

At length, a knock sounded at their door. "Ready for dinner?" Matthew asked from the hallway.

Callie opened the door and, seeing him, drew a quiet breath. He was freshly shaven, and had changed into a clean white shirt and collar. It even appeared that he wore a new black suit. He was so handsome, she found herself speechless.

And, equally important, he looked at her most cordially. "You look very nice, Callie," he remarked. "That's a beautiful collar."

"Thank you," she managed, realizing she'd put it on for his benefit. "Come along, Glenda, Rolland. You must be starved."

As they made their way down the steps, Callie thought that she must buy new clothing for Rolland and Glenda. In such a fine hotel, even their best outfits looked shabby and outgrown. And when they entered the crowded dining room, she saw that the other diners likely thought the same.

For a long time they studied the menus in silence, then ordered the day's special, which was the least expensive— roast beef with peas, carrots, potatoes, and gravy, with strawberry-rhubarb pie for dessert.

"We'll have to see about accommodations on a Missouri riverboat this afternoon," Matthew said as they waited to be served. "I'm told it's best to take cabins, and was warned to carry much of our own food, if possible. It's a three-day journey at best. Perhaps Rolland wouldn't mind sharing a room with me."

Rolland glanced at Callie, who nodded in acceptance.

Matthew turned to Glenda. "Can you bear being parted from your older brother at night?"

Glenda had to laugh. "I can."

"I thought so," Matthew said with a small grin. "I have an older brother and a younger sister myself, though they're far older than you now."

"It's very generous of you to share your cabin with Rolland," Callie told him.

Matthew smiled, the cleft in his chin broadening. "I thought it would be more comfortable for him."

She wondered if he meant to interrogate Rolland about her family, and Matthew must have read her mind, for he said, "I'm eager to become acquainted with the rest of your family, Callie."

She straightened her back against her chair, but made no reply. As it was, he'd had no chance to ask further about Rolland's and Glenda's appearance, and she hoped to avoid it at all costs.

"If I'm not intruding, tell me about your family in Independence," he suggested.

She swallowed, for Glenda and Rolland were watching her closely. "We've actually never met them," Callie explained. "They're our father's relatives, who've lived on the frontier most of their lives. Our cousin attended Harvard and has a trading post in town as well as a farm on the outskirts."

That much she knew from her own father. Even at eight years of age, she had recognized his low opinion of his nephew Adam for returning to the frontier after a Harvard education. He'd also had a low opinion of his brother Benjamin, whom he'd called "my brother, the frontiersman."

Matthew raised his dark brows with interest. "I should like to meet your Harvard cousin if time permits."

Just then the waiter arrived with their dinners, and she was glad for the interruption.

Once the waiter had served them, Matthew asked, "Shall we give thanks?"

Callie bowed her head quickly and, aware of other diners watching, scarcely heard a word. She should have been accustomed to his praying aloud before meals, but it still took her by surprise that he would do so in a crowded public room.

"Amen," Glenda echoed with enthusiasm when the prayer ended.

Matthew smiled at her. "So be it."

Glenda nodded and returned his smile as if they shared a fine secret.

Rolland glanced at Callie, who took up her fork and knife with haste and cut into her beef.

When she glanced up, Matthew merely said, "Our dinner looks very good, doesn't it?"

"Yes. Yes, it looks very good indeed."

To her surprise, it was his last question during what turned out to be a most pleasant dinner. Instead, it was Glenda and Rolland who questioned him about growing up as a printer's son in Sturbridge Village and becoming a minister.

An hour later they walked through the town of St. Louis, where songs like "Buffalo Gals" and "Oh, Suzannah!" drifted through tavern doors. They passed by trading posts and less rustic shops of all kinds, and found the sidewalks abustle with clerks, gamblers, shopkeepers, and settlers bound for Oregon and California.

Seeing St. Louis from this new angle, the Mississippi River appeared even more impressive. Now it seemed there even were more boats maneuvering about, even a daguerreotype flatboat to make pictures of people and places from ashore or on the water.

Seeing it, Matthew said, "I should like to stop at a daguerreotype shop to have a picture made of us."

"Are you serious?" Callie asked him.

He smiled most charmingly. "We shall probably never

again be in St. Louis, and it would make a fine remembrance."

"It would be expensive," she warned, not certain she wanted him to have a picture of them.

"I can well afford it," he assured her, and she felt he had done so much to help her that she could scarcely refuse him this wish.

At the daguerreotype shop, the man seated Glenda and Rolland before them, while Callie and Matthew stood in the rear. Quite suddenly it seemed to Callie that they must appear to be a family, a thought that was as comforting as it was painful, especially when Matthew smiled down at her so warmly. Finally the daguerreotype light holder flashed, and their picture had been taken.

Down the street, they stopped at a mercantile for ready-made shirts and trousers for Rolland, and lengths of gingham for Glenda—one blue and one pale yellow. Callie added blue and yellow hair ribbons to the order, and a small sewing kit. At the last moment, it occurred to her that Glenda might need a church dress, and she decided on a length of shiny light blue cotton with a matching white fabric for a collar and cuffs.

"Oh, Callie! I can't remember ever having three new dresses!" Glenda exclaimed. "When shall we make them?"

Callie smiled at the girl's delight. She would be pretty in the dresses, especially once her auburn hair was washed. "We might start cutting tonight in the hotel room, then sew up the seams up as we travel along on the river."

"Can you really sew a frock?" Glenda asked. "I can only make plain things."

"Yes, a seamstress friend taught me," Callie answered, reminded again of Becca. "I made this very dress with her. We'll use the frock you're wearing as a pattern, only cut it fuller and longer."

Glenda beamed, and Rolland and Matthew seemed equally pleased for her.

On the other side of the mercantile, they inspected foodstuffs suitable for taking on the riverboat and decided on cheeses, crackers, hard biscuits, and tinned meat and fish.

All in all, Callie thought, they hadn't seen much of St. Louis, but despite her worries, it had been pleasant.

The mercantile owner offered to hold their purchases while they arranged for their passage to Independence, and they set out with satisfaction for the Missouri riverboat landing.

As they neared the muddy brown river, it wasn't difficult to understand why the Missouri riverboats looked so grimy. Callie drew an unhappy breath, and Matthew must have noticed, for he nodded with understanding

"At least we were forewarned at the hotel," he said.

Glenda and Rolland were too excited to be disturbed about dirty boats as they watched Callie and Matthew buy tickets for a steamboat called the *Missouri Queen*. Instead, they asked the ticket seller if buffalo would stop the boat on the river as they did years ago.

"Don't happen much lately," the man answered. "Ain't nearly as many buffalo about as in the '30s and '40s."

The transaction completed, Callie turned from the steamboat office window and had a terrible premonition that Mr. Stane might be following them! She turned, unnerved, but there was no sign of him.

"Let's return to the hotel right away," she said uneasily.

"You're pale, Callie," Matthew remarked. "Are you well?"

"Only . . . eager to begin cutting out Glenda's frocks. It would be nice for her to have a new one before we meet our relatives."

The next morning they boarded the *Missouri Queen*, a squat, snub-nosed steamboat with twin smokestacks on either side of the wheelhouse. In the filthy cabins they found scanty bed linens, poor washing facilities, and pillows filled with corn husks. The boat, which would twist 250 miles westward on the muddy Missouri, carried not only a crowd of passengers, but a heavy cargo that made it ride low in the water.

As the *Missouri Queen* gave a blast of its horn and chugged away, Callie looked about the deck nervously for Mr. Stane. But if the butler were aboard, he wasn't to be seen.

Once the steamboat's smoke had trailed into the air, they all stood at the ship's rail and watched the city of St. Louis disappear. Matthew had been making friends with Glenda and Rolland, and now they discussed the river and whether a storm lurked in the sky's dark clouds. Likely her sister and brother wondered why they had to be so careful—and why she was so unendingly nervous, Callie fretted.

Hoping Mr. Stane was not aboard, she returned to the cabin to fetch the yellow gingham pieces and her sewing kit. When she climbed back up the steps to the deck, she watched most guardedly for the butler, but still saw nothing of him. Outside, Glenda and Rolland stood with Matthew, discussing the pirogues, mackinaws, and bull boats that made their way up and down the river. She settled herself on one of the deck's benches and worked Glenda's yellow gingham dress, looking up occasionally to see her sister and brother obviously enjoying their conversation with Matthew Hansel.

Later, when Glenda came to help sew, she said, "Oh, Callie, I know we're not to speak of it, but I do so wish you'd marry Reverend Hansel."

"Whatever put that in your mind?" Callie asked.

"He'd be ever so nice to have in our family."

Callie tried to forget the familial feeling she'd half-enjoyed in St. Louis. "His being nice has nothing at all to do with my feelings for him, Glenda. A woman doesn't marry a man merely because he is nice."

"He loves you, though."

"How do you know?!"

"The way he's always lookin' at you," Glenda said. "Just see over there this very moment."

Callie glanced up toward the railing where Matthew and Rolland had admired the Missouri countryside. Now Matthew's back was to the rail, and he was without a doubt admiring her.

She turned to her sewing quickly, stitching up a yellow gingham seam. No matter how hard she tried, she couldn't stop caring for him. And Glenda was right about the way he looked at her. Perhaps when she saw Langsdon in Independence, she'd tell him it was impossible, utterly impossible, for her to go on like this. . . that she cared for Matthew, and her brother would have to think of a new plan for the trip to California.

During the three-day trip, they ate mostly the food they'd bought in St. Louis. Since the fine spring weather held, they stayed out on the deck for fresh air. The river was too dangerous to run in the darkness, so they spent much of the nights on the deck as well, looking out at the stars, which Matthew pointed out for them.

"The Milky Way . . . and there the Pleiades or Seven Sisters, supposedly the seven daughters of Atlas, pursued by the great hunter, Orion . . . Venus, the evening star, the harbinger of love. . . "

"The harbinger of love" was far from what Callie wished to hear of now. Instead, she wished she could block out the sight of him with Glenda and Rolland.

The last night aboard the *Missouri Queen*, Matthew came to sit beside her on what she'd come to think of as her bench. After they'd admired the night sky for a long time, he said, "I like Glenda and Rolland. I like them a great deal, Callie. If it's your responsibility to them that keeps you so distant from me, I want you to know I'd be pleased to have them as part of our family."

"Matthew, please—"

"Hear me out, Callie. I'd accept them as our family with pleasure and treat them as well as it's possible for a human to treat others. I promise, as God is my witness."

Moved by his kindness, she was almost tempted to give in. But she'd given her word to Langsdon, and he'd been working out the plan all the way from New York.

She hid her face in her hands, torn in two irreconcilable directions. "That's only part of it. When we're in Independence, I hope I can explain. Perhaps things will be different then."

"Whether you tell me in Independence or not, the entire matter is in God's hands."

She straightened up on the bench. "I don't want to hear that . . ."

He caught her by the shoulders and waited until she looked him full in the face.

"Two weeks before leaving New York, I prayed He would send me a wife to love, one who would love me as well, and it wasn't a week later when I saw you at the Burlingtons' party. I was taken with you then, and you know how I came to love you on the train trip. And I fully believe, because of the way you kissed me by the creek, that you love me too."

Unable to deny it, she removed his hands from her shoulders gently. "I can't love anyone now, Matthew. I can't. Please believe me and let it be."

He caught his breath as she backed away. "You won't stop me from praying about it, Callie. Nothing will ever stop me from praying about you and seeking God's will in this."

She supposed this was the moment she should tell him

that she wasn't even a Christian. How could a minister marry her? She was entirely unworthy.

She rose from the bench. "I'm going to my cabin. But I thank you, Matthew, and I'm sorry—"

Now, she told herself as he stood up with her. *Now was the time to tell Matthew she was already married.* But instead of heeding Langsdon's order, she turned and hurried away.

10

Benjamin wrote the letter with more haste than usual.

I have word that several of my brother Charles's "other" children are on their way to California, and I would not be surprised if they stopped at the farm for free room and board on the way through Independence.

Earlier, I hired a New York investigator and have just received his answer. Langsdon Murray is an ex-convict who is wanted in New York City for grand theft. I have no idea whether his sister Callie is of the same inclination, but Langsdon is now going by the name of Talbot. I pray that this missive arrives in time to prevent trouble to your household. Forewarned is forearmed, as the saying goes. I have mixed feelings about what we will do if they come here. I continue to commit the matter to prayer.

In haste, but with love,
Father

The *Missouri Queen* churned through the muddy river toward the wooded Wayne Landing, and Callie clung to the rail, looking for Langsdon on the wooden wharf.

When her eyes lit on him, she knew he'd spotted her in the same instant. He stood under a cottonwood tree, where he'd tied up two bay horses and a farm wagon—and he looked straight at them. She nearly raised her hand to wave, but he made no effort to acknowledge her or Glenda or Rolland.

Suddenly Glenda pointed and called out with girlish excitement, "Look there, it's Langsdon!"

Callie gulped with dismay and wasn't surprised to hear Matthew inquire from beside her, "Your family?"

"Yes," she replied too quickly. "Yes, a member of the . . . Talbot side of the family."

Though the damage seemed to be done, she turned and gave her sister and brother a silencing glance, hoping they would be more circumspect.

When she looked out at the landing again, it struck her as peculiar that Langsdon, who was supposedly her husband, had not acknowledged her. She'd wait just a moment longer.

"If you need me, I'll be lodging at Smallwood Nolan's Hotel," Matthew told her. "I hope to call on you, Callie, and to meet your family."

She felt like weeping. "No, please—"

He was waiting for his trunk to be delivered from his cabin, and she saw she must seize the moment to make the break from him, no matter how much it pained her. "It's impossible, Matthew. Impossible. Thank you for . . . for everything." She gave a sob that startled both of them. "And please . . . please forgive me!"

His brown eyes full of concern, he reached for her shoulders. "What is it, Callie? What are you saying?"

Twisting away, she grabbed her carpetbag, caught up her skirts, and ran for the gangway. "Hurry!" she called back to Glenda and Rolland. "It's nearly supper time, and they'll be holding it for us! We don't want to keep them waiting!"

The moment the gangway bumped onto the wharf, she hurried down it off the *Missouri Queen* and rushed toward Langsdon.

Instead of smiling, he glared at her and staggered forward. "Welcome home, wife!" he yelled so all could hear. "Where's your weddin' ring? You been pullin' yer old trick . . . lettin' men think you ain't married?"

Heat rushed to Callie's face. "Langsdon, please!"

"Don't be tryin' no sweet talk, woman," he shouted. "Now come along! You and them brats!"

Callie darted a look back at Glenda and Rolland, who appeared as dumbstruck as she felt. Matthew was hurrying down the gangway too, and there was no mistaking his terrible shock.

"Langsdon," she whispered, "whatever are you doing, talking like that? Have you been drinking?"

"Hush!" he returned, his eyes narrowed. "Anyone could see from the lovesick look on the poor minister's face that you hadn't told him yet. We make a clean break from him here and now, or there'll be trouble ahead. Don't look back or I'll whack you across the face, and there won't be a thing he or anybody else can do about it."

She stared at him aghast. Why was it so important that Matthew should think she was married? What was Langsdon hiding? Or was it her attachment to Matthew that Langsdon feared?

Glenda and Rolland had caught up with them, and Rolland asked, "Somethin' wrong?"

"Get in the wagon fast," Langsdon ordered. "We're puttin' on an act to get rid of that minister. Your sister didn't do what I said, and it's makin' matters harder for all of us."

Callie allowed Langsdon to boost her up onto the front seat of the farm wagon, while Glenda and Rolland scrambled up in the back, sitting just behind the front seat so they wouldn't bounce out. They were scarcely settled when Langsdon urged on the horses with a "Git along, boys! Git along!"

When she dared to glance back, the wharf by their steamboat was abustle—roustabouts clanking barrows across the wharf and drayage wagons taking on or off loads. And in the midst of it all stood Matthew—dear, dear Matthew—staring after her as if he'd been turned into a pillar of stone.

It was a bumpy four-mile ride from the river landing to Independence, and Langsdon kept the broad-backed bays moving through the woods at a steady pace.

"When I tell you to do something, it's always for a good reason," he reminded Callie grimly. "It was one thing to use Hansel to provide your train ride to St. Louis. It's another thing entirely if he tries to interfere with our lives now."

"I don't understand!" she protested.

"Independence might not be such a small town, but if Hansel's a blabbermouth, word about you will get around."

Callie held onto the splintery seat as they jolted along. "I didn't have the heart to tell him I was married. I just couldn't—"

"I suppose you're in love with him?"

She bit down on her lower lip, then cast a glance at her brother. He looked so determined for their plan to succeed.

"No answer is as good as admittin' it," he said, "and I warn you, Callie, there's no room for that minister in our plans." He whipped the reins across the horses' backs, and they ran faster, making the wagon bounce even harder.

Callie kept her eyes on the ruts worn into the road. No matter how her heart ached over Matthew, Langsdon likely had reason to be angry with her. His plans were like the ruts in the road, already in place and easiest to follow, and doubtless worked out for the benefit of all of them. Wasn't that what she'd dreamed of, to reunite their family? Wasn't that why they'd come so far west already?

"I'm sorry," she apologized. "I've never met anyone like Matthew Hansel. He's truly a fine man, Langsdon. He even offered to take in Glenda and Rolland if I married him—"

"He's a man nonetheless, no question about that. I saw him kissin' you by that creek."

Remembering his kiss—and not for the first time—she had to agree. There was nothing unmanly about Matthew Hansel.

"Well, that's over," Langsdon announced, "and don't you lose sight of the fact that it's ended!"

She felt a piercing sadness. "It's unlikely that I'll ever in my life see him again."

They bumped along the dirt road in silence, and at length her brother said, "I'll find you a good husband, a man with some money, in California. There's still a shortage of young women, I hear, though not what it once was. Like you said back in New York, you're not even a Christian."

She didn't feel too sure about Langsdon finding her a good husband, but she had to agree to the rest of what he'd said. In the end, that was what would matter most to Matthew: she wasn't even a Christian.

As they rode from the beauty of the forest into the shabby town of Independence, she felt even more despondent. The town was crowded with shanties and log buildings, much smaller than St. Louis, but abustle with business. Loud music drifted from the taverns, and tawdry signs hung in front of the trading posts on the dirt streets: "Goods for Santa Fe trade! Goods for Oregon and California! Used and new goods, cheap prices!"

Squalid men wearing dirty buckskins peered at her and Glenda with more than necessary interest, and Callie whispered back to her sister, "Be sure to ignore them."

Glenda nodded. "It's no different than some in Centerville, Callie, except there's lots more of them!"

From the stern look on Rolland's face, it appeared that he, if not Langsdon, stood ready to protect them.

"Provisioning town," Langsdon remarked. "Expensive. The big log place over there is the Talbot tradin' post. They got plenty of money from it, and a farm to boot."

After they'd passed it, he added, "No decent hotels in town, and what there is have high prices. That's why I figured we'd stay with the Talbots."

Rolland asked, "Where've you been staying?"

"Men's boardin' house on the other edge of town."

"Have the Talbots invited us?" Callie asked, hoping they'd know something of Becca and Thomas.

"Haven't met 'em yet," Langsdon answered. "But I can be charmin' if I like. I'm countin' on you three to do your part too. Now that I think of it, it might be just as well you didn't tell Hansel we were married. It'll save us pretendin', to let these Talbots know we're brothers and sisters, and keep the married story for the wagon train, where it's most important."

"Good," Callie replied, "I'm sick of lying. Matthew wouldn't speak of me anyhow."

"Unless he makes inquiries," Langsdon muttered. "Unless he makes inquiries."

So that's what Langsdon feared, Callie thought. He wanted them to disappear like a fog in a woods.

"We're supposed to walk in honesty," Glenda observed from behind them with her usual sweetness. "Let us walk honestly, as in the day."

Her sister's words rang true to Callie, but Langsdon cast an annoyed glance back at Glenda. "Where'd you get that sayin'?"

"It's from the Bible," she replied sweetly.

Langsdon flicked the reins over the horses. "Then let's not hear of it again. As long as I'm in charge of this family,

I'm makin' the rules, 'n I don't want to hear any Bible preachin', you hear?"

Callie pressed her lips together to stop herself from interfering, and was glad when they left the raucous town behind them. Set back from the road there were now frame houses and a few brick buildings with trees and vegetable gardens between them, and the beginnings of farm land.

At length, Langsdon drove the horses up a lane lined with oaks and black walnut trees to a sprawling log house with lilacs abloom by the front porch.

"Is this the Talbot house?" Callie asked.

Langsdon nodded. "Too rustic for my taste, but it's big. Course they got eleven children."

"How'll we ever fit in?" Rolland asked.

"They got a small cabin on the other side of the land," Langsdon replied. "I looked in. It's dirty, but there's an old stove and bed frames and such."

"Tell us about these Talbots," Callie said.

"Adam's the father . . . in his forties. Wife's about the same. Children range from married to little ones."

Callie grew more and more nervous, wondering if they'd be welcome. "Have you met them?"

Langsdon shook his head and reined in the horses at the hitching post. "I been stayin' out of sight, pricin' provisions at the other tradin' posts and figurin' out how we're goin' to make the trek to California. It won't be easy without spendin' all our money."

"I'd be glad to help with any farm animals and the provisions," Rolland offered, his voice full of excitement.

"We'll see," Langsdon said. "We'll see how matters go."

They climbed down from the wagon and saw two older girls on the front porch. They'd been shelling peas and watching two little ones, but now they rose to their feet.

"They've all got red hair like us!" Glenda exclaimed.

"Not like mine," Langsdon objected, though his brown hair had reddish highlights. "And I'm thankful for it."

As they approached the porch, one of the older girls asked, "Are you . . . are you kinfolk?"

Nervous as she'd felt, Callie gave a laugh. "How did you guess that?"

"You're the spittin' image of our married sister, Sarah," the girl answered.

To Callie's surprise, Langsdon laughed himself. "We're Talbots, all right."

Callie straightened Rolland's white shirt and was glad that Glenda looked so nice in her new yellow gingham dress.

The girl called back to the open front door, "Mama, come see who's here! More Talbots!"

Just then the mother hurried out the door. She was tall and a bit plump—and the only blond-haired one among them. "Hello, I am Inga Talbot," she said, her slight German accent reminding Callie of Becca. "Kate says you are Talbots?"

"New York Talbots," Langsdon announced most charmingly, then introduced all of them. When Inga Talbot extended her hand, he pressed his lips to it, making her beam with pleasure. Langsdon looked pleased himself. "I hope you received our letter."

"Letter?" Inga Talbot repeated. "We have no letter."

He shook his head. "Must be delayed in the mails or gone up in one of those infernal steamboat explosions."

Lying, Callie thought. *He never wrote them a letter.*

Langsdon went on rapidly, however, introducing all of them with his best manners.

Still delighted, Inga said, "This is Kate and Jocie, and the little ones are Alicia and Alex. Come in and be welcome. My husband and the other children are in town or out on the land . . . around everywhere, but they will all be here for supper. We have *rolladen* and *apfel strudel*, and that means they all come on time for sure!"

In the wide log entry, they could smell the beef *rolladen* roasting and the apple cake cooling.

Langsdon said, "I should think such heavenly smells would bring in the whole neighborhood."

"*Ach*," Inga laughed, blushing, "you are a man after my heart. My husband, Adam, should take lessons from you." She turned to her children. "Kate and Jocie, bring in the little ones, and we finish the peas in the kitchen. First, we need *apfel* cider for everyone."

Langsdon surely knew how to charm women, Callie thought. Worse, in the beginning, she'd been taken in by him herself.

Inside, the vases of wildflowers and the bright scenic water colors relieved the darkness of the wood furniture, chinked log walls, and horsehair settees and chairs. Great braided rugs lay on the wooden floors, and homespun curtains were tied back from windows that gave good light.

"It feels just as a home should," Callie told her, ignoring Langsdon.

Inga smiled. "Thank you. I think so myself. It was my father-in-law's house until they went to California, but I have slowly come to feel it is ours."

"A fine house," Langsdon remarked, looking about with approval. "A very fine house."

It wasn't until later, when Callie had a moment alone with Inga in the kitchen that she asked, "Have you heard anything of my friend Becca Schumakker from New York? I gave her your name and told her we might meet here if she came."

"No," Inga replied. "I've seen nothing of her. Perhaps she will yet come. It is only the beginning of the season for the covered wagon trains to set out."

As the children arrived during the afternoon, it became more and more complicated to remember all of the names. There was Kate, who was eighteen, and Jonathan, seventeen; Jocie was sixteen and Madeleine fifteen; Kurt fourteen, Efrem eleven, Eva ten, Willie nine . . . and Alicia and Alex, three and two years old.

By supper time, Langsdon had the family charmed, telling the news of New York and of adventures he'd had on the way to Missouri.

Adam Talbot—a gentle giant with graying red hair—didn't question their relationship, though he eyed them suspiciously. When supper was over, he apologized. "I'm sorry, but with such a full house, we can only put you up in the children's rooms for tonight."

"We didn't expect that," Langsdon protested. "I had hoped, though, that we might rent the little log cabin on the far side of your property while we're here."

Adam shook his head. "It's run down . . . been out of use for years. Besides, we couldn't accept rent from family."

"We could fix it up in no time," Langsdon offered, "and you'd have something in return for your trouble. We'll be needin' to buy a mattress for the covered wagon anyhow, and we could use that for Callie and Glenda. Rolland and I need to buy bedrolls, and we can sleep in them."

"I won't hear of you buying them," Inga said, ignoring her husband's frown. "We have plenty at the trading post. If you can fix the cabin, we have the best of the bargain."

Callie suspected that Langsdon usually got the best of every bargain, but for tonight, she was glad to sleep in Kate and Jocie's chinked log room in the house. As for Adam, she guessed he knew exactly where she and the others fit into the Talbot family, but that he'd decided to be hospitable.

The next morning, they set off in Langsdon's wagon for the small one-bedroom log house with rags, brooms, buckets, dust mops, and hammers and nails. With Kate's help, Callie and Glenda went after the cobwebs and dirt, while Rolland, Kurt, and Efrem repaired the door stoop, kitchen shelves, and window frames, then cut back the oak branches that scraped against the roof and front windows.

Just before midday, Inga stopped by in a wagon with little Alex and Alicia, took down the old homespun curtains to wash at her house, and left behind enough beef stew and buttermilk for all of them, as well as white sunbonnets for Callie and Glenda.

After they'd eaten, Langsdon drove the buggy to town to get the free mattress and bedrolls, and returned with far more: a coffeepot, tin mugs and plates, and iron pots and pans—not to mention a ham, rice, coffee, dried peas and beans, smoked beef, dried fruit, and other provisions that Adam had given to them.

"He's decided to let bygones be bygones," Langsdon explained to Callie. "Feels a little guilty their side of the family wasn't kinder, I'd guess. I told him being born wasn't our fault."

By early evening they were settled, and Inga sent out bedding, a colorful quilt, and a red and white checked table-cloth, as well as cornbread, a basket of fried chicken, peas and carrots, and hot apple tarts.

"You're too good to us," Callie protested. "I feel as though we're imposing."

"Not at all," Inga answered. "It's our pleasure to help."

Apparently Langsdon had succeeded in changing Adam's opinion of them as well, for he arrived in a wagon with sacks of salt, bran, sugar, flour, cornmeal, and baking powder. "Don't remember the old cabin looking so good in a long time," he said, admiring their work. "Inga's right. You're doing us a favor, fixing it up."

Callie hoped so, but couldn't quite believe it.

Langsdon stood, sleeves rolled up and hands on his hips, smiling as if he had accomplished all of the work himself.

It was just his way, Callie decided, all the more determined to make the cabin as nice as she could for the Talbots.

"This was the first cabin on the land," Adam told them. "Later it was used for Talbot newlyweds until they got their own places. A honeymoon cabin."

"We'll fix it up so Jonathan can use it when he gets married," Langsdon said, making seventeen-year-old Jonathan blush and everyone laugh.

Suddenly Callie thought of sharing the cabin with Matthew Hansel. Impossible as the notion was, there was no harm in thinking of it since she would probably never see him again.

The sky poured rain for the next few days and, Callie imagined more and more what life with Matthew would be like in the honeymoon cabin. Dreaming about him made the cleaning and cooking a pleasure. In her spare time, she sewed up the dresses for Glenda, teaching her sister as they worked. When Inga came calling between downpours, she always brought more provisions, even an inkwell with India ink and quills, "In case you want to write friends," she said. "I am glad to let you use it."

"You're too good to us," Callie protested.

"We have been blessed," Inga replied. "In church they say we are blessed to be a blessing to others."

"I wish I could be more like you."

"You are making your sister's dresses without complaint," Inga pointed out. "I think maybe you even like it."

Callie nodded. "I do. We've been—" She stopped just in time, having almost said, "We've been apart for so many years that it's a pleasure."

Langsdon had told the Talbots that they'd been orphaned

in New York—giving the impression it had been recent—and that they preferred not to discuss it yet.

Late Saturday afternoon, he drove home in a brand new covered wagon pulled by six strong brown draft horses with black manes and black tails. The rain had finally stopped, and Callie, Glenda, and Rolland rushed out of the cabin, excited.

"Them bays must of cost a lot!" Rolland said.

"Plenty, but not near as much as chestnut horses," Langsdon replied with satisfaction. He climbed down from the wagon. "Most favor the flashier chestnuts, but I'd just as soon have darker horses when I'm passin' through Indian country."

He tossed the reins to Rolland. "They're yours to take care of. See to it you do a good job of it."

Catching the reins, Rolland's hazel eyes widened with awe. "I'll do my best, Langsdon. I promise. I figured we'd be usin' oxen."

"Smart emigrants are usin' horses now . . . makin' the trek in two months instead of five or six," Langsdon explained. He walked around to admire the horses and wagon himself. "Plenty of fresh horses to buy on the way nowadays. We'll finish provisionin', then leave in a week or two when it's not so muddy and prairie grass is good for grazin'."

Adam had sold them the wagon at half the usual cost, and it was solidly built of ash with elm wheel hubs, oak spokes, wrought iron reinforcements around the tongue and hounds, and wheel tires of iron. Five hickory bows arched over the wagon bed to support the canvas cover, and there were even hooks on them for hanging their clothes and other belongings.

"Now it looks like we're really goin'!" Rolland said.

"Still have plenty to buy," Langsdon said. "I got us two

good rifles to use for shooting game on the way. Two rifles . . . and a handgun for protection."

Callie didn't like the rifles and felt even more uneasy at the sight of Langsdon holding the handgun, but she didn't dare say so. When she asked Langsdon about money, he answered gruffly, "You do your work and I'll do mine."

That night they ate supper at the big log house again, and Callie wished she'd grown up in such a congenial family—a real family with married parents, and all of them living together like this, even if it was noisy and not quite perfect.

Once they'd discussed the new team of horses and their covered wagon, the talk shifted to the numbers expected to make the long trek. In 1850, there'd been fifty thousand on the trail, but the last three years only five thousand, which would make matters easier. The biggest problem now was the great herds of sheep and cattle being driven west and overgrazing the grass on the trail. Next came talk of the eccentrics: men with wheelbarrows averaging twenty-five miles a day and a Negro woman walking and carrying all of her possessions on her head.

If they could make it, so can we! Callie thought.

"As I see it, after last summer's terrible shortage of grass," Langsdon said, "we'd best be in the advance guard, ahead of the herds and the wave of migrants crowdin' the campgrounds. Probably be more of 'em after last year's Dred Scott Decision, expectin' war in the land."

Adam nodded. "You never want to be in the rear guard, where the Paiutes do most of their harassing or where you'd be worried about being snowed in the mountains, like the Donner party in '46."

"*Ach*, Adam, don't even mention them," Inga said.

Callie didn't like to hear about them herself. The whole country knew of the Donner party being snowed in. To survive starvation, some had actually practiced cannibalism.

Rolland interrupted. "What is the Dred Scott Decision that everyone's talking about?"

"Dred Scott, a slave from Illinois, sued for his freedom since he lived in a free state, north of the Missouri Compromise line," Adam explained. "But the Supreme Court said a slave has no right to sue and that the Missouri Compromise has always been unconstitutional. Our family, as you might guess, is appalled. I fear the decision will lead us to a civil war before long."

Callie expected Langsdon to say again that he had no intention to fight for Negroes, but he kept his mouth shut and sent Rolland a look that clearly told him to drop the subject.

Adam must have noticed, for he said, "You'll like our family in California, even if I do say so myself. Wish we were half as fine Christians as they are."

"Come to church with us tomorrow morning," Inga suggested. "It is a small church, but filled with love."

"Oh, could we?" Glenda asked. "I've missed going to church ever so much, traveling here."

"Of course," Inga answered, beaming. "We go together."

Apparently Inga assumed they always attended church, Callie thought, and she didn't have the courage to disabuse her of the notion. And—and what if Matthew Hansel were in attendance? Perhaps she could explain Langsdon's deception at the wharf . . . perhaps things could still be made right.

Adam had been carving the roast for second helpings, and he said in an offhand manner, "Just before closing tonight, a man was in the trading post asking about you, Langsdon. Scrawny fellow with a British accent."

Callie turned to her brother in despair.

Langsdon, however, appeared unperturbed. "Wonder

who it might be. Haven't had time to meet many people here."

"Claimed he knew you from New York City," Adam added, serving Rolland another thick slice of beef.

"You tell him where I was?" Langsdon asked.

Adam shook his head. "Believe me, I wouldn't tell a man of his disposition the name of a hound. He made a pretense at composure, but when you've raised a family this size, you know rage when you see it."

"A Britisher, you say?" Langsdon replied, affecting a look of puzzlement. "Likely a dejected fellow, maybe run away or run off from his own country. Maybe I can give him a hand."

Nothing else was mentioned about Mr. Stane, and once Callie put thoughts of him aside, it was a most pleasant dinner. She sat at the huge oak trestle table between Kate and Jonathan, who were lively and full of good humor. Since they often worked at the trading post, they knew everything of interest that went on in Independence, and though a few years younger than Callie, they were good company.

When dinner ended, Inga gave them the leftover fruitcake and loaf of yeast bread to help with breakfast in the cabin. "We meet you at church a few minutes before nine tomorrow morning," she said, then made sure they knew its location.

Adam insisted they take a spare lantern, even though the moon was full, and they left the main house with heartfelt thanks.

When Langsdon pulled the horses and covered wagon up in front of the log cabin, however, he rasped, "We pack up now as fast as we can. We leave tonight. No arguments!"

Callie stared at him in the moonlight, then suddenly knew what the trouble was. "It's Mr. Stane, isn't it?"

"No questions! No arguments!" Langsdon replied. "I got a feelin' for such things."

A feeling for avoiding who-knew-what-all troubles he'd gotten himself into! she thought. She clenched her fists, furious at the idea of leaving in the middle of the night like fugitives. "You're not afraid of a scrawny old butler, are you?"

"I'm afraid of no one," Langsdon barked into the darkness, "but I'm not waitin' around for a wretch like Stane to shoot me in the back. He plans to kill me."

"Why would he?" she asked.

"We had business dealin's, and he's a man who holds a hard grudge," Langsdon replied as he tied the horses to a tree trunk. "Now, you want to come along to California or not? I can go faster without you."

Callie hesitated, thinking of the kindness they'd had from the Missouri Talbots. As for business dealings between Mr. Stane and Langsdon, could it have to do with the stolen paintings?

"I'm for California myself," Rolland replied to Langsdon. "The land's all played out in Missouri. That and the summer fevers are why so many leave, according to Jonathan."

"I want to be with Rolland," Glenda put in.

She had no choice, not if she wanted to hold the family together. "We'll go then," said Callie. "But I did want to wait in case Becca and Thomas came."

"No waitin'!" Langsdon snapped. "We leave tonight!"

The full moon and their two lanterns lit the blur of the next few hours: spreading out the mattress and bedding in the wagon, carrying out the provisions and packing them right. Langsdon hung the rifles on the hooks on the hickory bows and made Callie and Glenda pack the cottage's tin mugs and plates, as well as the pots and pans in the wagon's grub box which sat on the rear. Rolland packed in sacks of grain for the horses, so they could travel on after the grass gave out.

"What will Inga and Adam and the rest of them think of us leaving like this, taking some of their things?" Callie asked.

"I don't care what they think!" Langsdon replied.

"But they'll warn their relatives in California," Glenda said. "They'll tell them what we've done."

Callie stopped in her tracks, not having considered that.

The thought even stopped Langsdon, but not for long. "Callie, you write 'em a letter sayin' we're sorry that we had to leave so fast, but that somethin' came up . . . a chance to leave with a wagon train right away instead of imposin' on them longer, that's what you say. They've been so fine to us, we don't want to impose any longer. Remind 'em we fixed up the cabin. And tell 'em we decided to go to Oregon!"

"That's another lie!" she objected. She swatted angrily at one of the many mosquitoes that had invaded the cabin during all of their running in and out. Already her arms were full of bites.

"I'll dictate the letter," he stated.

Callie cringed at the thought, but with Langsdon at her shoulder, she got out the inkwell and paper Inga had brought for "writing to friends." She sat down at the table near the lantern, her heart full of guilt as Langsdon stood over her and dictated.

Dear Inga, Adam, and our fine cousins,

We are sorry to leave so suddenly, but we have no choice. We have just been invited to join a faster wagon train in the morning, and we are eager to get going before the oxen and mules eat all of the prairie grass.

We thank you for your help in provisioning and for the use of your cabin, which we have fixed and cleaned up. We hope you will understand our haste, since our lives would be in danger from snowstorms if we leave too late. You will be surprised to hear that we've decided to go to Oregon, where we hear the farming is best of all.

Thank you for the fine dinner last night and for

your many other kindnesses, which we hope to repay if
you ever come to Oregon.

Sincerely,

"Sign your name," Langsdon told her.

She glared at him. "It's lying. You know the letter's full of
lies. I expect you've forced other women to write letters for
you. You seem so at home at it."

His blue-gray eyes flashed with fury in the lantern light.
"Sign it or you stay here alone."

She signed her name reluctantly, then Glenda and Rolland had to sign theirs. Finally, he wrote with a fine flourish,
Langsdon Talbot.

While he and Rolland finished readying the wagon, Callie scribbled a quick note to Becca.

My dearest friend,

It breaks my heart, but we are leaving Indepen-
dence like thieves in the night. No matter what you
are told, our plans remain unchanged. How I long to
see you again.

Your loving friend,
Callie

She folded the letter, stuck it in an envelope with Becca's
name on it, and hid it behind a closed window curtain.
There was just time for another note to hide behind the
curtain with it.

Inga and family,

I'm truly sorry to run off like this! Thank you so
much for your many kindnesses.

Callie

Somewhere, Langsdon had gotten a good chestnut stallion named Major, as well as a bridle and saddle.

"Where did you get him?" Callie asked, for the horse
looked vaguely familiar.

"Let's go!" he ordered, ignoring her question and riding alongside the wagon in the moonlit night.

A nervous Rolland drove the six horses, and Callie and Glenda sat in the wagon behind him, hanging onto the wooden sides to keep from bouncing about so wildly.

The horses, their heads bobbing, pulled them through the moonlit night for hours until they came upon the "jumping-off meadow" for the California and Oregon trails. Instead of joining one of the covered wagon circles, Langsdon muttered, "We go on."

He rode on ahead of them, and they followed until, at long last, he reined in his horse. "We'll stop behind that copse of trees for a few hours' rest."

Rolland guided the team to a halt, and Langsdon tied the horses to a tree so they'd be ready to go again.

"That's no way to treat good horses," Rolland objected.

"We'll treat 'em right later," Langsdon replied. "Give 'em some grain, then lie down and get some sleep."

When the pink rays of dawn rose in the east, Langsdon was already mounted on the chestnut stallion. When he woke them, he said, "We'll eat that bread as we ride on."

"Aren't we going to join a wagon train?" Callie asked, quickly getting out the bread Inga had given them.

"Up at the Kansas River, we'll find one."

They rode on and on, Callie and Glenda putting on their new white sunbonnets against the sun.

Callie might have thought it a glorious excursion across the rolling countryside if the ride weren't so hard—and if she didn't feel so much like a fugitive. As if that weren't daunting enough, she wondered if she would ever find Becca—if she and Thomas would indeed come.

Once they passed a covered wagon train drawn by oxen, and an emigrant called out, "You goin' it alone?"

Langsdon didn't answer, but Callie couldn't miss the

pitying glances of the emigrant women.

"It's safer in numbers from Indians when you got women along!" one called out. "Some tribes been on the warpath!"

Callie and Glenda gave them stiff waves as they jolted past the line of slow-moving covered wagons.

"Do you think Langsdon really means us to join a wagon train?" Glenda asked. "You know how everyone says the Indians have gotten mad at emigrants for killing their buffalo and all."

Callie shrugged, unwilling to voice the terrible fear that was beginning to take hold of her. There had been no discussing anything with Langsdon since they left, but Mr. Stane seemed a mild threat compared to enraged Indians.

Day by day, they rode on through the rolling countryside, starting at daybreak and making a late camp off in a copse of trees or hidden down by a creek, always by themselves. There were only occasional covered wagon companies ahead of them now, and Langsdon asked the riders in passing if they'd seen the last horse wagon train that had set out. None had.

At the Kansas River ferry, they encountered a wagon train encamped for the next morning's crossing. "Seen a horse wagon train ahead of us?" Langsdon asked again.

"Yep," the captain answered. "Likely a day or two ahead."

Callie felt a surge of relief. It was bad enough seeing so many grave markers along the trail already without thinking of traveling through the territories of Kansas and Nebraska by themselves. It did seem there'd be safety in numbers.

The captain added, "We'll give ye a jump on us crossing the river in the morning since there's only one wagon of ye."

"Appreciate it," Langsdon said.

They made camp ahead of the other party, and Langsdon

told Callie and Glenda, "Make plenty of cornbread. We'll live on that and ham till we catch up with the others."

Early the next morning, the horses pulled the wagon up to the river ferry, and Rolland and Langsdon unhitched them. Callie did not like the looks of the dilapidated ferry, nor of the disheveled Shawnee and Delaware Indians who were pulling their wagon onto it, then putting wedges under the wheels. Likely they were angry at having lost this part of the Indian Territory a few years ago.

"Grave markers on both sides of the river," Glenda said.

"I'd just as soon not think of it," Callie answered. She couldn't swim, and she doubted that Glenda could, either.

Callie caught her breath as Langsdon and Rolland began to swim their horses across the rushing river downstream from the ferry. Suddenly the ferry jolted loose and was moving across the river with them on it. She clung to the wagon and closed her eyes, feeling the rush of the river under them.

"It's a thrilling sight," Glenda exclaimed. "Do look." She must have seen Callie's fear, for she added in a caring tone, "Perfect love casts out fear, Callie. If you trust God, you won't be so scared."

Callie was glad for Glenda's courage, but she didn't know how God could help her. When the ferry bumped against the opposite shore, she finally opened her eyes and was glad to see the Indians pulling the wagon onto land. Moreover, Rolland and Langsdon had gotten the horses safely across the river.

They hitched up the horses quickly and rode through the green prairie, shifting from west to northwest. Langsdon rode alongside the wagon with his guidebook. "Platte River next. Guidebook says about 220 miles from here."

That evening they came across a camp that appeared to have been left the last night. "We'll have to ride on a few more hours to catch up with them tomorrow," Langsdon said.

"It's too hard on the horses," Rolland protested.

"When they're done in, we'll get new ones," Langsdon said. "There's horse traders up by the Platte River."

"He's heartless," Glenda whispered.

Callie nodded. "Wonder if he'd leave us behind too, if we got done in?"

They had no more than stopped speaking than Langsdon approached with a determined expression on his face. He pulled something from his pocket and handed it to Callie. "Wear it from now on," he ordered. "And no arguments!"

A gold wedding ring!

Glenda and Rolland stared at Callie as she slowly slipped it on her ring finger.

"And you two," Langsdon said to Glenda and Rolland, "keep your mouths shut, whatever you do."

The next evening they saw the wagon train circled for the night in the distance.

"That's Captain Wood's train . . . all horses!" Langsdon said. "I'll ride ahead to let him know we made it."

As Langsdon rode forward, Rolland urged on their tired team. "Almost there, boys! Almost time for you to rest."

When they approached, Langsdon and other men pulled several of the other covered wagons aside to make space for them in the tight wagon circle. "Pull 'er in here!" one of the men called out.

"It'll be better, being with the others," Callie said. Suddenly she saw two familiar figures helping to pull the nearest wagon aside—one was Yorker and the other, Reverend Matthew Hansel!

11

Callie caught up the skirt of her blue calico frock and climbed down from the wagon. There was no point in trying to hide. Even in the last rays of sunshine, she saw that Matthew's brown eyes were wide with amazement. He no longer wore a black suit and clerical collar, but a new set of buckskins, in which he looked ruggedly handsome.

"Miss Murray!" Yorker yelled, and all of the nearby emigrants looked at her.

"She's Mrs. Talbot," Langsdon informed him coldly. He turned his glance on Matthew as well as the other men. "I hope everyone will keep that firmly in mind. She is my wife."

Even Yorker seemed intimidated. Once he stopped staring, he continued to push the other wagon aside to make room for theirs. But he did say to Matthew, "Ain't that beans, Reverend Hansel? I sure guessed wrong there!"

Matthew gave Callie a look of disbelief himself, and she whirled away. Recalling the drunken husband scene Langsdon had played at the Wayne Landing, she once again felt mortified.

Glenda whispered, "Why must you pretend to be married to Langsdon?"

"Single women of my age aren't welcome on wagon trains."

"Why not?" Glenda asked.

"People think a single woman will cause trouble, even if she doesn't mean to."

Glenda blinked, not quite understanding.

"Come, let's help Rolland with the horses," Callie suggested. "It appears that Langsdon is too occupied with his fine stallion to help us here."

She darted another glance at Matthew, but he was speaking to several other emigrants, his back to her. What must he be thinking?

By the time their wagon was in place and the horses were staked in the corral formed by the wagons, darkness had fallen and lanterns glowed all around.

At length, Langsdon arrived with Captain Wood, who carried a lantern himself. By way of introduction, Langsdon said, "My wife, Mrs. Talbot, and her sister and brother, Glenda and Rolland Murray."

Callie managed a polite, "How do you do?"

The bearded captain nodded at her. "My wife, Annie, is also with us. Since we have so few young wives in this company, you might enjoy each other's company."

In the lantern light, she saw he was a short, middle-aged man with a military bearing. "Thank you," she said. "I look forward to meeting her."

"And I look forward to your tending to your chores," Langsdon told her, his voice terse. To the captain he said, "I got a jealous streak, and with good reason. It'd be best to keep your wife away from a bad influence."

Callie felt her mouth drop open while the captain eyed her, then turned back to Langsdon. "Can't say that I blame you, Talbot. Just so there's no fighting, or your wagon will be turned out. Our aim is to get to California fast, not to become embroiled in marital disputes."

"I'm in agreement with you there," Langsdon replied. "I

hope you heard that clearly, woman."

Callie clenched her fists. *The nerve of him! The appalling nerve!* Furious and feeling a bit feverish, she retorted, "I trust you will stay away from the captain's wife and the other women then, too."

Now Langsdon looked as angry as she felt. "We'll stay to ourselves as much as possible!"

The captain gave a nod to Callie, Glenda, and Rolland. "Welcome," he said, likely from force of habit. "You'll find we travel fast, though we do break for a decent nooning so most of the day's cooking can be done then."

"The faster, the better," Callie answered, after which the captain hastened away. She climbed into the wagon, still indignant. "I'm going to bed," she told them. "I don't feel well."

"What about our supper?" Langsdon asked.

"Since you're such a jealous husband, I should think you'd fear I'd poison your food!"

Glenda broke in with a conciliatory voice, "I'll get out a ham, and there's still cheese for tonight. Tomorrow noon, we can start to do real cooking."

"A good thing you're along," Langsdon told her, loudly enough for Callie to hear.

In the wagon, Callie wondered why he'd made such a point of his jealousy. Then suddenly she knew—it was to keep Matthew and others away. Worst of all, her anger had played right into Langsdon's plans. If only she didn't feel so exhausted.

The next morning, the emigrants rose before dawn. People shouted, children cried, pots and pans clattered, dogs barked, and harnesses jingled. Callie pulled on her blue calico and a shawl, and hurried out to start their cook fire. Casting a glance at Langsdon's and Rolland's bedrolls under the wagon, she was glad to see they were already empty.

Before long, the tantalizing aromas of coffee and frying bacon filled the cool air. As Callie and Glenda cooked breakfast, it didn't take long to see that Langsdon's tactic last night had been successful. The other families, although glancing at them and nodding politely as they went about their morning chores, kept their distance. Heartsick, Callie wondered what they must think of her.

At length, however, Yorker ambled over in his new buckskin outfit. After nodding at Glenda, who was frying the bacon, he asked Callie, "You really married ter that Talbot fellow?"

She'd been stooping over the campfire, stirring the porridge, and nearly lost her balance. "I . . . can't talk about it, Yorker."

He pinched his pointy noise thoughtfully. "You ain't married then, just like I told Reverend Hansel."

"You told him that?"

Yorker nodded. "Yer too smart ter hook up with a snoozer like Talbot, even if you are wearin' a weddin' ring. When you been a New York streeter long as I was, you know a snoozer when you see one. Wouldn't want ter buy a horse or a wagon from the likes o' him."

She changed the subject quickly. "Why did you leave Illinois? And how did you find Reverend Hansel?"

Yorker grinned. "I ain't beans at store work . . . too restless. I knew he was stoppin' in Independence, so I made my way along as fast as I could."

Yorker's grin faded. "The reverend wasn't any too glad about my leavin' my orphan train family. He helped me write 'em a letter, but he didn't beat me none."

Callie stirred the porridge a bit too vigorously. "Are you in someone's wagon here?"

"No, me and Reverend Hansel, we're on horseback. Tried to talk 'im into just the two of us ridin' on alone to

California, but he says we're stayin' with the wagon train in case of Injuns and other dangers. He bought me a horse, an' I'm mighty sore from ridin', but I aim ter help 'im. Besides, he's with the train fer religious work. You know, marryin' 'n buryin'."

"You're going to help with that?!"

Yorker laughed. "No, not that! We're both outriders, too, meaning we ride up 'n down the wagon train ter watch for wagon breakdowns 'n other troubles. Reverend Hansel's a good rider, and he's been teachin' me."

"That should keep you busy," she replied.

"He's sure broken up about you bein' married, Miss Murray . . . I mean, Mrs. Talbot."

She swallowed with great difficulty. "I'm sorry to hear it, Yorker, but I am glad to see you."

Yorker glanced at Glenda. "Expect that's yer sister."

"Yes. Glenda, this is Yorker, one of the boys from the orphan train."

Just then Langsdon rode over on his chestnut stallion. "What you doin' here?" he demanded of Yorker.

"Admirin' yer bride," Yorker replied, undaunted. "Ye got fine taste in women, Mr. Talbot. Very fine taste. She's beans, all right. So is her sister."

Langsdon shot him a look of pure loathing. "Be on your way, if you please. We're about to eat our breakfast."

Yorker stalked off, calling back, "Yer a snoozer, Mr. Talbot, just like I thought. I know 'em a mile off."

Langsdon gave Yorker another fierce look, then shot one at Glenda, who was trying to cover a smile. Frowning, he helped himself to a mug of steaming coffee.

Callie dished porridge into a tin bowl for him, then into another bowl for Rolland, who'd been seeing to the horses.

"What was that brat doin' here?" Langsdon asked Callie.

"I expect he was just being friendly."

"See to it that you're not friendly with anyone," he warned her. "Now eat, all of you, and be quick about it."

Callie forced herself to swallow the porridge, wondering if Matthew had sent Yorker to talk to her. Maybe if she could send a message with Yorker . . .

Langsdon must have guessed her thought. "Don't get any clever ideas, *Mrs.* Talbot, or you either, Glenda. We're all in this together, the four of us."

None of them answered.

Before long, Captain Wood called out "Catch up! Catch up your teams!"

Everywhere, women and children doused the cook fires, and the men hitched their horses to the wagons. As the morning sun sent its pink rays over the eastern horizon, Captain Wood bellowed, "Wagons, ho-o!"

Callie and Glenda donned their sunbonnets and joined Rolland on the front seat. The line of twenty-five wagons in front of theirs rolled along. Rolland called out, "Giddup, boys! Giddup!" and their wagon rolled along behind the others across the prairie.

Somehow Langsdon had set himself up as one of the scouts, likely because there was a dearth of young men. When he had ridden off, Rolland asked, "What are we going to do about Langsdon's scheming?"

"I'm just praying that when we get to California, things will be different," Glenda replied. "Remember what Inga and Adam told us about the California Talbots? I know it'll be better there."

"What if they don't want us?" Rolland asked.

"Don't even think such a thing!" Glenda answered.

Callie made no reply, but the question continued to bother her as the horses pulled their wagon over the rolling plain of wild flowers and bright green grasses. The sun slowly dissipated the morning chill, and after a while she took off her shawl. If they didn't have so many problems, it would be a fine morning, she decided—especially if their wooden seat had springs.

She saw Matthew and Yorker riding their horses toward them from the front of the wagon train, doubtless on their outrider duty. As Matthew neared them, she turned so her sunbonnet hid her face.

"Everything fine here?" Matthew asked.

"Everything's fine," Rolland replied, "except for eating the other wagons' dust."

"You'll be moving up in the rotation of wagons every day," Matthew told him as he rode on. "That way everyone has a chance of being first or eating dust."

"A fair way o' doin' it," Yorker added.

The days that passed held both bad and good aspects; the scenery remained pleasant, but the other emigrants made no move to be friendly; streams swollen with spring rains were treacherous to cross, but a few now had bridges unlisted in the guidebooks. When they reached the Nebraska Territory and stopped at a horse ranch, some of the emigrants traded for fresh horses.

"Not us," Langsdon said. "Our horses got to last longer."

As usual, Callie avoided speaking with him. Not only was she angry with him, but she felt poorly, especially in the evenings.

Before long they sighted the South Fork of the Platte River, a fearsome sight since the river was over a mile wide. For days, they traveled near the river, albeit on dry, rough land. The hills and bluffs showed the outcroppings of rocks, and the first prairie dog "town" was a scene of excitement, and not only for the children.

One morning, Captain Wood called to everyone in the circle of wagons, "We'll be fordin' the Platte right here."

"Here?" Callie repeated. The river was at its very widest,

and she was feeling more and more exhausted. Langsdon was scouting ahead.

Just then, Matthew Hansel rode by their wagon. As usual, Callie turned away quickly, glad for her sunbonnet's wide brim. He must have nodded to them, for Rolland gave him a pleasant, "Mornin'," and Glenda said a sweet, "Good morning, Reverend."

"The captain says to water your horses well before we cross," Matthew told them. "If they stop to drink in the river, they're apt to go down in quicksand."

"Help us, Lord!" Glenda called out fervently.

Matthew smiled. "Glad to hear that you pray. I thought you might be a believer."

Likely he meant that Glenda might be the only one in the family who was, Callie thought angrily.

She looked out again and saw that Matthew had ridden his bay gelding out into the water to help guide the first wagons across the river.

"No stopping!" he shouted. "Move on! Move on!"

When it was their turn to cross, Rolland yelled, "Giddup, boys! Giddup!" He slapped the reins over the horses' broad brown backs to keep them going, and ripples flowed out from around them as they moved along. The water rose higher until the river reached the hubs of the wagon wheels, and it seemed they floated in the midst of a great muddy sea.

"I can't swim!" Callie called out in terror as Matthew rode toward them. "If we go down, none of us can swim!"

"I can," he told her. "You'll be fine, Callie, I promise. I'll be right alongside your wagon. I'll take care of you."

Her eyes met his, and she quickly looked down at her hands and saw the gleam of the wedding ring. He'd save her even though she seemed to have betrayed him?

The Platte turned out to be shallow, and the horses

pulled them and the wagon through steadily. When they reached the other shore, Matthew was still behind them, urging the other wagons on.

After their crossing, the trail led higher and higher, angling over to the North Fork of the Platte. The countryside still held green grass for the horses, but the ground was hard, hammering at the wagons. Each evening when they made camp, Rolland had to mend wagon wheels and hammer in wooden wedges to tighten the iron rims.

Surprisingly, they encountered no Indians.

There were no trees now, either, and Callie and Glenda gathered dried buffalo chips. It was a repugnant chore, but there was nothing else to be used for the cook fires.

"When will we see the buffalo?" Glenda asked Langsdon one evening after he'd ridden in from scouting.

"Soon enough," he assured her. "One of the scouts spotted some old bulls. He says we'll see herds soon enough."

The next day, however, a different sight appeared on the horizon, and the cry echoed down the wagon train. "Mountains! Look, it's the Rocky Mountains ahead!"

Callie pressed down the brim of her sunbonnet and squinted ahead into the fading sun. There they were, the famous Rockies, standing like a mighty gray fortress, their peaks jutting up against the red sky.

"We're making progress," she told Glenda and Rolland, though it would likely take a week to reach the imposing sight. Despite her weariness, she began to feel hopeful.

The next day a hailstorm hit in the night, pelting the poor horses, who put their heads down and took the painful pounding stoically. The emigrants, however, were not so stoic about it, for the hailstones also tore the canvas covers of the wagons. When they started out in the morning, everyone and everything in the wagons was wet, and the horses picked their way through a sea of mud.

Two days farther west, the ground became higher and dry again. During their nooning, the scouts rode in crying, "Buffalo! Buffalo stampede!"

Callie stood up in their wagon and looked out over the plain. Thousands upon thousands of the dark beasts were angling straight for them, churning up a great cloud of yellow dust.

"We'll be trampled to death!" she cried. Already the earth shook beneath them, and her knees felt weak.

Up ahead, the scouts tried to turn the far end of the stampeding herd, and Captain Wood cried, "Ride on straight ahead as fast as you can! Everyone in your wagons! Wagons ho-o! Wagons ho-o! We have to outrun 'em!"

"Giddup, boys! Giddup!" Rolland yelled, and their wagon tore off with the others, jolting across the land.

The cloud of yellow dust was almost overhead, and Callie was certain they'd be trampled by the thundering beasts.

Glenda beseeched God for assistance, and Rolland slapped the reins over the horses, spurring them on. It seemed impossible that the herd wouldn't flatten them in minutes.

"They're turning the herd!" Rolland shouted, looking back over his shoulder. He spurred on the horses. "The scouts are turning the herd to go behind us!"

At long last, the covered wagons slowed to a halt, the horses' brown coats lathered. Callie peered out the back puckering hole of their wagon and saw Langsdon, along with Matthew and some of the other men, shooting buffalo on the outer edges of the herd to turn the beasts eastward.

"We're safe!" she told Glenda. "We're safe!"

"Thank Thee, Lord!" her sister cried out.

"Seems to me that the scouts and outriders turned the herd," Callie answered as weariness overcame her again.

"God uses people to do His work, too," Glenda

explained. "Didn't you know that?"

"Guess I didn't," Callie replied to satisfy her sister. But she thought to herself, *If God is so wonderful, why doesn't He halt this agonizing lie I have to live with Langsdon?* The more she considered it, the angrier she was. Worst of all, she still felt weak, too feeble to even take it up with her brother.

The next day the wagon train stopped for the travelers to cook as much buffalo meat as they could. Even the leftover strips were hung on a campfire frame to dry into jerky.

In the afternoon Glenda made Callie rest. Lying down seemed to help her, despite the bumping wagon. As they traveled on and on, Callie tried to forget their narrow escape with stampeding buffalo. Infirm as she felt, she tried to keep her attention on the arresting rock formations they passed. Courthouse and Jail Rocks were first, and then, in sight for a full day, the fantastical Chimney Rock, resembling a giant upside-down funnel. The line of rust-colored formations led onward to the rock castle called Scott's Bluff.

Had Abby Talbot sketched them when she'd traveled west twelve years ago? Callie wondered about her half sister and worried about how the California Talbots might receive them. When she slept, she had nightmares about them, nightmares she couldn't remember in the daylight.

Before long, the emigrants sighted snow-capped Laramie Peak and then Fort Laramie in the distance. As they rode closer, they saw that the old fur-trading fort was surrounded by an encampment of Indians.

At last they were what Captain Wood considered near enough, and he called out, "Circle the wagons tightly, and keep your horses in the corral! It's likely Sioux."

Langsdon rode back from his scouting position, and Rolland asked, "Are Sioux warlike?"

"They got their women and children with 'em," Langsdon replied. "We'll stock up on provisions and trade horses."

Moments after the wagons were circled, the Indians rode over for trading, bringing moccasins and skins with them. They eyed the wagon camp closely.

"Break out your trading goods," Captain Wood said, "but keep your eyes on 'em. They think different than we do and don't see a thing wrong with taking what appeals to 'em."

Callie was so tired of her high-laced leather boots that she got out the beads that Langsdon had laid in for trading. When two Indian men approached the wagon, she pointed at a pair of moccasins.

"Langsdon will have a fit!" Glenda gasped. "And what will the others say?"

"I don't care! They're probably talking plenty about me already, and I'm sick of these high leather boots! I ache all over as it is!"

After Callie had affected her trade, Glenda pointed at a pair of moccasins herself. "Now we'll be in trouble together," she said, her eyes twinkling.

Callie smiled herself, then realized it was the first time anything had amused her in a long time. Later, when Langsdon sneered down at them for wearing moccasins, she laughed, harder than she'd intended.

"You deranged?" he asked.

Callie laughed again, just to spite him.

Days later, when their new horses pulled the wagon to the North Fork of the Platte River, everyone was glad to see that a bridge had been erected for this second crossing of the Platte. They passed Independence Rock and headed onward into the Rockies, and the days became a wearisome blur for Callie.

As they toiled higher and higher into the mountains and pine forests, the air turned colder, and she felt somewhat better. Before long they were heading for South Pass, the backbone of the country, and were glad to find the pass more like a broad plain between two solid walls of mountains.

They passed through Rattlesnake Creek and near Rattlesnake Mountains, and Callie stayed in the wagon. Despite Langsdon's anger, she refused to cook for fear of snakes, which had begun to fill her feverish dreams.

After a while, she took in little of what passed, only that Glenda often put cold compresses on her forehead and forced her to eat porridge and drink water. As from a great distance, she heard talk of a deadly desert before them. Forty-mile desert. Then everything dissolved into a feverish blackness.

That night Glenda opened the back flap of the wagon. "Langsdon let me bring Reverend Hansel to you since you're so sick," she said. "I thought a prayer from him might help."

Callie stared at Matthew and dimly saw Langsdon behind him.

"Callie," Matthew said gently, "I'm so sorry to hear you're not well. Is there anything I can do?"

She slowly eased off the gold wedding ring, and threw it with the last of her strength at Langsdon, hitting him on the forehead. "I hate you! I hate you!" she cried out, then fell back exhausted.

"She's crazed from her fever!" Langsdon charged, jumping down from the back of the wagon to retrieve the ring.

"Callie," Matthew whispered, "the Lord Jesus Christ loves you. For that matter, I still care for you, too. I can't help myself. . ."

Langsdon grabbed Matthew by his buckskin collar and shoved him away furiously. "I knew I shouldn't trust you! I knew it! Don't you ever come near here again, or—"

"Langsdon, stop it!" Glenda shouted.

CHAPTER ELEVEN

Callie closed her eyes, blotting out her brother's words and clinging to Matthew's. *I still care for you, too. I can't help myself.*

As she slipped in and out of consciousness, she was scarcely aware of the jolting wagon or of being half-carried beside it along ledges. She vaguely heard the landmarks of the journey: Green River, Fort Hall, Raft River, Humboldt River, Humboldt Sink, the Sierra Nevada Mountains. She seemed closer to death than to life, but she still clung to Matthew's wonderful words. After a long while, however, she could no longer separate them from her fearsome nightmares.

After long, long weeks of fading in and out of consciousness, she heard the emigrants raise a great cheer. "The Sacramento Valley! We made it! Two thousand miles to California!"

California. . .

Despite the fearful dreams she'd had of the Talbots, the word gave her hope. As they made their way down into the valley, she began to feel better, even sitting up in the wagon.

"Your fever's broken, Callie!" Glenda told her, tears in her eyes. "You're going to live! Oh, how I've prayed for you! Rolland prayed, too. And Yorker keeps inquiring how you are. I think Matthew sends him."

"Matthew?" Callie whispered. "I want to see Matthew."

Glenda shook her head. "We can't call for him. Langsdon says he'll kill Matthew if he comes near you again!"

12

Sitting under the California pepper tree in the courtyard, Benjamin Talbot opened the letter whose familiar script and return address revealed it was from his son Adam. The envelope and even the pages inside were so muddied that they might have sailed up the Missouri River without a mail boat, Benjamin reflected. Eager to learn the Missouri news, he put on his spectacles, smoothed out the stained pages, and read:

Dear Father, Aunt Jessica, and sisters and brothers,

Unfortunately your letter about Langsdon and Callie arrived after they had made their late night departure. Some might say that we were badly taken in, but we are trying to remember that we are to give thanks in spite of all things.

The gist of the matter is this: They arrived in Independence with their younger sister and brother, Glenda (fourteen) and Rolland (fifteen), whom we think were, like Callie, ignorant of Langsdon's schemes. I was suspicious at the outset, but decided to give them the benefit of the doubt. They did tell us from the beginning that they meant to go to California, and Langsdon said you had encouraged them to come, which we assume is a falsehood after having read your letter. They seemed delightful relations, most willing to fix up the old cabin while they stayed in it. We all pitched in to help, and we must admit that the cabin is once again livable, though not due to Langsdon's efforts. In retrospect, I see that he avoided as much labor as possible. Instead, he did the running and planning for the rest of them, doubtless considering himself the "brains of the outfit."

We accepted them as family and let them buy a covered wagon, rifles, gun, and other purchases at cost. We gave them numerous provisions, often shared meals with them, and helped in every way possible, only to have them disappear in the middle of the night, stealing our best saddle horse, Major, not to mention tools, lanterns, sacks of grain, and a multitude of other items. After they left, Inga discovered a note from Callie (hidden behind a curtain) thanking us for our kindnesses and apologizing for their running off in the night. There was also another letter to a friend named Becca, who has since passed through here with her new husband on their way from New York to California.

We do not mind the thefts nearly as much as Langsdon's betrayal of our trust. I hope you will be more careful than we were. It is especially interesting that the evening before they disappeared they had agreed to attend church with us the next morning.

As if they hadn't duped us sufficiently, they left a letter saying they were going to Oregon, where the farming is said to be better. Langsdon Murray (I don't believe his legal name is Talbot) is no farmer! He blamed their middle-of-the-night departure on a sudden inducement to join a fast wagon train the next morning and their concern about imperiling their lives with snowstorms if they left too late in the season.

    They stayed with us for nearly a week, and Inga believes that the cause for their early departure was my mentioning a Britisher in town who asked for them. We asked Callie's friend Becca if she knew of such a man, and she said it sounded like a Mr. Stane, a butler in Uncle Charles's former New York mansion, where Callie worked with Becca. She also told us that Mr. Stane, in a moment of fury, swore vengeance against Langsdon. Becca believes they were both involved in a theft of paintings from the mansion, and Langsdon did not give Mr. Stane his share of the funds. When Becca left New York, both of the men were wanted for grand theft by the authorities.

    We understand that the Britisher is now on his way to California too. It is a most unfortunate saga. Recalling my college-day visits in Boston with Grandfather, who was such a highly respected minister, I know what a sad chapter this is for our family. I suspect Langsdon is the major culprit, but as Grandfather always said, those who are given over to evil slowly draw the innocent into their schemes and eventually lead them down the same path with them.

    On a happier note, the family is well. . . .

Benjamin lowered the pages to his lap with heartache and a growing anger. This particular evil had come through his brother Charles, who'd been full of lies and arrogance since his school days, then had sunken to complete rebelliousness and bald-faced defiance. Even before stealing funds from the bank where he'd been vice-president, and before taking a mistress who'd born him the five illegitimate children, he had caused their family endless strife and heartache.

Benjamin pounded his fist against the tiled seat and was even more irate when a pain shot through his hand. It seemed that he'd forgiven his brother the biblical seventy times seven already, and now Charles had reared his unrepentant head from the grave through his illegitimate children. After a lifetime of contending with the shameful consequences of Charles' rebellion, it was too much for him to continue to assault them now.

As if he didn't have enough on his mind, what with searching the state to find a new pastor because of Reverend Daniels' objection to the church's revival! It had been galling last Sunday to hear his public resignation from the pulpit, saying he felt God was calling him to move back East immediately. Everyone knew the true reasons: first, his Boston fiancée refused to live in the "uncivilized west" and had issued her last ultimatum; second, he was against too many prayer meetings and evangelism, especially if they were carried out by the laity.

Oh, Lord, why is it that life is so full of aggravations? Benjamin asked, though he already knew the answer. He lived in a fallen world because of man's propensity to disobey God. In any event, there was no use worrying the family about this letter yet. They already knew about the likelihood of Charles's illegitimate off-spring coming, from their first letter and from the New York investigator's report. *Lord, turn them to Oregon,* he added. *California has more than its share of scoundrels already!*

They took a riverboat westward along the picturesque Sacramento River, and Rolland scrutinized the rich delta. Already, prudent miners had turned to farming and appeared to be prospering in the rich soil. "This is the place for me," Rolland decided. "This is where I'll settle."

"Not for a while," Langsdon told him. "You'll need

funds to buy that land. Play my way 'n you'll have that money."

Langsdon had been more close-mouthed than ever after their day's stop in Sacramento, where he'd disappeared for a while, doing what he called "takin' a survey."

"What do you mean, 'play your way?'" Callie asked.

"You'll find out," Langsdon answered. "I got you all this far, didn't I?"

It was true, he had gotten them together and this far, but Callie remained silent.

At noon, they arrived in San Francisco Bay, where wraithlike fingers of fog still shrouded the hillsides that surrounded the water. When the riverboat docked, Langsdon and Rolland reclaimed their horses and covered wagon from the boat's lower deck. Once ashore, Langsdon stopped by the Wainwright and Talbot Shipping and Chandlery warehouse to ask for directions to the Talbot ranch, and came out looking satisfied.

"Were the Talbots there?" Callie asked nervously.

Langsdon shook his head. "The old man takes Saturdays off now, and the son-in-law, Daniel Wainwright, was out on church business. It's a big and prosperous place. Their Rancho Verde sounds big, too."

Callie sat on the front seat of the covered wagon, jolting along with Glenda and Rolland as they rode through the overcast city of San Francisco, heading southeast toward the Talbots' ranch. At length they left San Francisco's gloom and broke into the sunshine. The horses' heads bobbing before them, they rode for a stretch through golden hills and flat-bottomed valleys with clusters of dark green live oaks before the ranch came into sight.

"That must be it," Langsdon said, riding on Major slightly ahead of the covered wagon.

Callie gazed at the distant Spanish-style buildings. Their

white-washed walls glistened in the mid-afternoon sun-shine and, as the wagon drew closer, she could see smaller white houses as well as barns and outbuildings. With the overhanging trees, the bright blue sky up above, and hun-dreds of cattle on the surrounding hillsides, Rancho Verde was a most charming place.

Langsdon was gazing at the cattle on the golden hillsides himself. "Appears these Talbots are even richer than the ones in Missouri. Let's hope their knack for making money runs in the family."

Callie inhaled sharply. Her feverishness on the journey had not dimmed the memory of fleeing in the middle of the night from Inga and Adam's cabin, nor of their many kindnesses. "This time, there will be no more lying," she told Langsdon firmly. "I will not pose as your wife."

He gave a scornful laugh. "You can surely be my sister again. I'd never consider your faint-hearted type for a wife! Pretendin' to be concerned with a feverish wife for a month was trouble enough for a lifetime."

"I'm sure it was," she returned. "Not that I recall any sincere sympathy from you."

He slowed his horse until it was beside her, then warned, "The one thing you must do—every one of you—is to act like we're a close family. Once we're set up and no longer need them, you can frown and criticize all you want."

They eyed him in silence until at last Glenda inquired, "What will you do about employment, Langsdon?"

"To begin, I'll see what there is to turn my hand to in San Francisco. Likely see if there's something to do at their shipping and chandlery warehouse."

"You mean you'll truly work?" Callie asked with disbe-lief.

Langsdon gave another scornful laugh. "As little as pos-sible, which is doubtless what you thought."

"What of your plans to mine gold?" Rolland asked.

Langsdon affected a smile. "I talked it over in that tavern in Sacramento and decided I don't care to do any digging. You will not, however, tell that to the Talbot family . . . that or anything else to cause me or the rest of us trouble."

Having made himself clear on the subject, he urged the chestnut stallion on and distanced himself from them and the covered wagon.

Most likely he was working out what he'd say to gain these Talbots' favor, Callie guessed. Working out lies again.

"We have to forgive him," Glenda said quietly. "If we don't, we'll only worsen the tangle of sin."

Callie knew of no way she could forgive him. As far as she was concerned, Langsdon had taken on all of the bad traits of both their mother and father. What's more, he'd ruined her one chance for happiness.

If only she might see Matthew to explain. Surely he'd understand her posing as Langsdon's wife so they could ride with the wagon train. The last time she'd seen him, he and Yorker were riding off north of San Francisco to the new college formed by the Presbyterians and Congregationalists. She'd watched until they were far off, her heart broken.

As the horses moved along steadily before them, Rolland sat holding the reins thoughtfully. "Wonder why Langsdon didn't come to California alone. Why did he even bother to bring us along?"

Callie had no more than shrugged when an answer began to come to her. "Now that I think about all that's happened since he first came to see me in New York, I wonder if he's not running from trouble. Maybe we've served as a cover for him." It wasn't the first time the thought had occurred to her.

"You mean he's disguised himself by having a family

along?" Rolland asked, his hazel eyes turning to her.

"It wouldn't surprise me," she replied.

Rolland gave a nod. "And maybe he thought he could get favor from others by having us with him."

"That's likely, too," Callie replied. "Though there's probably more to it than that."

"I'd guess he thinks it makes him a 'good person' for taking charge of us," Glenda said. "My family in Centerville said that bad people like to hang onto at least one good thing about themselves for bragging on to others and to themselves."

"It's true. The one thing he can say is he got his family together," Callie replied. "And I *am* grateful for it."

Rolland pressed his lips together. "A bad thing I didn't tell you is that Langsdon stole Major from the Missouri Talbots. He stole the saddle and bridle, too, and the sacks of grain we brought with us. Tools, too."

"He didn't!" Glenda said.

"I'm not surprised," Callie replied. She looked up and saw him just ahead tying Major to the hitching post. "Hush, he'll hear us."

When they got down from the covered wagon, Langsdon said, "These Talbots might have heard harsh things about us from their Missouri kin, even though we wrote we were going to Oregon."

"How could they have heard anything harsh?" Rolland asked, mocking him.

Langsdon eyed him with suspicion. "Because people are always lookin' to criticize others. Anyhow, if they've heard anythin' bad, let me handle it. I'll do the talkin'."

Benjamin was sitting in his white-washed adobe parlor reading the newspaper when he heard voices outside by the front gate. Saturday afternoon visitors, he decided. He put down the paper and rose from his black horsehair chair to peer out the window. Maybe the visitors would include a minister, since Daniel had been sent up to the university to find one. Outside the window, however, he saw two young men and two young women approaching the house.

"Someone's come visiting!" he called out to Abby and Jessica in the kitchen.

"I'll be there in a minute," Abby replied.

"I'll greet them," Benjamin announced. "I'm already up."

He headed for the front door and opened it wide. It was then that he saw the group clearly—led by a young man who looked exactly like his younger brother, Charles!

Benjamin stiffened with anger. *Oh, Lord, help me to deal with this!*

"Good afternoon," the young man said, his voice precisely like his late father's. He added most charmingly. "Would you be the honorable Benjamin Talbot?"

Benjamin swallowed, then managed a small smile at this nephew who was not only an ex-convict and a horse thief, but was wanted in New York for grand theft. "Honorable, I doubt, but I am indeed Benjamin Talbot."

"Ah, but we hear you are most honorable," the young man objected in an ingenuous tone. "We're Talbot kin from New York. Children of your younger brother, Charles. I'm Langsdon, and this is Callie and Glenda and Rolland."

"How do you do?" Benjamin replied. Part of his mind longed to say *We were just leaving the country for the Sandwich Islands*, but the better part of it asked, "Won't you come in?"

"Thank you," Langsdon replied cordially. "Since we're kin, we felt it would be discourteous not to pay you a visit."

Benjamin pressed his lips together, leading the way

through the white-washed entry into the parlor. He hoped his terse invitation did not imply a lifetime of free room and board. He considered saying, *We've heard all about you horse thieves from my son in Independence*, but something stopped him. Likely his years of drilling in good manners, he reflected sourly. Good manners, while as laudable as his mother had taught him, sometimes led to great inconveniences.

He turned and gestured to the horsehair sofa. "Won't you sit down?"

"Thank you, sir," Langsdon replied. He had his father's fine figure and the identical engaging grin that Charles had employed to charm everyone. He even had the same brown hair and blue-gray eyes. Now he said, "We've heard so much good about you, that it's not surprising to find you're kindly and hospitable."

Benjamin drew an incredulous breath. *Flattery will get you nowhere with me, young man*, he was sorely tempted to say. *I know your type from dealing with your father for years.* Instead, he said, "Well, well," sounding to himself like an idiot. To top that, he added an inane, "What brings you to California?"

As they settled on the sofa, Langsdon smiled at his siblings, as if reminding them to smile too. "Times are bad in New York due to the financial collapse," he began, "and we hear there are better opportunities in California."

"It doesn't hold the opportunities it used to," Benjamin replied, "but there are always openings for those who are truly industrious."

"That we are," Langsdon replied most sincerely. "Rolland, here, wants to take up farmin' and has plenty of experience at it. And the girls know all about hard work. We thought you might know of positions."

Still standing, Benjamin surveyed them.

Rolland had nodded at his brother's mention of farming, though he looked discomfited about their visit. The girls appeared abashed as well. As for appearance, Rolland resembled neither of his parents, but he looked like an honest, determined person. Callie was a beautiful auburn-haired young woman, whose face resembled Abby's, and Glenda had a sweetness about her, a bit like his own sister Jessica had once looked, only with redder hair.

"Let me call Abby and your Aunt Jessica from the kitchen," Benjamin said. "If you'll excuse me—"

In the kitchen, he hissed, "Charles's children have come! Four of them."

Abby's blue eyes widened, but Jessica took off her white apron with a flourish. "Good. I've been praying about them and what we should do if they came. I believe the Lord wants us to be hospitable and—"

"Exactly what they expect," Benjamin told his sister.

"Then it won't come as a surprise to them, will it?" she asked. "Now stop looking so infernally willful, Benjamin! It's the same stubborn expression you wore when you were two years old, and it doesn't get one anywhere."

Likely she was right, he decided, but that wasn't enough. "Langsdon will flatter you fiercely, Jessica," he warned.

She laughed. "Now that's something I've dealt with from men for almost seventy years. There's not a one yet who's gotten the better of me from it."

"Charles did," Benjamin reminded her. "He always got the better of you, and you know it."

She gave him a long look, then nodded. "You're right about that."

"And Langsdon's the spitting image of him. I don't feel the least bit good about it," Benjamin added, though he knew full well that feelings should have nothing to do with the matter.

Abby appeared nervous herself, but Jessica took hold of her elbow and urged her along. "As I recall, you're the one who claimed these half sisters and half brothers were family."

"That was before I expected to actually have them in the house," Abby countered nervously. "And I didn't expect Langsdon to look like my father." After a moment, though, she closed her eyes, straightened her spine and looked resolute.

Likely prayed, Benjamin reflected, *just as I should.*

When they returned to the parlor, he introduced them, and wished he could feel as welcoming as Abby and Jessica appeared to be. He let Jessica take the lead in the visit, and not too surprising, she soon had Callie, Glenda, and Rolland telling about themselves. It was heartening to learn that Callie had escorted an orphan train to the Midwest, but despite their explanation, worrisome to learn that she and Langsdon had plucked Glenda and Rolland from foster homes. It was also worrisome to see Langsdon glower at them when he wasn't eyeing the oil paintings, Persian carpets, and everything else of value.

"We would be pleased to have you stay with us," Jessica said, to Benjamin's chagrin. "We have enough spare bedrooms if you can double up."

Benjamin noticed Callie dart an uneasy glance at Langsdon. She was unsure about staying, that much was certain.

Langsdon, however, replied, "We wouldn't want to put you out, but if you do have extra room, it would be a great help to us until we get settled. You don't perchance have a position open in your shipping and chandlery in town? It's a business of interest to me."

"No, not at the moment," Benjamin replied firmly. "The only opening I know of is for a new minister for our church."

Langsdon's blue-gray eyes darkened. "I don't have any leanings in that direction."

"Nor do many," Benjamin replied. "Nor do many."

"Let's have coffee and cake," Jessica said. "We made six applesauce cakes this morning."

"Thank you," Langsdon replied. "Just so we don't put you out none."

"We were about to try the cake ourselves," Jessica said. She bustled back to the kitchen to fetch it.

Benjamin watched Langsdon settle back on the sofa with unconcealed pleasure. They were hungry, likely half starved to death after their covered wagon trek, even if they did hurry it along with horses.

After they'd consumed the entire applesauce cake, Rolland and Langsdon went out to the covered wagon for the trunk that held their clothing, and Aunt Jessica rushed back to the kitchen, saying she smelled something burning.

Benjamin feared she smelled the heat under his collar, for it was mighty aggravating to sit in his own house and listen to Langsdon Murray's duplicity like an out-and-out simpleton.

Abby smiled at Callie and Glenda. "Let me show you to your room. It's one where my husband, Daniel, and I stayed while our house was being enlarged."

Callie wondered if her half sister was aware of their relationship. She felt increasingly uneasy as Abby escorted her and Glenda through the huge central hallway to the bedroom wing of the house. Finally, to fill the silence, Callie spoke. "Rancho Verde and the house is a beautiful place."

"I thank you for Uncle Benjamin. The house is called *Casa Contenta* . . . house of contentment," Abby said. "Before we had a schoolhouse, Cousin Betsy, who's Uncle Benjamin's youngest daughter, taught school to our children and some of the neighbors' children in this hallway."

"It's certainly big enough for a schoolroom," Callie responded. "It looks as big as the ballroom—" She'd almost slipped and said *in your old mansion*, but quickly changed it to "in a great house." Flustered, she looked about at the chests and the tall English clock, whose dark wood contrasted well with the white-washed walls. On the plank floor lay an enormous Persian carpet. But one of the loveliest features of the huge hallway was its intricate coral and green border stenciled above the green wash at sideboard height.

"Actually, this was used as a ballroom when the Californios—the original owners—lived here," Abby was saying. "Ballroom-sized central hallways were common in Californio houses. They had such a passion for dancing, it was said they'd dance right through an earthquake."

"Truly?" Callie asked as they moved on.

"Truly," Abby replied with a smile. "That's why the floors squeak so."

Callie had been too nervous to notice. "I guess they do."

"Do you dance here?" Glenda asked.

Abby shook her head. "The Talbot men don't care that much for dancing."

"I'm glad to hear it," Glenda said. "In the family where I lived, they said dancing was sinful."

Callie blinked, hoping to avoid a religious discussion.

"Some Christians do say that," Abby allowed without delving further into the subject. "Here's your room now. It has a nice view of the courtyard."

They stepped through the arched doorway into the sunny white bedroom. A colorful wedding ring quilt with a dark green border lay on the double bed, and dark green draperies were tied back at the arched window. Trailing green leaves and coral flowers were painted in a matching arch over the window and over the heavy oak bedstead's headboard.

"Did you paint the decorations?" Callie asked Abby.

Abby's blue eyes sparkled. "How did you guess?"

"We heard you were an artist."

"I try," Abby replied, "but there's not much time now with children. What else have you heard about me?"

Callie searched her mind, then simply shook her head.

After a moment, Abby said, "Church tomorrow. I hope you'll want to go."

"I do," Glenda answered promptly.

Callie pretended not to have heard, and she rushed to the window to look out over the courtyard and distant hillsides.

"Tonight we meet in the parlor before six, then have supper," Abby told them. "After such an arduous journey, I'm sure you must want to rest."

"Indeed we do," Callie agreed. She was glad to hear her brothers arriving down the hallway with the trunk before Abby could ask additional questions.

Benjamin was just settling back again in his parlor chair when he heard someone ride in on horseback. Glancing out the window, he saw Daniel quickly hitch his horse to the pepper tree out front. In a hurry, as usual.

His adopted son rushed into the parlor, breathless. "Whose horses and covered wagon are those out by the hitching post?"

"They supposedly belong to Langsdon Murray—also known as Talbot—and family," Benjamin replied in a depreciating tone. "According to Adam's latest letter, however, I expect that the chestnut stallion belongs to Adam."

"You don't say!" Daniel answered.

"I do. But there's a good deal more to this than a mere

horse, and I am trying hard to keep that foremost in my mind."

Daniel raised his dark brows. "I admire your fortitude."

"Not mine," Benjamin replied. "It's the Lord who just barely keeps me from losing my temper. Jessica's invited them to stay with us until they get settled, which could be years. Pray for me, Daniel!"

"I shall."

"We'll see what they do when I mention attending church with us tomorrow morning," Benjamin said. "When Adam and Inga invited them, they ran . . . though there was more to it than that."

Daniel shook his head. "Ah, I almost forgot. Another letter from Adam arrived at the warehouse this morning. It's out in my saddlebag."

"Sit down for a minute; the letter will keep." Benjamin said. "I could benefit from your comforting presence."

Daniel gave him a small smile and sat down on the sofa. "How is Abby taking this, having her father's other children right here?"

"With caution and leaning on the Lord for acceptance. At least, that's my observation. Looks to me as if there's a great bit of turmoil among our visitors. Not surprisingly, Langsdon immediately accepted your Aunt Jessica's offer to stay with us. After devouring an applesauce cake, they are now ensconcing themselves in our guest rooms."

"I'm not surprised."

"And what did you race in here so excited about?"

Daniel caught a deep breath. "I interviewed an impressive young minister who just came into town. He'd been up at the university asking about positions. Since the elders gave me general authority, I invited him to be a guest preacher at our church tomorrow, and he's accepted. He's also accepted an invitation to stay at my house, and should be arriving shortly. He's brought along a young New York friend who has traveled with him."

"What's the minister's background?" Benjamin asked.

"Grew up in Sturbridge Village. From there, Princeton Theological Seminary, a small church in Massachusetts for three years, guest preaching at the big New York churches, a friend of Charles Loring Brace and the Children's Aid Society. Most important, he has the love of the Lord about him."

Benjamin raised his brows. "Sounds interesting. What's the young man's name?"

"A good biblical one—Matthew Adam Hansel."

Callie sat up in the bed in her chemise and petticoat, blinking her eyes at the white-washed bedroom. It took a moment to recall where she was: the Talbot house in California! It didn't seem quite possible to actually be here. Already the long journey from New York was taking on the aspect of a dream, an experience out of time and place that had nothing to do with reality. But beside her, Glenda was sleeping as sweetly as a babe, and in the central hallway, as further proof, the clock bonged out five o'clock.

Callie slipped out of bed and tiptoed across the wooden floor to the old oak armoire, hoping that the wrinkles had fallen out of their frocks. It was important to make a good impression on the family at tonight's dinner. They'd been kind enough thus far, but it was only a beginning, since Langsdon had implied they might have to rely on the family for some time.

The armoire doors squeaked as she opened them, and Glenda sat up in bed. "Oh, is it time to get dressed?"

"We have an hour, but I wanted to tidy my hair and make certain that we look especially presentable." She glanced through the dresses. "Everything is still fiercely wrinkled."

"I'll pull on my old calico and press whatever we need while you do your hair," Glenda offered. "I expect there's a flatiron in the kitchen. I'd better see if Langsdon and Rolland have things that need pressing, too."

At six o'clock, Callie and Glenda hurried from their room, catching a glimpse of themselves in the ornate hallway mirror. Glenda looked fine in her new pale blue frock with its trim white collar, and, despite losing weight during her fever, Callie was pleased at how well she looked in her navy blue frock with the lacy collar and cuffs.

They entered the parlor, where Rolland, Langsdon, and Uncle Benjamin were already waiting. They'd no more than exchanged greetings when there came the sound of other guests arriving at the front door. Callie put on an agreeable expression and turned toward the newcomers, but the smile froze on her face.

Matthew Hansel and Yorker!

A short distance behind them were Abby, who'd stopped to remove a stone from under the heel of her shoe, and a bearded man, likely her husband.

Still dumbstruck at the sight of Matthew and Yorker, Callie finally remembered to breathe normally.

Uncle Benjamin, as host of *Casa Contenta*, was extending a hand toward Matthew. "You must be Reverend Hansel. It's a pleasure to meet you. Daniel has spoken well of you. Let me introduce—"

"We've . . . we've met," Callie blurted, her heart pounding hard.

Uncle Benjamin stared at her in surprise.

Matthew nodded, a pinched expression on his face. "I'm glad to see that you are looking well again, Mrs. Talbot."

"*Mrs. Talbot?*" Uncle Benjamin echoed.

She avoided Matthew's eyes, focusing instead on his clerical collar, which seemed to expand in size.

Langsdon spoke up quickly. "Had to pretend she was my wife on the covered wagon trip, or they wouldn't have allowed us to join the company. You know the rules." He turned to the rest of them to explain. "We came in the same covered wagon train as Reverend Hansel."

"Ah, yes," Uncle Benjamin replied belatedly. "The old rule that no single females of marriageable age are allowed unless accompanied by parents."

Blood rushed to Callie's face, and she stared down at the Persian carpet, wishing she could die right here before them. "It was an outright lie, but we saw no other way. I'm . . . sorry for deceiving you. I'm truly sorry."

She still avoided Matthew's gaze, but Yorker said, "Yer still Miss Murray? Hey, ain't that beans!"

"Yes, I'm still Miss Murray." Darting a glance at Matthew's face, she saw no joy—only confusion.

Her situation was beans, all right. Hard uncooked beans, impossible to swallow. She still loved Matthew, and he was rightfully disgusted with her.

Aunt Jessica stepped into the parlor. "Supper is ready," she announced. "Jenny brought most of it over . . . pot roast . . ."

She was greeted by such a heavy silence that she eyed them with concern, but to her credit, asked no questions.

Uncle Benjamin finished the introductions, and another awkward silence followed.

"Dinner smells wonderful," Abby said, starting for the dining room. "Let's hurry along before it grows cold."

The men waited for Callie and Glenda to precede them with Abby into the dining room. Still heartsick and ashamed, Callie passed Matthew with downcast eyes. At the large trestle table, he sat several places over, but on the other side. She avoided his gaze, her hand shaking as she helped herself to green beans, mashed potatoes, and a fine slice of beef as the serving plates were passed. Did he remember their kiss as she did? Did he ever think of her?

"Reverend Hansel, would you honor us by saying grace?" Uncle Benjamin inquired.

"Thank you," he replied. "It's my pleasure."

Callie bowed her head nervously, shaking so she could scarcely take in Matthew's words. There was something about "look down on this home with love" and "daily bread" and "returning thanks to Thee."

As they ate and Matthew conversed with the others, it became clear that he was to preach a sermon at the Talbots' church tomorrow morning. And he was staying at Rancho Verde with Abby and Daniel.

"I'm sure we will all enjoy your sermon," Uncle Benjamin said. "Langsdon, you were on the same wagon train, so I dare say you've already heard Reverend Hansel preach."

Callie glanced at Langsdon, who at least had the grace to blush. "I fear not," he replied. "First I was out scoutin', then Callie was so feverish we had to care for her night and day."

"Well, then," Uncle Benjamin added in an unequivocal tone, "you'll have that privilege tomorrow morning."

Langsdon hesitated as if searching for an excuse, and for once, Callie hoped he'd come up with one. She had no wish to face Matthew in such a setting, or any other, again.

"We would be less than good hosts if we didn't take you to church with us," Uncle Benjamin continued. "We eat breakfast at seven-thirty and leave at eight-thirty." He chuckled. "I used to have to rouse my boys from bed occasionally for church, and I wouldn't want to have to rouse all of you."

Callie concentrated on eating her dinner, scarcely tasting it. When she glanced at Langsdon, it appeared even he was caving in about attending church the next morning.

Now her uncle turned to the minister with a smile. "I look forward to hearing you tomorrow morning, Reverend Hansel. As Daniel must have told you, we are searching for a new minister. Our last one was called back East by his impatient fiancée. Do you have any such entanglements?"

"No," Matthew replied. "I have no one but my father in Sturbridge Village, Massachusetts, and my brother and sister and their families there, also. While I miss them, God has called me to California."

"You're of an age to marry," Uncle Benjamin observed.

Matthew nodded. "You needn't be concerned about that. I believe God will send someone."

"A strong Christian woman," Uncle Benjamin put in.

"Yes," Matthew responded. "I've learned that lesson well. I would marry none else."

Callie's heart sank even lower.

The conversation shifted to the great spiritual awakening back east, and when Uncle Benjamin spoke of the excitement at their own small church, Callie noted that Matthew was equally excited about the news.

After dinner they all adjourned to the parlor, and her uncle said with dismay, "I almost forgot! I have a letter for you here, Callie. With so much taking place, I forgot to give it to you. It was enclosed with a letter from my son Adam in Missouri."

Still filled with despair, Callie accepted the letter.

Her uncle continued. "Adam wrote that a Mr. Stane had been looking for you, Langsdon. According to all accounts, he took a fast steamship down the Mississippi, and had inquired about the new railroad crossing Panama, as well as the coastal steamers to San Francisco. He may have even beat you here."

Callie stared at Langsdon, whose face was now pale. She

had an inkling that their uncle already knew more about Langsdon and Mr. Stane than he intended to tell.

"An old friend from New York," Langsdon replied.

"Adam didn't conclude he meant to see you about friendship," Uncle Benjamin said.

Langsdon lifted his shoulders with a show of indifference. "To put it more accurately, Mr. Stane is an old business acquaintance."

Callie didn't wish to hear another word of it, and she opened the letter in her lap. Glancing down at the signature, she was amazed to see Thomas Warrick's name. Her eyes flew to the top of the page.

> *Dear Callie,*
>
> *Becca and I came through Independence after you'd left. I'm back here now with your fine Missouri kin, staying in the old cabin where you were, until I recover my senses.*
>
> *Becca and I decided to make a life for ourselves and follow you. The Talbots told us you had just left, and they thought you still meant to go to California, so we set out.*
>
> *It hurts to tell you this news, for I know it will hurt you, too. We had a short but good married life. Becca died after falling from the wagon and hitting her head the first day out along the Platte. We started with such high hopes, but I brought her back in a casket to be buried here where it's more civilized. The Talbots most kindly got her into their church cemetery, for she was a true believer, as I am now, too.*
>
> *That's all I can write. I don't know what to do. Adam Talbot offered me work at the trading post and maybe that's best for me now.*
>
> *I know your heart will ache over Becca, but like she said before she died, "Turn your heart over to Christ*

and I'll be waiting in Glory for you." Them were her last words, then she smiled a long way off and was gone from the living. I will never forget that smile. She saw something or someone wonderful.

> *Yours sincerely,*
> *Thomas Warrick*

Callie rose to her feet, tears welling in her eyes. "Excuse me, please. Excuse me!"

She ran from the parlor, hot tears rolling down her cheeks. It was her fault . . . her idea for them to leave New York and to come to California. She was the one who'd caused Becca to die. She'd not only killed Matthew's love for her, she had all but killed her very best friend!

13

Benjamin Talbot drove the carriage to the front door of the hacienda, then climbed down to help Jessica up the carriage steps. He'd eaten breakfast early with his sister and now he inquired, "Any sign of our guests?"

She nodded with amusement as he hoisted her up into the carriage. "You made required church attendance rather clear last night."

"I meant to," he replied, "especially after Adam wrote they fled in the night instead of going to church with him."

"Try to be kinder to Langsdon," Jessica urged him. "You know he and the rest of them didn't have the advantage of a good home as we did as children."

He nodded. "You think I've been too hard on them?"

"Bordering on it," she replied as she settled back on the seat.

"I was just trying to be clear on the rules here," he replied, but he knew in his heart that there was more to it. "It's impossible for me to look at Langsdon and not see Charles before me again."

"It is at that," she agreed, "but they're entirely different people, Benjamin. They're entirely different souls, too."

He turned to the hacienda door, where Langsdon, Rolland, Callie, and Glenda were letting themselves out.

"Good morning," he said as they approached. "It is a

good one with sunshine already, isn't it? And you are all dressed up nicely."

Callie looked peaked, as if she'd spent a bad night. For his part, Langsdon looked stubborn; clearly he was attending church under protest. Rolland appeared more pleasant, and Glenda beamed like the sunshine itself.

"Langsdon, why don't you sit up on the driver's box with me?" Benjamin suggested.

Langsdon gave a nod and, after helping the others in, climbed up on the box.

"Git along, boys!" Benjamin called out to the horses.

As they clip-clopped along the path, he told Langsdon, "You watch, these horses will go straight to the church without much direction. Somehow they always seem to know when it's Sunday morning."

He sat back, the reins loosely held over the four horses, and inhaled the fresh morning air. "A beautiful morning."

Langsdon grunted, looking out at the countryside with him.

"Langsdon," Benjamin said, "I want to ask your forgiveness. I haven't treated you as well as I should. You look so much like your father, it's hard for me to see you as a separate person. There were difficulties between your father and the rest of the family, but it's not fair for me to prejudge you. I'd like to start over again with you. I ask your forgiveness."

Langsdon shot an incredulous glance at him.

"Do you forgive me?" Benjamin inquired.

Langsdon shrugged, then stared away at the countryside.

Benjamin spoke as kindly as he knew how. "It's important for people not to be in a state of being unforgiven, just as it's important to keep short accounts with God, asking His forgiveness." He hesitated, then put it plainly. "As you may know, there are two camps in which to end one's life, and I'd like to see you in the loving fellowship where Christ is your Redeemer, rather than in Satan's eternal abyss."

Langsdon eyed him with fury. "I'm goin' to church to please you, but it don't give you license for preachin' at me too."

Benjamin swallowed. "I was just hoping to make it plain. It's a very simple decision one makes for Christ—yes or no."

"It's plain to me," Langsdon snarled, "and I'm not interested. You're lucky enough to get me goin' to church today."

Benjamin drew a sorrowful breath. "I see."

Moments later, a rider on a brown saddle horse cantered toward them, and the bony stranger on it peered hard at them. Langsdon straightened up on the seat as if he'd seen a phantom, but the stranger rode on.

Lord, forgive me if I haven't done right, Benjamin prayed with dismay. *I put Langsdon and his salvation in your hands!*

As the horses drew to a halt, Callie glanced out the carriage window at the small white church. Other horses already stood at the hitching post swishing their tails; some were saddle horses, and others were still hitched to their wagons and buggies.

"It's a little church," Aunt Jessica remarked, "but it's a loving place. When we're in it with the other believers, I always feel closer to God."

It occurred to Callie that she had never in her life felt close to God . . . unlike Aunt Jessica . . . or Becca. Her eyes filled with tears again at the thought of her old friend.

"A good crowd this Sunday," Aunt Jessica said, looking out at those arriving. "Our revival continues."

They climbed out of the carriage, Uncle Benjamin helping them down the steps. Langsdon was too preoccupied staring up at the road to help them, then watching as more people arrived in their farm wagons and buggies.

Whatever is wrong with him? Callie wondered. He looked like such a dark thundercloud that he'd ruin matters for all of them. As if things weren't bad enough with the news about Becca!

Callie followed the rest of them to the church steps, but Langsdon said, "Go ahead. I'll come along later."

Uncle Benjamin asked him, "What's the trouble?"

"Nothin'," Langsdon replied. "Just need a little more fresh air."

"Won't be hard to find us in there," Uncle Benjamin told him. "It's not a big New York City church."

Inside, Abby and Daniel and their children sat in a pew near the front, and Matthew Hansel was seated on a chair behind the pulpit. He wore his black robe, as he had the first time Callie had seen him in the New York church. He seemed faraway, though, as if he were praying without closing his eyes.

Callie followed Aunt Jessica to the second pew and sat down, leaving room for the others. The side windows stood open, and a fine morning breeze wafted toward them.

Suddenly a loud commotion erupted outside, and someone yelled, "He's stealin' a horse! That man's stealin' Sven Olson's horse!"

Callie clutched her heart, recalling Langsdon's dark look and his turning up with Major in Independence.

People rose from the pews to peer out the church window as hoof beats pounded up the road, followed by four loud gunshots.

For an instant there was silence, then people shouted, "He's shot! They're both shot!"

Callie started for the window just as someone yelled, "It's the fellow who came with Benjamin Talbot! The one after him shot himself, too!"

Langsdon and Mr. Stane . . .

The white walls of the sanctuary whirled all around her before she sank down onto a pew.

Two days later, the Talbot men unloaded Langsdon's and Mr. Stane's closed caskets from the wagon and carried them to the old Californio graveyard behind the walls of the Talbot complex. A cluster of oak trees overhung the graves, and the rest of the family congregated in their shade.

Abby held her arm around Callie. "I'm so sorry it happened, Callie. I can't tell you how sorry."

Callie nodded sorrowfully. "I am too."

For the past two days, she'd reexamined all that had taken place since the day Langsdon had called on her in New York. She'd put that together with what Uncle Benjamin had told them with reluctance: the New York bank robbery, the theft of the Burlingtons' paintings with Mr. Stane, the theft of Adam's horse and far more in Missouri.

Her brain and body were numb with grief, despair, and humiliation, and her eyes were beyond tears as she walked with the others to the open graves.

"Mr. Stane must have had a vengeful heart," Abby remarked. "To think that he'd come all the way to California after Langsdon . . . and then shoot himself too."

"He had a great deal of pride."

"Don't most of us?" Abby remarked. "Trying to follow our own ways instead of God's."

Callie felt a twinge of guilt and turned to look at Matthew, who stood in his black robe at the head of the graves. *What can he say about two thieves . . . one who'd shot the other and then killed himself?* she wondered. *What can a minister possibly say?*

Once they were all assembled at the side of the graves, Matthew opened his Bible. He read aloud about God knowing everything about each of them and about man knowing God, then continued, "I am the Lord which exercises lovingkindness, judgment, and righteousness in the earth: for in these things I delight, saith the Lord."

Matthew looked up at them. "Judgment belongs to the Lord," he said. "It is not our duty to condemn men, but to proclaim the good news of salvation in Jesus Christ, our Lord.

"We commit the bodies of Langsdon Murray and Ian Stane to the earth from whence they came. Their lives on earth have reached their conclusions. They will stand before the great white judgment throne, and we can only say with humility and all sincerity, 'May God have mercy on their souls.'"

Matthew looked at all of them—Callie, Glenda, Rolland, Yorker, the entire Talbot family. "Langsdon Murray and Ian Stane are no longer able to hear us, but each of you can. I would remind you that we must each come to a decision about committing ourselves to Jesus Christ as our Savior . . . a decision about death or eternal life. If there is anyone here who wishes to repent of his sins and make a decision to follow Christ, let him come forward now. You need not be perfect, nor baptized, nor a world-renowned sinner."

Callie felt a powerful pull at her heart. Without hesitation she stepped forward, tears of remorse running down her cheeks. *Forgive me*, she prayed, *forgive me for my pride and lies. . .*

As she stood there, she began to feel surrounded by a heavenly warmth and knew in her soul that it was God's wondrous love.

A moment later, Rolland stepped up beside her, then Yorker, and there were joyous murmurs all around.

"We prayed that something good would come of this," Matthew said, "that God would use even this to His glory. It reminds me of a time in history over eighteen hundred years ago. When evil appeared triumphant over Christ's life, he rose from His grave."

He looked at Callie and Rolland and Yorker. "God has used this sorrowful funeral service to bring eternal lives to your souls and His love into your lives."

For the first time in her life, Callie felt something far greater than happiness . . . she felt joy.

Behind her, Uncle Benjamin sounded joyous himself. "We all prayed mightily to be used in the Great Awakening. How the angels in glory must be rejoicing with us right now!"

That evening the supper table was a scene of more rejoicing. Matthew had seated himself next to Callie, and though what they said was of little importance, she felt his presence in a new and quiet way. Instead of the mere thrill at his nearness that she'd felt on the orphan train, there was something far deeper—a nearness of souls.

As they finished their apple pie and coffee, Uncle Benjamin spoke from the head of the table. "Last spring I prayed for a sign from God . . . *any* sign besides the letters from Langsdon—when those very letters were the beginning of God bringing the three of you here, which eventually led to your salvation."

He shook his head. "I presume the lesson I should take from it is not to ask for signs since God is likely to be already in action right under my nose, and I'm too thick to know it."

Her gray-haired uncle looked the picture of wisdom, yet he was still learning, Callie marveled. "There must be a lot to being a Christian," she ventured quietly.

"Indeed there is," he replied.

"And sometimes a great deal to learn over and over," Aunt Jessica said.

A thoughtful silence filled the white-washed dining room, and Matthew added, "It seems to me that much of the learning and relearning has to do with trusting God. Come to think of it, that's a fine topic for Sunday's sermon. Trusting God is a lesson I've just relearned myself."

Failings or not, Callie was glad that they'd asked him to pastor their church for a time.

Matthew turned to her with a warm smile. "My most recent lesson was well worth the relearning." He spoke almost formally. "May I take you for a stroll in the court-yard, Callie?"

A blush crept to her cheeks. "I— Yes, some fresh air would be fine."

"If you would excuse us, please," he said to Uncle Benjamin, who sat blinking at them before his eyes widened.

"Ain't that beans!" Yorker declared. "Not that I didn't know it all the—"

"Never mind, Yorker," Abby interrupted. "I'm sure you'd like another slice of pie. Perhaps some of you others would like more pie or coffee."

Uncle Benjamin gave a nod. "Yes, of course, you're excused. As it is, Daniel and I have some Rancho Verde business to discuss. I'm sure Rolland and Yorker will benefit by staying with us."

Outside in the courtyard, brilliant red, pink, and orange hues splashed against wispy clouds in the western sky.

"A fine evening," Matthew observed as they strolled along.

"Yes," Callie agreed, "a fine evening."

For a long time neither of them spoke again, until at last she turned to him and said, "You'd been praying for me, hadn't you, Matthew?"

The cleft in his chin broadened as he smiled. "I've

prayed for your salvation from the moment I suspected you didn't know Christ."

"I thought you'd guessed nearly at the beginning. . . ."

He shook his head, his brown eyes holding hers. "The minister's letter, which I assume Langsdon concocted, took me in. But I did know that if God wanted us together, it would happen in His way and in His timing. I trusted not in my own understanding but in Him."

Her words came in a whisper. "You mean . . . you still . . . ?"

"I still love you, Callie, and I always will."

"And I love you, Matthew. I do."

He gathered her into his arms, then lowered his head most decisively, and his lips touched hers with tenderness. With the sunset behind him, it seemed that the God who'd made the sun and the earth had also surrounded them with His love.

When they parted, she whispered, "I'm truly sorry for misleading you. I promise, no more deception."

"You were forgiven a long time ago," he answered. "I saw in St. Louis that your accompanying the orphan train was part of a ruse. Then later, I was so stunned by your supposedly being married to Langsdon that I rethought everything from our first meeting onward. I remembered a good many clues, especially your uncertainty at being around a minister and an evasiveness when I mentioned Christ."

"I felt guilty about it," she confessed. "I should never have listened to Langsdon, but I didn't know how else to get our family together. I didn't know what else to do."

"How could you have known? You may have had prayers at the orphanage, but I assume you'd never heard the Gospel until you came to church that first time in New York."

She shook her head. "We'd just begun morning devotions at the Burlingtons'. . .and Mr. Burlington did speak of Christ."

"That was likely the beginning of your spiritual battle.

Eventually you'd have to arrive at a decision . . . either following the world's ways, like Langsdon, or following Christ."

"You didn't know what the outcome would be?"

Matthew gave her a radiant smile. "I knew that if God meant you for my wife, you'd have to be a believer before we married. It was merely a matter of overcoming impatience and waiting for you to come to Him."

"And finally I did."

He nodded "And finally you did!"

Suddenly she realized what he'd said: *If God meant you for my wife. . .*

"And did . . . did you think He meant me. . . ?"

Matthew nodded. "I know He did. That's why I'm asking for your hand in marriage."

"Yes," she whispered. "Oh, Matthew, yes!"

Returning his smile in the brilliant sunset, a wondrous peace swept through her . . . the peace he'd spoken of in that first sermon. In the midst of their love and joy, there was peace like a river in her soul.

ABOUT THE AUTHOR

Elaine Schulte is a wife, mother of two sons, and a writer whose short stories, articles, and novels have been widely published. Her first novel in the California Pioneer Series is *The Journey West*, in which Abby Talbot comes to California with her Uncle Benjamin's covered wagon train in 1846.

The second book is *Golden Dreams*, which brings Abby's best friend, Rose Wilmington, around Cape Horn by clipper ship in 1848 into the beginnings of California's gold rush.

The third novel is *Eternal Passage*, in which cousin Louisa Talbot Setter flees an abusive past in Virginia in 1849, enduring the dangers of sailing by gold ship and trekking through the jungle of Panama. Finally she sails by coastal steamer to California, only to learn that she cannot outrun her past.

In *With Wings as Eagles*, the fourth book in the series, Betsy Talbot, who was eleven years old in *The Journey West*, becomes the schoolteacher in a mining community while her father, Benjamin Talbot, continues to fight the lawlessness in San Francisco.

Elaine tells us, "The major characters in *Peace Like a River* are fictitious, as is usual in my novels. However, The Reverend Charles Loring Brace did found the Children's Aid Society, which between the years of 1854 and 1904 transported over 100,000 children from the streets and orphanages of New York City to the Midwest. I quoted from Brace's writings in his dinner speech. Most other accounts about the orphan trains tell of the first year when the children rode in box cars. Such travel was so hard, that by 1858, they rode west in railroad coaches.

"Also, Jeremiah Lanphier and the Second Great American Awakening are accurately portrayed, and over a million converts were indeed added to the churches of America in 1857-58. According to the May 27, 1858 issue of the *New*

York Christian Advocate and Journal, revival also broke out in California. As is usually the case, the Second Great American Awakening began with one person.

"Having grown up in Merrillville, Indiana, I had hoped to place part of the story there. The records of the Children's Aid Society show thousands of children placed in Indiana in the late 1850s, but no specific towns, so I created a fictitious Centerville, which turns out to have been an earlier name for Merrillville. Also, many orphans were placed in Ohio and Illinois, but there are no longer records of specific towns, thus I used fictitious towns in those states as well.

"The quote, 'We lived the same as Indians 'ceptin' we took an interest in politics and religion,' came from Dennis Hanks, a cousin of Abraham Lincoln, who was an early Hoosier himself. Before the time of this story, Lincoln called his early childhood place 'a wild region with bears and other wild animals still in the woods.' It's a way I enjoy thinking of it."